THE GOOD SAMARITAN

Lois Hunter is happily married to Ken, a City banker. They have a nice home, two well-adjusted sons, and live in a beautiful part of the country. Both are into good causes and local activities. A privileged, satisfying, richly rewarding life one might think. Why, then, with so much going for her, does Lois develop an attachment to a beggar she sees outside a supermarket? Seeing Oliver and his two puppies sitting on the pavement on a cold afternoon touches her heart and she resolves to help him despite the protestations of Ken and her sister Wendy. Shortly after they meet, Oliver disappears, to re-emerge six months later, injured. Once again he becomes the object of Lois's solicitude and this time she invites him to stay on their land. All this not unnaturally produces strain between Lois and Ken, and Wendy, too, is critical of her sister's philanthropy—until she meets Oliver and, in turn, becomes as obsessed by this mysterious stranger as Lois.

THE GOOD SAMARITAN

Nicola Thorne

CHIVERS PRESS
BATH

First published 1998
by
HarperCollins
This Large Print edition published by
Chivers Press
by arrangement with
HarperCollins Publishers
2000

ISBN 0 7540 1345 6

British Library Cataloguing in Publication Data available

Printed and bound in Great Britain by
REDWOOD BOOKS, Trowbridge, Wiltshire

CONTENTS

A certain man went down from Jerusalem to Jericho and fell among robbers, who also stripped him and having wounded him went away, leaving him half dead.

And it chanced that a certain priest went down the same way and seeing him, passed by.

In like manner also a Levite, when he was near the place and saw him, passed by.

But a certain Samaritan, being on his journey, came near him and, seeing him, was moved with compassion.

And going up to him, bound up his wounds, pouring in oil and wine; and setting him upon his own beast, brought him to an inn and took care of him.

And the next day he took out two pence and gave to the host and said: 'Take care of him; and whatsoever thou shalt spend over and above, I, at my return, will repay thee.'

Luke 10: 30–35

PART 1

A Certain Samaritan: Lois

CHAPTER ONE

The young man crouched on the pavement outside the supermarket, a small brown puppy clasped in his arms. There was no cap on the ground in front of him and for a moment Lois, in the act of entering the store, thought he was just sitting there resting. He didn't appear to be begging; he sat gazing rather apathetically, almost uninterestedly, at the people like herself hurrying by. She took a trolley and, glancing back, thought that the expression of the man resting his head against the plate glass of the front of the store was infinitely sad, infinitely pathetic, somehow haunting. The thing that struck her was that it was so cold.

Lois pushed the trolley into the store, took out her shopping list and marched purposefully along the aisles until the trolley was nearly full. Ken was arriving with business friends for the weekend and although most of the preparations had been completed, much remained to be done.

One of the last items on her extensive shopping list was dog food and, impulsively, remembering the puppy in the cold outside, she added a couple of tins of one of the cheaper brands.

When she emerged it was getting dark. She had half expected that the young man would have sought the shelter of a warmer place, but he was still there. The puppy which before had been wriggling on his lap was fast asleep. The head of the young man rested on his shoulder as though he too was asleep.

Lois wheeled the trolley towards him and, suddenly feeling foolish, passed quickly by. A few yards further on she stopped and retraced her steps. Feeling even more foolish and self-conscious, she leaned towards the man, proffering the tins of cheap dog food.

'For the dog,' she said.

'Thank you.' The young man started, as if he had been dozing, and took them from her. As he did, another canine head appeared from under his coat and Lois exclaimed in surprise.

'Oh, you have two!'

'But you've brought two cans,' the young man said, struggling to make himself upright.

'I only saw one dog.' Lois fumbled in her coat pocket and produced two one-pound coins.

'Thank you,' he said again. 'That's most kind.'

'Have you nowhere to go?' Lois asked him urgently.

'Oh, yes,' he looked surprised. 'I've a van I've left outside the town. It's broken down.'

'And you live in the van?'

'For the time being.' The young man smiled. 'I'm on my way to Cornwall.'

'I see.' He had a pleasant, open face and the

4

soft burr in his voice of someone who came from the north of England. 'But it seems terrible . . .' she looked around and lowered her voice almost to a whisper, though no one could possibly have heard her, the car park being adjacent to the supermarket and engines starting and stopping all the time. 'It seems terrible that you have to *beg.*'

'What can you do,' he said, 'if the money runs out? They only let you have so much. After that if you can't find work you have no alternative.'

'I wish you luck,' Lois said, straightening up.

'Thank you,' his smile was charming if a little wan. 'You've been very kind.' Lois stooped and patted the heads of the two puppies, who were gazing adoringly, trustingly up at her. Suddenly her eyes filled with tears and she hurried away without saying goodbye.

*   *   *

Of course they did it for effect, she thought, driving through the autumn mist towards home. She wondered where he'd left his van. *If* he had a van. They brought dogs and cats along with them for sympathy. The British public was notoriously gullible.

The Range Rover was stuffed with goodies for the weekend and, as she came to the gates of the house, which swung open at a signal from the car, Lois Hunter tried to put the

5

beggar and his two dogs firmly out of her mind.

Temporarily she was successful. Friday evening was a busy time at Higham Hall. Ken was expected with two business friends and their wives at about seven. The preparations for the evening's meal had been well in hand before she left, but there was a lot to do for the shoot the following day. On Sunday there was to be a big lunch party when their number would be swelled by people who lived locally. Then the house guests would depart in the late afternoon, leaving Lois and Ken to enjoy their only quiet evening together that week.

As she stopped outside the kitchen door the stable lad ran forward to help her, and Beverley came out of the back door wiping her hands on a cloth. Beverley was a cheerful young woman, a little younger than Lois, the wife of the estate manager Neal who looked after the couple of hundred acres of land that surrounded the Hall, and the adjoining farm. She was a cordon bleu cook and assisted Lois in all the preparations for the sociable weekends that were such a feature of the Hunters' lifestyle.

'Hi!' Beverley said, coming up to the open door of the Rover. 'Got everything you wanted?'

'Just about,' Lois grinned back. 'I ticked off every item I had on the list. Did Ken ring?'

'They've left London and they should be on

time. The Goodacres are making their own way. They may be here a bit early.'

Pheasant shot the previous weekend was on the menu. One of Beverley's soufflés to start and a fine claret selected by Ken to go with the main dish.

Lois looked around at the sun setting over the roof of the main house. Yet it was only five o'clock.

'It's beginning to get dark early,' she said, taking one of the supermarket boxes firmly in both hands, and then she remembered the man with the two brown puppies and the contrast in their lifestyles struck her with such force that she stopped in her tracks.

Beverley, also with a box between her hands, stopped with her.

'Anything the matter?'

Lois shook her head and proceeded into the kitchen where Ted the stable boy had put his boxes on the big kitchen table. 'I'll leave you to unpack, Mrs Hunter.'

'Thanks, Ted. I think we've got everything out.'

'Shall I put the car away, Mrs Hunter?'

'If you would.' She smiled at him and began to unpack the boxes, ticking off the items against the list she'd put on the table. From the range behind her came a wonderful smell. She stopped and breathed in.

'Isn't life wonderful?' she observed, turning to Beverley who was busy stirring something

7

on the Aga.

'Something happen to you today?' Beverley asked, sticking her finger into the pot and licking it. 'Not enough salt.'

'There was a beggar outside the supermarket. He was quite a young man . . . not too young, not a teenager. Between twenty-five and thirty. He was quite well dressed. The thing that touched me was that he had two little puppies on his lap.'

'Oh, they all do that,' Beverley said offhandedly. 'It's to get sympathy.'

'I know. I mean, I know that's what people say, but he didn't quite seem like that. Not a real beggar. I think he was simply hard up. He said he was on his way somewhere and the van had broken down.'

'*What* van?' Beverley's tone was sarcastic.

'He said he lived in a van and was on his way to Cornwall from the north of England. He had a northern accent. Quite pleasant . . .' Lois looked up from her checklist and caught Beverley looking questioningly over one shoulder at her. 'What I'm trying to say, without sounding patronizing, is that he was just like us.'

'You should have asked him to dinner,' Beverley said derisively. 'Ken *would* have been pleased, with the Goodacres and the Browns coming.'

John Goodacre was the Chairman of Ken's bank and Henry Brown was an important

8

official at the Foreign Office.

'Ken's not as stuffy as you think,' Lois said defensively, 'but I think he might have drawn the line at my friend.'

'Oh, a "friend", is he?'

'I spoke to him for two minutes, if that. I don't expect I will ever see him again.'

'I don't expect you will.'

'I felt sorry for him, that's all.' Lois sighed deeply. 'Having spent over a hundred pounds at the supermarket and having given him two cans of dog meat, I couldn't help contrasting our lifestyles and feeling rather guilty about the luxuriousness of mine.'

*   *   *

It was almost as though she had forgotten him—it had been such a busy week—but then as she rounded the corner of the supermarket from the car park she saw that he was still there, as if he had never moved. The sight of him seemed to stab her conscience and she stood unobserved for a few moments looking at all the passers-by who ignored him, people with laden trolleys bent on their business.

Lois collected a trolley and paused alongside him. The puppies looked thinner. Instead of being fat and wriggly like thick sausages they lay supinely on his lap, expressions dejected, heads resting on their paws as though they too found life hard with

9

the winter closing in. Lois thought he looked more unkempt than the week before; then he had been clean-shaven, whereas now he had a stubble of black beard.

'Still here, I see,' she said, looking down at him. He raised his eyes and appeared not to recognize her, but he shuffled about and made some attempt to straighten himself up. As he did, the dogs looked at her too, their pathetic little faces gazing up at her. Being a passionate animal lover she thought she really cared more about the dogs than him. Of course to imagine that he would remember her meant assuming that there were not many other people as generous as she had been. In fact, there were probably a good few more. When she thought of the couple of pounds and the two tins of cheap dog food, Lois Hunter felt ashamed of herself.

'We had a little chat last week,' she said. 'You told me your van had broken down.'

'I'm waiting for a new part.' He coughed and the movement unsettled the dogs, who tried to get off his lap. A light of recognition came into his eyes. 'Oh, I remember you now. Yes, we had a talk.'

'Do many people ...?' Lois stopped and looked around.

'More than in the city. You'd be surprised.'

'But I thought you didn't—'

'I am not a professional beggar,' the man said testily. 'I am temporarily short of cash and this is the only way I can continue to exist. Don't think I like it.'

'Of course not.' She felt humiliated, momentarily lost for words. Now it was as though she was the disadvantaged one. Lois moved quickly on and pushed her trolley through the automatic doors of the store.

This weekend, for once, they weren't entertaining. Ken was in Switzerland and wasn't due home until Saturday. Saturday night there was dinner with friends in a nearby village and Sunday they would have to themselves. She did a light shop but in it she included a pound of ham, two loaves of bread, butter, cheese and eggs that she didn't want, plus, of course, tins of dog food. These she put in a separate carrier bag, two in fact. She also extracted a note from her wallet and tucked it carefully inside one of the bags. Then she changed her mind and added another.

But when she came out he had gone, moved on; no sign of him or the dogs.

Lois felt a sense of hopelessness as she stowed the goods in the Range Rover and climbed into the car. She had offended him, humiliated him. This is what people like her did. They meant to do good, but they did it clumsily. They forgot that even beggars had their pride.

It was getting dark; dark and cold. She drove out of town and at the roundabout took the road that, five miles later, would lead to

11

her home. The town of Stinsbury sat on a hill and the road wound down through one of the beautiful valleys of North Dorset. She was half a mile outside the town when she saw a figure stumbling ahead of her, shoulders hunched as though he was carrying something. A few yards further on she stopped and, as he drew level with the car, he looked up.

'I'm sorry,' she said, leaning out of the window.

'Sorry for what?'

'I was rude.'

'I didn't think you were rude.'

He seemed about to walk on, so she said, 'Can I give you a lift to your van?' She pointed to the heavy bundle in his arms. 'That must weigh a ton.'

He stopped again and looked at her.

'Aren't you afraid?'

'What of?' She looked surprised.

'Of me. I'm a beggar. You know nothing about me.'

'Hop in,' Lois said with a smile, indicating the far door. 'It's a chance I'll have to take. Besides, you told me you weren't a real beggar. That's the version I prefer to believe. What's your name?' she asked as he climbed in and shut the door.

'Oliver.'

'I'm Lois. Lois Hunter.'

Oliver didn't reply but continued to look in front of him as if concentrating on the road.

Perhaps driving with strangers made him nervous. Perhaps he was the one who was afraid of her.

'It's a few miles down the road,' he said after a few minutes. 'It isn't far.'

'Far enough on a day like this.'

'I'm used to it.'

'Did you ...' she paused. 'Did you collect much today? Maybe it's rude to ask.'

He shrugged. 'A few pounds.' He looked at her. 'I make about thirty pounds a week.'

Lois felt shocked.

'How can you live on that?'

'Once I get to Cornwall and begin looking for a job, I can start to claim benefit again.'

'I see.'

'Here!' Oliver said sharply and Lois braked hard. To her left was a piece of waste ground on which she sometimes saw the trailers and caravans of tourists or gypsies in the summer. It was in a pretty spot at the bottom of the steep hill leading to Stinsbury. All around were fields and woodlands, scattered cottages and farms, and about two miles further on Higham Hall with its old manor house, its farm and adjoining buildings, its two hundred acres of land.

The van was parked up against a hedge that divided the lay-by from a field belonging to one of the farms. There was a caravan a few yards away which was shuttered and uninhabited. Oliver's abode, however, wasn't a caravan but a medium-sized, closed delivery van, windowless at the sides. It seemed dreadful to think of it as someone's home.

'Well, thanks very much,' Oliver said, preparing to get out.

'May I see it?'

'You've seen it.' He sounded defensive and stepped carefully on to the ground, clutching the puppies and a heavy plastic bag, probably full of tins of dog food from kind well-wishers. On an impulse she jumped out after him.

'Honestly, I'd like to see how you live. Somehow,' she paused, 'it doesn't seem right.' She realized immediately that she sounded patronizing, but Oliver beckoned and she followed him to the van. He let the puppies go and they scampered around, yelping happily and relieving themselves against the hedge. Feeling in his pocket, he produced a set of keys and opened the back door of the van. It was almost too dark to see inside; nevertheless, Lois peered in. She could make out very little, but what she did see appeared clean and tidy. Something about him convinced her that Oliver was a fastidious man.

'No lights?' she asked.

'In the front; the battery's gone. I have a paraffin lamp which I light at night, but, like the birds, I tend to go to sleep when it's dark and wake up when the day breaks.'

'And where do you cook?'

14

'On a Primus stove. But sometimes the supermarket gives me sandwiches left over from the day, or stuff from the delicatessen counter. One day they gave me a bottle of wine that someone had returned because it was off.'

Lois laughed. 'And how did it taste?'

'It tasted off,' Oliver said ruefully. Then he laughed too. Suddenly the ice was broken and Lois began to think that a bond had formed. 'Anyway, thanks for the lift.'

'Look, I bought some more goodies today for the dogs and something for you. I also wanted to give you . . . a little more money. I would really like to help you, because it's getting cold and dark, and this place'—she looked round and shivered—'will be terribly bleak in winter.' She took a few steps back and looked doubtfully at the van. 'What exactly needs repairing?'

For answer Oliver went round to the front, raised the bonnet and pointed inside. 'No engine.'

'Oh, I see. That's pretty serious, isn't it?' She looked across at him. 'How did you get here without an engine?'

'I got here with an engine, but it conked out. A bloke from the junk yard down the road came to look at it and said it would cost too much to repair, almost the same price as a new engine. So he took it off me for scrap and said when he came across a good second-hand one he'd let me have it for a few quid.'

'That was trusting of you.'

Oliver folded his arms and continued to gaze at the van.

'I have to trust people, Mrs Hunter. You can't get by in this life without trust. Take yourself, for example: you trusted me. Not many women would give a stranger a lift on a dark night. You didn't hesitate.'

'I feel I know you, in a funny way. I mean, anyone who is so fond of animals ...' Her voice trailed off and she looked around for the pups but they'd disappeared. 'Aren't you worried about them running out into the road?'

'They've too much sense.' Oliver looked behind him. 'They were both rescued, so they're living on borrowed time too. I found them in a canal, with their legs tied together. They missed drowning by seconds.'

'Oh!' Lois covered her face with her hands. 'How *awful*. How can people be so cruel?'

'People *are* cruel. Surely you know that?'

'But you said you trusted them.'

'I don't trust everyone.' Oliver gave a brittle laugh. 'Not by a long chalk. But I trusted the bloke who took my engine to give me a replacement, and,' he glanced at her sideways, 'I trust you.'

'Well,' said Lois, lifting her wrist and studying her watch in the waning light, 'I must be going. If you'd like to come to the car I'll

16

give you the stuff I bought for you.' She fished in the pocket of her trousers, producing two crumpled ten-pound notes. 'I would like you to take this—for the puppies,' she added quickly, looking awkwardly up at him. 'I do hope the man appears with the new engine and you can get on your way.'

'It had better be soon,' Oliver said. 'The police will move me on. I've already been warned.'

'But you can't move without an engine!' Lois exclaimed.

'You'd be surprised what the police can do when they put their minds to it.'

Lois held out her hand.

'If I don't see you again, good luck.'

'Thanks, Mrs Hunter.' He walked with her to the car, opened the door and held it for her. 'You really have been terribly kind.'

Again she looked round for the puppies, but they were still nowhere to be seen. She climbed into her car and drove off, aware of a curious feeling of emptiness inside.

*   *   *

Lois and Ken Hunter had been married fifteen years. Lois was now thirty-six and Ken forty. They were considered a harmonious and contented couple. Their fourteen-year-old twins, Tony and Peter, were at boarding school. Lois and Ken both came from well-off

17

families. Lois's late father had been a distinguished surgeon and Ken's, also now dead, had been a senior partner in a City bank, one of whose eighteenth-century founders had been a Hunter. After university, Ken joined the bank as a trainee and because of the family influence was now a partner. Lois had trained as a beautician, and after her marriage she threw herself into local activities in the village near the large, comfortable family house that had been a gift of both families as a wedding present. They had added the farm and more land to it later on.

Neither was an intellectual, but they were intelligent, alert and interested in current affairs. Of the two, Ken was more conservative, in every sense of the word. They enjoyed the social and sporting life of the county. Ken was a good shot, both were keen golfers, and they followed the local hunt.

They had a pied-à-terre in the Barbican where Ken lived most of the week, Lois joining him for social functions and City dinners.

It was a good life and they were happy people. There was little to distinguish the Hunters from other affluent couples like them.

Ken and Lois were sitting by the fire in the lounge after Sunday lunch. They often went to church, but that day they hadn't. When the children were home or they had guests, Sunday lunch took the form of the traditional roast, but today, following a dinner party the night before, they had cold ham and salads and Ken was now nodding over the Sunday papers. Lois was looking at the TV guide to see if there was anything worth watching on the box. Outside, the rain was pouring down. Winter was already setting in. Lois thought of Oliver, his forlorn van, and the two hapless pups. Once again she felt uneasy.

'How much would an engine cost?' she asked, and Ken, jerking himself awake, looked at her.

'An *engine*? What sort of engine?'

'An engine for a car—a van, as a matter of fact.'

'What on earth do you want to know that for?'

Lois tossed aside the TV guide and poured coffee from the pot on the table by her side. She passed Ken his and then poured herself a cup.

'There's a poor man living in a van which has no engine. He wants to go to Cornwall. If he could get his van working, he could be off and find a job.'

'But how do you know this man?'

'He was begging outside the supermarket.' Lois paused and, brow furrowed, flicked back her hair as though she was trying to recall the occasion she'd first set eyes on Oliver. 'He wasn't actually *begging*. He was sitting on the pavement outside the supermarket. What touched me was that he had two small puppies who were snuggling up to him to get warm. I think it was the puppies that really got to me . . .' She looked defiantly across at Ken. 'Still does.'

Ken finished his coffee and put down his cup.

'But how do you know where he lives?'

'I gave him a lift home. I met him on the way . . .'

'You picked up a strange man!'

'Listen, Ken. I trusted him. He's not your typical beggar. His name's Oliver and I really think that if he can get to Cornwall he will find a better life. The engine in his van broke down and he's waiting for another from a scrap merchant who took the old one.'

Ken leaned back and studied the fire. He was a tall, thin, attractive man with blond hair, slightly balding. However, it seemed to enhance his good looks—or, rather, in the opinion of Lois it did. He had blue eyes and a pleasant, friendly, confident expression, and she always felt proud of him and glad to be seen in his company. Ken was the thoughtful type and he appeared to be thinking deeply now.

'Did he ask you for money for the engine?'

'Oh, no, not at all. There's something quite *dignified* about him.'

'I don't see how you can be dignified *and* a beggar.' Ken tried to sound reasonable.

'A lot of people on the streets don't like

20

being there. Ken, compared to us, Oliver has nothing. Do you think a couple of hundred pounds would buy a new engine?'

Ken rubbed his chin.

'I think you could get a second- or perhaps third-hand one for about eighty pounds, but I'm not sure that's what you should be doing. He probably wants the money for drugs.'

'Ken, don't be so unfair!' Lois exclaimed angrily. 'You just have all these preconceived ideas about people, based on prejudice.'

'My dear Lois,' Ken impatiently crossed one foot over the other and balanced his chin on the tips of his fingers, 'I don't know what else to think about someone who sits on the pavement outside the supermarket, apparently waiting for pennies, or perhaps pound coins, to drop into his lap. I haven't seen him and I don't know him, but I have seen a lot of people like him and I know—we all know—the reason they're there is that most likely they are drug addicts and want the money to feed their habits. How long have you known him?'

'I don't *know* him,' Lois protested. 'I've met him a couple of times, talked to him, seen his van. I'd very much like to help him get a start in life, Ken. It would make me feel better. I mean, if eighty pounds . . .'

'Well . . .' Ken shrugged and, now fully awake, put his hands behind his head. 'If that's what you want to do, ask him how much it will cost and then say you will pay whoever

21

provides the engine direct. Don't just give him the money.'

'Ken, darling, you *are* brilliant.' Lois rose, flew over to him and kissed him. Then she perched on the arm of the chair and stroked his face. 'And kind. Do you know that *Brief Encounter*'s on in a few minutes? Would you like to see it again?'

* * *

The following morning Ken went back to London, driving himself as usual. After a day doing chores and seeing to some matters locally, Lois climbed into the Range Rover and, with a sense of purpose, headed for the small town of Stinsbury. She approached with some excitement the place where she had last seen Oliver and his van. She was excited because it felt good to be helping somebody, helping to change their lives and not just being a smug lady bountiful, salving her own conscience by doling out a few tins of dog meat and some coins. Once Oliver had his van going he would be out of her life.

It gave her a feeling of wellbeing. She would really be helping to put someone on their way. It would be nice, too, for the puppies to have a proper home.

When she saw Oliver she would say it was her husband's suggestion—put the onus on Ken—and then offer to go with him to the scrap merchant and select a new engine. Of course he wouldn't be with the van at the moment. He would most likely be outside the supermarket, or on his way home, and she realized it was important to be tactful, not patronizing. She might even suggest that, if he wished, he could pay the money back when circumstances permitted. That would save his pride. It was about four o'clock and she reckoned that in this appalling weather he'd be back around five in time to give the dogs a run round, light his lamp and prepare his frugal meal. What a wretched existence! What a . . .

Lois nearly drove past the lay-by because she hadn't recognized it. Expecting to see a small brown van parked on the right-hand side, she now realized the space it had formerly occupied was empty. She braked, stopped and stared. There was no doubt that she was in the right place because the deserted caravan was still there, but of the van there was no sign.

Lois pulled into the lay-by and went over to inspect the spot where she'd examined the van with Oliver a few days before. The ground was damp and flattened, the grass where the van had stood was a slightly different colour. There was no doubt that it had stood there but did so no longer.

Lois went slowly back to her car and sat for some time thinking. Maybe the police had moved him on. She drove on up the hill and into Stinsbury, turning at the top into the car park by the supermarket. Perhaps the car dealer had moved the van to fit a new engine. But she knew she was kidding herself, and as she looked at the space where he used to sit, she saw it was empty. Oliver and the puppies had gone, and although in a way she was glad, she knew she would miss him. Somehow, there had been unfinished business between them.

CHAPTER TWO

Lois adjusted her stirrup and, with Ted holding on to the reins, she gained a foothold and leapt agilely on to the back of her horse, Whisper.

'All right now, Mrs Hunter?' Ted enquired.

Lois prodded the stirrup with her foot and nodded.

'Fine thanks, Ted. You'd better get mounted or you'll be late.'

Ted, already in his riding clothes, raised his hand and returned to the stables, re-emerging a few moments later on his horse.

Lois sat a little apart from the rest gathered in front of the house for the weekly meet of the Stinsbury Vale Hunt. Her stirrup still felt a little uncomfortable, the left one higher than the right, despite the adjustment. She wriggled a bit more in her saddle to try and get equilibrium.

The hunt met at different venues. Today it was their turn. She and Ken didn't ride every week, and sometimes she rode without him. These days, however, some of the pleasure had gone because of the protesters belonging to the anti blood sports lobby, some of whose members were sure to show up on every occasion, waving their ridiculous banners and hurling insults.

Lois was incensed by the anti blood sports lobby. Most of them didn't know what they were talking about; what a menace the red fox was in the countryside to lambs, chickens and other innocent prey. In effect, it was a kindness to cull them, better and more compassionate than letting them die of disease, creeping away to suffer painfully in their lairs.

Of course the fanatics said that was what the wounded fox did; but how did they know? How the hell did they know?

The previous season they'd only killed two foxes; most of them had gone to ground, got clean away and, although she didn't enjoy the kill, the master of the hunt made sure that the cornered fox was speedily and mercifully despatched.

Lois loved the hunt: loved the dressing up; the customs and formality; the quaint time-honoured courtesies of the participants; the rituals; the stirrup cup drunk just before they set off, and being offered around now by Beverley.

Beverley didn't hunt, but Neal did. The hunt was a democratic affair, not merely for the rich or upper classes as some antagonists insisted. Most of the members of the Stinsbury Vale Hunt were farmers, their workers and families. Anyone could join in and have a good time.

For Lois there was nothing to compare to a brisk gallop across the bare fields on a bright winter's morning, the ground still hard with frost, the frozen cobwebs glinting in the hedges like snowflake crystals.

There was a movement among the riders towards the gate. The hounds, which had been milling around, formed themselves into a more or less orderly pack. Beverley collected the empty stirrup cups and then riders and hounds set off towards the gates. As anticipated, the hunt was met with banners and placards held aloft by a small body of protesters, among whom were several familiar faces. The customary policeman was standing at the back of the small crowd to ensure that things didn't get out of hand. He was actually laughing and joking with some of the protesters, he knew them so well. By now the whole thing was almost a ritual and the majority of the riders could ignore it. But Lois hated it still, a small knot always forming in her stomach as she ran the gauntlet of the well-disciplined but, nevertheless, abusive mob.

'Killers!' 'Murderers!' The usual epithets were flung at the riders as, heads down, they pressed on towards the fields where, in time, they would be able to escape their persecutors. Ken usually rode alongside Lois as they ran into the mob, and they trotted together for a while exchanging grimaces. Then, as they came to the field, Ken drew ahead—he always liked to be among the leaders of the pack—and, with a sigh of relief as the knot untightened, Lois cantered into the field. Behind her, Ted leapt off his horse and shut the gate and, as Lois glanced back at the mob who had gathered to send catcalls after the hunt she glimpsed, or thought she glimpsed, a familiar face: dark hair, stubbled chin, burning eyes, his mouth framed by his hand opened wide as he called abuse.

The shock of recognition seemed to jolt her memory and she slowed down, slightly turned Whisper and looked again as the man lowered his hand and said something to a female companion at his side. No, it wasn't him; but it was very like him.

She wondered what had happened to Oliver. Since that time the previous October he had completely slipped her mind, yet now she had no difficulty recalling his name and here she was thinking about him again and, of course, his dogs. They would now be grown-up, no longer wriggling puppies whose soulful expressions had so touched her heart. It was the dogs she'd been interested in, concerned about. Not Oliver.

Ahead of her she heard the master's call. The pack had speeded up. It seemed they'd scented a fox and the hunt was on.

*　　*　　*

The day was drawing in when, tired but exhilarated, Lois, with Ken and Ted, returned to the stables. The hounds had been taken back to their kennels, the horses had been collected in their boxes by their various owners. Everyone had had a good day—except, possibly, the fox, who had been chased a fair distance but had managed to evade his pursuers by going to ground.

In a way, Lois wished that that was always the case. The fox gave everyone a good run and then got away. Surely that would take care of the protesters? But maybe it wouldn't. If they didn't have that to protest about they would find something else. They would go off and disrupt the construction of highways or find some other troublesome way of saving the planet. There were a hard core of professional protesters who would never be appeased.

Usually after a meet the Hunters invited people back for sandwiches and drinks, but today Lois's sister, Wendy, was arriving. In fact, judging by the car parked in the drive, she

28

had already arrived.

Leaving Ted to rub down Whisper, feed and stable her, Lois shouted the news of Wendy's arrival to Ken and ran into the house where Beverley confirmed that Wendy, together with her boyfriend, had been there some time. They were in the drawing room having a cup of tea.

Briefly Lois discussed dinner with Beverley and then flew along the hall and threw open the drawing-room door. Wendy and Tim were lying on the couch, arms round each other, shoes off, eyes on the TV screen. By their side was a table with teacups, but the tea, by the look of things, had not yet been poured. Tim looked asleep, his head on Wendy's shoulder, but when she saw Lois, Wendy unceremoniously pushed him away and got up to throw her arms round her sister.

'Hi!'

'Hi!'

Hugs, kisses. The two sisters were close, only a couple of years between them. They were also alike to look at: short fair hair, blue eyes deeply recessed, high cheek bones. People often took them for twins. Wendy was two years younger than Lois, the spoilt, irresponsible one towards whom Lois had always felt protective—and still did.

Lois glanced towards Tim who got to his feet and came shuffling towards her in his socks, hand outstretched, still half-asleep. He was a large, friendly man, an auctioneer with a posh London auction house, an expert in antiques who liked to tour the countryside in his time off looking for bargains. Wendy was a publicist with a publishing company, having been for many years a journalist on a provincial newspaper.

'Sorry I was out,' Lois said.

Tim leaned towards her and kissed her on the cheek. 'How was the hunt?'

'Fine.' Lois glanced nervously at Wendy. Tim came from a county family and would like to have hunted, but Wendy was a firm opponent of blood sports, so the topic was almost always taboo when they came to stay. Lois was rather sorry that Wendy had arrived on a day when there was a meet. Usually she tried to avoid it. Wendy, however, had turned her attention to the tea tray and was pouring from a large silver pot.

'Tim and I are getting married,' she said, looking up.

'Wendy! That's wonderful.' As Tim was still standing near her, Lois clasped him by the arm and hugged him again. 'When?'

'Well . . .' Tim smiled ruefully at Wendy. 'Wendy wants to do it straight away at a register office.'

'We've waited long enough,' Wendy said, passing a cup to Lois.

'I know my parents would like a big wedding, and so would your mum.'

30

'Yes, but they're not getting married.'

'It *is* a big occasion.' Tim, cup in hand, sat down. 'I'd like it too.'

'A big wedding would be fun.' Lois leaned forward eagerly in her chair. 'We haven't had a really big wedding . . .'

'Since yours,' Wendy said. 'But I am so much older than you were.'

'That doesn't matter at all, does it, Tim?'

Tim shook his head.

'Of course I want what Wendy wants, and a wedding is more important for a woman, but, yes, I think a big wedding would be nice.'

'What do you mean, it's "more important for a woman"?' Wendy looked at him sharply and moved away from him. 'It seems to me that it's more important for *you*, if you want to make a fuss about it . . .'

'Darling,'—Tim reached out for her hand—'I want to do what you want to do. Really.'

'I think I'll go and change.' Lois, sensing a row, got up and made for the door. 'Do help yourself to more tea.'

*   *   *

'I can't think why they're getting married,' Ken said later in the privacy of their bedroom. 'They've done nothing but argue all evening.'

'They always do.' Lois undid her necklace, removed her dress and, putting on a robe, sat down in front of the mirror and began to

31

cream her face. 'I think they like to have something to quarrel about, and what could be better than what sort of wedding to have?'

'Beats me.' Ken got into his pyjamas and went to the bathroom from where Lois could hear the sound of him brushing his teeth.

It had been a nervy evening with Wendy and Tim bickering and another couple they'd asked to dinner, the Woodhouses who lived along the road, clearly ill at ease. As if that wasn't enough the topic of hunting came up because the Labour Party had announced that if they won the election they would abolish it, and that led to Ken and Wendy screaming at each other, the Woodhouses looking terribly nervous and Tim drinking too much until he could barely stagger away from the table.

'I do *like* Tim,' Lois said as Ken came back into the bedroom and got into bed. 'But sometimes I wonder if he's right for Wendy. He's so laid-back and easy-going.'

Ken pulled the duvet up to his chin. 'She's leaving it a bit late.'

'What do you mean?'

'Darling, she's only two years younger than you and you've got two children of fourteen. She must feel the biological clock ticking away.'

'I don't even know that she wants children.'

'I think you should have a talk to her.' Ken gave a huge yawn. 'Try and sort her out. Although, frankly, I doubt if that's possible.'

Ken and Wendy didn't really get on, or rather there was a sort of love/hate relationship because they differed about so many important things. Ken called Wendy a champagne socialist, which in a way she was, and then there was the blood sports thing. On the other hand, she was pretty and amusing, and Ken liked pretty, amusing women.

'Personally, I think they should rush off to the register office, if that's what she wants, and get it over. It's odd, don't you think,' Lois turned to look at Ken, 'for a man to want a large wedding when the woman doesn't? It's usually the other way round.'

*　　*　　*

The boy was nineteen but he looked a lot younger. He had been on drugs since he was about fifteen and was an habitual offender. He stole to be able to feed his habit. Even a place like charming, rural Stinsbury with its ancient church and abbey, its mainly well-heeled, law-abiding citizens, its small specialist shops and twee boutiques had a drug problem. There was a youth centre attached to the church, but there was little other entertainment; no cinema, no regular bus service to the nearest town of any size, which was Salisbury, nearly thirty miles away.

There was absolutely nothing for the youth of Stinsbury to do in their leisure time unless they were extremely disciplined or motivated, or had especially caring parents, and so every week, every day when it sat, the court was bursting with young people with problems. The chairman of the bench was the headmaster of the local school and he always liked to come down hard on drug addicts. He thought the only thing to do was to punish them heavily, lock them up, put them away. He had a major problem in his own school, so his methods couldn't have been so successful. Many people were critical of his old-fashioned ideas and thought he should take early retirement and give someone more progressive and younger a chance.

The trouble with people with set ideas was that they always thought they were right.

The youth was put into temporary custody to await psychiatric and welfare officers' reports. He was immediately succeeded by a girl with a similar problem. She too was nineteen and had been before the bench many times. Lois sighed and made a note on the pad in front of her. She was, in fact, a little dispirited, depressed really. Not like her usual self at all. She was worried about Wendy and Tim who had continued to bicker most of Sunday. In the afternoon, thinking her sister to be alone—Tim having set out on a walk after lunch—Lois went along to the guest room, gently pushed open the door in case Wendy was asleep, and found the pair energetically making love. Fortunately, their loud grunts had obscured the noise she made on entry so she had speedily exited.

By dinner Wendy had returned to the fray, only this time she had agreed to a big wedding—indeed, seemed positively enthused by it, but now they couldn't decide when to have it or where. That night Lois had a headache verging on migraine. The lovers had left early in the morning to go to their respective jobs, and Lois had set out for her day at court.

She had been flattered when, a year or so ago, she had been asked to be a magistrate. It gave her a sense of responsibility as a citizen, a feeling that somehow she had arrived. It was true that they had first asked Ken, who was chairman of the local Rotary Club, but he had pleaded pressure of work beside his duties with the Rotarians and as joint master of the Stinsbury Vale Hunt. In fact, Ken had suggested Lois, which took a bit of the gilt off the gingerbread, but she had been accepted with enthusiasm, the senior magistrates assuring her that they had asked themselves why they hadn't thought of her before. It was worthwhile work, but it was also sad to see so many unresolved social issues that led to so many people appearing before the magistrates. Ken said that the Tories came down hard on crime, but Lois wondered if that was the answer.

She wondered, really, what was the answer to so many problems that, after all, didn't actually affect one.

She, Lois Hunter, had a loving husband, two wonderful children, a lovely home, no financial problems. Sometimes you felt you were so fortunate that you wondered what you had done to deserve it.

The answer was nothing. It had just happened.

* * *

The problems of the nineteen-year-old drug addict took up most of the rest of the afternoon. Finally she was put on remand to allow time for new reports from the psychiatrist and social worker. It was oppressive in the court and Lois was ready for her tea when they rose at four and gathered in the magistrates' room for a discussion and, usually, refreshments. But today she felt like getting away, so when John Garfield, the chairman, excused himself on the grounds of a meeting after school, Lois turned to her fellow magistrate Madge Cooper, who was gathering her papers together, and suggested tea in a local café.

'Good idea,' Madge said. 'It was terribly hot in that court today. We'll have to ask them to do something about the air conditioning.'

'I thought so too. I must confess, I nearly

fell asleep at one point as Mary Barnes went on and on.' She was referring to the girl's solicitor, a firm advocate of lost causes who had a touching faith in the innocence of her young clients, most of whom were habitual offenders.

Ensconced in a nearby teashop, the women ordered tea and a selection of home-made cakes.

'I really shouldn't,' Madge said with a wry grin, loosening her coat.

'Nor should I.' Lois took her fleece-lined jacket off and put it over the back of her chair. She wore a purple polo-necked sweater with a grey tweed skirt, a thick gold chain round her neck. As always, she looked perfectly turned out. Never saw her any other way, Madge thought, gazing enviously at her companion.

'You've no need to worry.'

'I have to be careful,' Lois insisted and smiled at Madge, who was a comparatively new friend, one she had made since joining the bench. She was a single woman who ran her own farm which she had inherited from her father and which had been in the family for five generations. She was about forty-five, not beautiful, not even especially good-looking, but with a friendly, humorous face, hair going grey, and a rather thick, stocky figure. As well as her farming, she was into a number of good causes, chairwoman of this and that organization, a leading light in the NFU, and

37

she also hunted with the Stinsbury Vale. Madge was unlike any of Lois's other friends, most of whom were comparatively wealthy, women with families and busy husbands; women like her.

It was true that one tended to meet people with similar lifestyles. Usually you met them through your husband or the children's schools. A lot of Lois's friends were London-based and came for weekends. Madge was a refreshing contrast to most of the women Lois knew; a brisk, practical woman, yet with a warm and sympathetic personality.

They discussed the cases they'd just dealt with, the problematical nineteen-year-old, which made Madge sigh.

'Sometimes I'm glad I didn't have children. It's a very depressing time to be young.'

'They needn't *all* be like that,' Lois said, sitting back as the waitress brought their tea and a plate of tempting, fattening-looking cakes. 'Mind you, I don't suppose we've reached the dangerous time with the boys. I hope we never do.'

Madge, tucking into her fresh cream cake, noticed her friend's anxious expression. She valued the friendship as much as Lois. It gave her a new dimension. Took her away from the farming community with whom she spent most of her social as well as working hours. She admired Lois: her looks, the classic English beauty, fair skin, so blonde, perfect white teeth, a flawless complexion. She was invariably well-groomed; always smiling, calm, so in control. There was an aura of glamour about her. Deep down, Madge thought herself a bit of a mess and would occasionally daydream about how nice it must be to be like Lois with a lovely house, a successful husband, two handsome, clever children and no money worries. Since the BSE scare hardly a farmer in Dorset had been unaffected by financial trouble; Madge had lost half her herd of Friesian dairy cows.

She finished her cake and licked the fork, eyeing the plate in front of her and wishing she dared have another. Lois, she noticed, had selected one of the least calorific cakes on the plate. Why was it that some people were incurably greedy even though they hated being overweight, whereas others always seemed to be able to keep themselves under control? Maybe if you were overweight and careless about your appearance, as she was, simply by not being able to say 'no', you lost the incentive to care about how you looked?

'But you're happy with the boys' school?'

'Oh, very happy. It's only one of the minor public schools, but we think that has an advantage. It's not so stressful academically and the pastoral care is awfully good. Ken went there, and he loved it. By the way, Wendy and Tim have decided to tie the knot.'

'That's lovely.' Madge smiled her warm

smile and sipped her tea. She decided, after all, to have another cream cake and reached for one.

'When?'

'We're not sure. They spent the whole weekend arguing about it.'

'But haven't they been together for some time?'

'Oh, ages.' Lois poured herself fresh tea. 'At least five years.'

'I suppose they want children?'

'Wendy didn't say. She wanted to go to a register office and get it over, but Tim is keen to have a big wedding.'

'Isn't that a bit unusual?'

'Tim is *very* conventional. His father is deputy sheriff of the county. Besides, I think he wants to show Wendy off. She'll make a lovely bride—if they get that far,' Lois concluded, a note of doubt creeping into her voice.

Madge put out a hand and snatched the bill before Lois had time to get to it.

'So you don't think they'll get married?'

'Sometimes I think they're a bit past it— past the romantic stage, that is. They're beginning to see the cracks in each other.'

'But doesn't that happen to everyone?'

'Yes, it happens; but after you've been married a few years you have children, usually, and a host of other things have opened up. When there's just two of you it's very intense.'

40

'I hadn't considered that.' Madge looked thoughtful. She shot out her arm and glanced at her watch. 'Oh, well, milking time.'

'I just want to pop into the supermarket.' Lois rose and put on her coat. 'Are you parked in the car park?'

Madge nodded and walked over to the counter to pay the bill.

'The evenings are getting lighter.' Lois drew on her gloves, looking up at the sky as they stood on the pavement outside. 'There's a touch of spring in the air. Madge, you must come and have a meal with us. It's been a long time.'

'I'd love that.'

'Maybe when Tim and Wendy are down again. Then you can give me some idea about what you think of the prospects for their marriage.'

'Oh, I wouldn't presume to do that!' Madge giggled as they walked towards the supermarket car park. 'I'm hardly an expert on the subject.'

'You're very shrewd though.' Lois glanced at her. 'I don't think you miss much.'

'That's a kind thing to say.' Madge looked around for her car while Lois fished in her pocket for her shopping list. Ahead of them the lights blazed from the supermarket window and, at that moment, she saw stretched on the ground a familiar semi-recumbent figure with a dog sitting by his side.

She pulled up suddenly, staring in front of her.

'What is it?' Madge immediately looked concerned. Lois continued to stare at the man. Oliver. No doubt.

'You've changed colour, Lois,' Madge went on. 'Are you all right?'

'Perfectly.' Lois, head down, hurried past the supermarket entrance. 'It's just someone I didn't want to see.'

'That's not like you.' Madge was looking round, curious as to who it was Lois wished to avoid.

'It's stupid . . .' Lois stopped beside her car. 'I'll explain it all to you one day.'

'Aren't you going to shop?' Madge asked.

'Not right now.'

Lois found as she put the key in the lock that her hands were trembling. Madge was still watching her with concern.

'Are you *sure* you're OK?'

'Perfectly sure. Perfectly OK.' Lois attempted a smile. Then she got into the car, opened the window and leaned out. 'See you next week. Thursday, I think it is?'

'Yes, Thursday.' Madge stood back and waved. 'Take care now.'

She watched as Lois drove off. Then she looked round again but could see no one except a beggar half lying, half sitting on the pavement in front of the supermarket, his hand in the frayed collar of a dog by his side.

42

＊　　　＊　　　＊

Lois couldn't explain what had got into her. She was still shaking. She put her foot on the brake so as not to drive too fast. She realized that her reaction to seeing Oliver was quite over the top. It was like seeing a ghost, and yet there was the fact that only a few days before she thought she'd seen him among the anti-hunting protesters shouting abuse. Now she was sure it was him.

She didn't want to get involved again, particularly if he was a hunt saboteur. Life was too happy, too secure, and she felt in some weird way that Oliver threatened it. She knew it was absurd and she wouldn't have been able to explain why. But that's how she felt.

She had been very near Oliver and she was sure he'd seen her. That made her feel worse. She slowed down and stopped the car by the side of the road, opposite the lay-by where he'd kept his van. But it was empty. The shuttered caravan had gone too. She sat for a while, taking deep breaths. Slowly she began to feel less agitated, her normal calm and good sense returning.

Oliver posed no threat at all, either to her or her wellbeing. Why, then, had the sight of him produced such confusion, the urge to flee?

She reversed her car into the clearing, turned and headed back up the hill towards Stinsbury. Her reaction had been quite ridiculous, and unless she faced it she would never understand the occasion or herself.

Lois parked the car, got out, fished in her pocket once again for her shopping list and walked up to the rack of trolleys.

Oliver sat upright, hands hugging his knees, looking at her. Lois paused beside him.

'Hello!' she said with a smile, looking down. 'It is Oliver, isn't it?'

'I thought you were going to ignore me, Mrs Hunter.'

'Oh!' She felt nonplussed. He had seen her.

'I suppose you were with someone and didn't want her to know that you knew me.'

'It wasn't like that at all!' Lois exclaimed. But still she didn't attempt to explain what had happened. 'How are you, Oliver?'

'Not so good.' He shook his head.

Lois looked at the dog, an engaging mongrel in whom it was difficult, but just possible, to recognize the pup it had been a mere six months before.

'Did you get to Cornwall?'

Oliver nodded. 'Things didn't work out.'

'I'm sorry. Have you ... have you still got the van?'

'That's why I came back here. I'm on my way home to the north. My pal who let me have a new engine last time—well, not new, a very old engine, as a matter of fact—has let me leave the van in his scrap yard while he looks for another one. Last year I was moved on by

44

the police.'

'I wondered why you'd left so abruptly.'

Lois bent down to pat the head of the dog. 'Is this one of the pups?'

He nodded.

'And the other?' Lois stroked its head again. It licked her hand and she recognized in its expression the adoring look of the puppy that had so moved her.

'I had to leave him behind. You can see the size of this one. Two is too much to handle. I left him in a good home.'

Lois nodded as if in agreement. 'Well, good luck this time, Oliver.'

'Thanks, Mrs Hunter.'

She moved away into the store. She felt she had to suppress her emotions, her irrational, confused emotions about this person. Because they were irrational and they were confused. She hardly knew him.

She had felt sorry for the puppies, and now she felt sorry for the dog one of them had become. This time she bought half a dozen tins of dog food in addition to the ones she got for her own dogs. She got a pound of ham and a loaf of bread, some bars of chocolate, and when she reached the checkout she put them in a separate carrier bag. Into the bag she tucked a twenty-pound note.

Outside he was looking expectantly at the door. He'd known that she wouldn't let him down. Even the dog looked eagerly up at her,

45

wagging its tail, as she walked towards them.
Lois reached down and Oliver took the bag
from her.

'Thanks, Mrs Hunter.' He peered inside the
bag.

'Oliver, I do hope this will help you on your
way. Frankly, I feel disappointed to see you
here again.'

'Maybe that's why you moved on?' He
looked quizzically up at her. 'The first time . . .
You were with a lady; I'm sure you didn't want
her to know that you knew someone like me.'

'I don't *know* you!' she cried indignantly,
aware of a sense of outrage. 'I think we only
met two or three times.'

'That's true. But you stood out. You were
very kind to me. I remembered you in
particular for being so nice, so understanding,
so kind to the pups. Few people would go out
of their way to give me a lift.'

Lois breathed deeply.

'I can give you a lift back now, if you like.'
She looked up at the darkening sky bearing the
threat of rain. 'From here to the scrap yard is a
pretty long walk.'

*　　*　　*

The man looked questioningly up at the
Range Rover as it came to a stop beside
Oliver's battered van. Oliver opened the door
and got out one side with his carrier bags; the

dog leapt for freedom and started running round the yard.

'This is Clifford, Mrs Hunter,' Oliver said, indicating the scrap merchant.

'How do you do?' Lois politely offered her hand, but Clifford wiped his greasy palm on his overall and shook his head.

'I've got grease all over me hands, ma'am.'

'So,' Lois pursed her lips and looked at the van, 'what does it need this time?'

'It's fit only for scrap. Care to buy it for a fiver?' Clifford grinned. He had a particularly engaging smile. Lois could understand why Oliver had trusted him.

'I don't think so,' Lois shook her head, the shadow of a smile on her lips.

'Can't be mended then?' Oliver looked downcast.

'It will only get you a few miles at most.'

'At least I can still sleep in it.'

'Yes, but I can't keep you here, mate. I'd have everybody dossing down here if news got round.'

'But how can he move it?' Lois felt distressed. 'Where can he go?'

Clifford shrugged and wiped his hands on a rag he had produced from the pocket of his dungarees.

'He can stay here for a day or two, but no longer. You best be on your way home, mate, if you ask me. Hitch a lift.'

Oliver shook his head. 'No chance at all of

saving it?'

'Look, if you give me a hundred quid, maybe I can fix it enough to take you, say, as far as Birmingham. What will you do then?'

'At least it gives me somewhere to sleep. Except that I haven't got a hundred pounds.'

'I really must go,' Lois said, suddenly aware of a sense of the ground opening under her, sucking her down into some swirling, subterranean tide. She turned to Clifford.

'Let him stay here for a day or so, to give me time to think about it. I don't want Oliver to be homeless, but I don't want to throw my money away. How much will a new van cost?' Hastily she corrected herself. 'That is to say, not a *new* van but one ... you know, that will get him home?'

Clifford frowned. 'You're talking about five hundred pounds minimum, Mrs Hunter.' He gestured airily at the motley scraps of metal surrounding them. 'I'll have to see which one I can make roadworthy, then I'll give you an estimate.'

'It's very good of you,' Oliver began, but Lois waved a hand towards him.

'I haven't *done* anything yet. I shall have to discuss this with my husband.' She paused and looked searchingly at him. 'Tell me the truth, Oliver. Why don't you hitchhike home? You could be there in a couple of days. Where was it you said you lived?'

'I didn't!' Oliver's expression remained

obstinate.

'You said you came from the north.'

'That's all I said, Mrs Hunter.'

'Well, if you want to be mysterious . . .'

'I don't want your help anyway, Lady Bountiful. They say charity is cold.'

'Oh, come on, mate!' Clifford expostulated angrily. 'Here's someone very kindly wanting to give you a leg up and you don't co-operate with her. I tell you, I'm not doing anything more for you if you're going to be difficult, and you can take yourself and your dog off here as soon as the lady's gone . . .'

'Just let him stay for a couple of nights,' Lois pleaded. 'I'll discuss it with my husband, talk to Oliver again, and think about it. We have enough people on the streets without adding to them. If you can come up with an estimate and telephone me, I'll let you know.' She turned to Oliver, aware of the pain and resentment in his eyes. 'Is that all right, Oliver? I won't ask any questions. I don't want to patronize you. I just want to do what I can to help get you on your way.'

As she turned towards the car, Clifford called: 'Don't forget to give me your telephone number, Mrs Hunter.'

'It's 434572,' Lois said as she got into the car.

Clifford stepped back and watched her drive out of the yard.

'That's a *very* nice lady,' he murmured,

looking sideways at Oliver. 'It seems to me that if you play your cards right you could be on to a good thing, mate. Fix you up with a nice van, she will, and see you on your way, maybe with a bit of extra cash.'

As Oliver remained silent, scowling, his lips pursed, Clifford turned away.

'You'd be mad if you looked a gift horse in the mouth, you daft bugger. The Hunters are about the richest people living round here. They're absolutely rolling with cash.'

CHAPTER THREE

It was not the best moment to bring this up, but Lois was beset by a feeling of urgency, of time passing. Ken had got home late and they were having a late supper. He wanted to relax and unwind, and so did she, but if she didn't let Clifford know, Oliver would be homeless. Already several days had passed since her visit to the scrap yard. On Saturday they had attended a wedding in Bristol, stayed overnight, driven to have Sunday lunch with friends in Gloucestershire, and then Ken had gone to a meeting in connection with the parish council.

The matter had been on her mind all weekend, but the right moment just seemed to evade her, maybe because she hated rows and was nervous about Ken's reaction. Usually she liked to talk things over with Ken because he was a good-tempered, level-headed sort of man, but this business with Oliver seemed slightly ludicrous even to her. Somehow she thought Ken would fly off.

She was right. Ken did.

'First of all you talked about buying this bloke a new engine, now you want to buy him a new car.'

'It's not a car. It's a van.'

Ken reached for the bottle of wine in the centre of the kitchen table and refilled his glass. Hers had remained untouched.

'Why does he have to have a van?'

'Because he lives in it.'

'Lois, forgive me, but I really can't understand the obsession you have with this vagrant . . .'

'I have *not* got an obsession with him,' she replied heatedly. 'I merely want to help someone who has nothing, whereas,' she looked wildly around her, 'we have everything.'

'But I thought he'd left the area?'

'He's come back. He wants to go home.'

'Then offer him the train fare, for goodness sake.'

'Ken, I just want your advice. I don't want your criticism. I'm sorry I ever mentioned it to you.'

'Darling!' Ken leaned back and held out his arms. 'Be reasonable. You mentioned it to me

51

because you said you wanted my advice and I gave it to you. It's not a question of money, is it?'

'No, of course money's not the issue.'

'If you'd wanted, you could just have written out a cheque and that would have been the end of the matter. For some reason you've taken this . . . this outcast to your heart.'

'I have not!' she said indignantly. 'Frankly, I was more concerned about the two pups he had.'

'And has he still got them?'

'He's got one and it's grown up. There is also something quite touching about him . . . I don't know how to explain it.'

'What sort of age is he?' Ken asked curiously.

'Oh, darling, it's nothing like *that*! I don't fancy him or anything.'

'They say middle-aged women do get fantasies.'

'I am not middle-aged and I am not fantasizing. If you'd seen him you'd probably have felt the same.'

'I'm darn sure I wouldn't.' Ken got up and, going to the stove, helped himself to more mashed potato from a saucepan. He held out the spoon to Lois, but she shook her head and pushed her plate away. 'What do you think I should do, Ken?'

'Offer him the fare home. Get rid of him.'

'I think you're being insensitive, Ken.'

'And I think you're a fool to get yourself involved with a beggar from the streets, someone you know absolutely nothing about. You'd think as a magistrate you'd know better. It's strange, isn't it, how he disappears and then reappears again? He must have realized you would be an easy touch.'

'The man who keeps the scrap yard helped him last time. I think he thought he would do the same this time.'

'And will he?' Ken sat down and helped himself liberally to pickle to go with his cold meat and mashed potatoes, a welcome late-night supper prepared for them by Beverley.

'Not without money. I have to let him know because he's letting Oliver stay in his scrap yard in the old van.'

'Why can't he go on staying there?'

'Because he can't. I mean, it stands to reason. If it got out that the scrap dealer had let someone camp on his land, every passing stranger would want to take up residence.'

'Exactly. What a sensible man. He's not getting involved and neither should you. This beggar, this Oliver, only came back here because he knew you were a softie. Now, please, my dear, do not bring up this subject again or I think perhaps I shall lose control of myself.'

*   *   *

That night they stuck rigidly to their respective sides of the large double bed. Often they made gentle love on their weekends together, but not tonight. Lois lay in the dark, aware from his breathing that he too was awake. She wanted to reach out but couldn't. She thought Ken was unfair, unreasonable, lacking in compassion.

Lois always voted Conservative like the rest of their friends—with the exception of Wendy, who supported actress-turned-politician Glenda Jackson, her local MP in Hampstead.

Yet Lois herself was disillusioned with the Conservatives. She was incensed at the number of beggars on the streets, of which Oliver was only one tiny manifestation. Who had ever seen beggars on the street ten years ago?

However, she agreed with Ken that the Tories knew how to run the country. He was a banker and had his finger on the financial pulse. The economy, he assured her, would go to pot under a Labour Government. They couldn't manage money.

The trouble with the Hunters was that they had too much of it. Lois had never known financial want and nor had Ken. Hopefully the boys would never know it either. Both her not inconsiderable fortune and Ken's were carefully invested. Her father had left both his daughters well off. It was ridiculous to bother about the trifling sum of money needed to repair the van, or even to buy a new one. She could have afforded a brand-new van without blinking. Given it to Oliver as a gift and told him to drive off.

So, why hadn't she? Simply because one didn't do that sort of thing. Charity wasn't enough. Look at all the handouts the Government gave. The thing was to help Oliver to stand on his own feet. That was real charity.

*　　　*　　　*

Ken was up before Lois the next morning. He had a swim in their indoor pool, made his own breakfast, and left before she was fully awake. Truthfully, she'd only got to sleep at about five and felt like a wrung-out rag when she tottered downstairs for a cup of tea, to find that Margaret, the daily woman, was already hard at work.

'Didn't sleep well, Mrs H?' she asked sympathetically, having flung her cigarette out of the kitchen door as soon as she heard the sound of her employer coming along the hall. Even then the kitchen reeked of smoke, but Lois wasn't fanatical about smoking as some people were. In truth, she was a tolerant person. Not really fanatical about anything. She knew quite well that Margaret smoked and nothing she could do or say would stop her. Besides which she didn't want to lose a good cleaner.

Lois, after exchanging a few words with Margaret, took her tea-tray back to bed, quite undecided as to what to do about Oliver. Ken, usually so helpful, such a good person to discuss things with, had got completely the wrong end of the stick. How ridiculous to entertain even a hint of jealousy about a beggar! There was not the slightest sexual attraction between herself and Oliver. Heavens, she'd hardly exchange a home and a husband like Ken, a way of life that she enjoyed, for someone who scraped a living off the streets.

It was insulting, and unsettling, even to think of it. Yes, it was very unsettling, somehow extremely so.

After her tea, Lois lay for a long time in her bath ruminating on life. She never really thought about it too much. She was a compassionate but not a very imaginative person. She never anticipated things that might happen to disturb the even tenor of her life: death or disease, losing Ken, or something happening to the boys.

Why, then, had she got so het up about a man in the street?

*   *   *

Lois had a sandwich lunch with Margaret and Bev, who had come in to discuss the programme for the week. Neal managed the estate while Beverley helped with the running of the house. She was an excellent cook whereas Lois was not. During the week, if Lois wasn't going out to attend a meeting or some function, dinner usually took the form of a tray on her lap in front of the TV. Invariably there were a couple of nights like these. Weekends were always frantic, and then she relied on Beverley's help.

Wendy had rung the night before to ask whether she and Tim might come down at the weekend to discuss the vexed question of the wedding. London or Stinsbury? There was something appealing about a large country wedding—Lois noted the word 'large' and already had a vision of a marquee on the lawn. Actually, she would quite enjoy it. Their mother would like it too. She led an active and fulfilling life in Sussex where she had a large bungalow overlooking the sea.

It was a more cheerful Lois, thinking about summer weddings—a visit to her dressmaker for a new outfit would be in order, and Ken always looked splendid in morning dress—who set out just before noon for the scrap yard to try and settle once and for all the matter of Oliver.

Yes, get him away, get him out of her system. He didn't belong. He didn't fit in.

Clifford, who seemed to be expecting her, welcomed Lois with clean hands and invited her to inspect a blue van similar to the brown in size which he just happened to have come across. He pronounced it a bargain at £1500.

'Fifteen hundred!' Lois gasped, looking doubtfully at the van. 'It seems an awful lot.'

'Frankly, Mrs Hunter,' Clifford puffed out his chest, 'I am offering it to you at an extremely good price because I think you have been very kind to Oliver and I want to do something to help him too. I am letting you have the van at cost, that is the price at which it was offered to me. There are not many ladies of your kind who would go out of their way to help a beggar.'

'Oh, I'm sure there are.'

'Not to *such* trouble, Mrs Hunter.'

'I was concerned about the dogs, that's all,' Lois said awkwardly. 'I mean, when they were little pups. I was just being sentimental about them.'

'I can understand that, but Oliver is very appealing too.' Clifford seemed inclined to chat and, arms akimbo, leaned against the side of the van on which Lois could now see an ugly dent that had been well patched up. 'He's not exactly your average beggar, is he?'

'I don't know what the "average beggar" is like. We really don't have too many about here.'

'They're a ruthless lot, I can tell you. Mostly feeding a drug habit. But you see, Oliver isn't on drugs.'

'Oh, isn't he?' Lois felt relieved, although— oddly enough—it was a possibility she had never seriously considered, even though it was not the first time the topic had come up.

'No, he is definitely not on drugs, Mrs Hunter, and, believe me, that is something. It's also the reason I wanted to help him. He doesn't speak much about his private life, but I think it's a sad one.'

'Do you know where he lives?'

Clifford shook his head.

'To tell you the truth, I know very little about him. He's not a person who talks much about himself. But that's not unusual. Travellers often tend to be secretive.'

'But I understood from Oliver, when I first met him six months ago that he was travelling from the north to Cornwall to see someone. He told me he was not a beggar but was reduced to begging for money because he couldn't claim his social security payments.'

'Well, I'm sure what he said then was true. He told me something similar.'

'So, what happened in Cornwall?'

'I have no idea, Mrs Hunter. As I told you, Oliver doesn't confide in me. But I suspect the trouble is mostly to do with his van, which also seems to be his home. He may come from the north, but he may not have a home in the north. Do you see what I'm saying?'

'I think so.' Arms folded, Lois began slowly to walk round the van. 'It's got a big dent in it.'

She pointed to the mark she had already noticed.

'That's why it's as cheap as it is, Mrs Hunter. If it were not for that mark, I'd be asking for something in the region of three thousand. The van was involved in a nasty smash, but all the serious damage has been repaired. To have a new body panel would have cost a lot more. You'd need a complete new section here, you see'—carefully he traced the outline of the front wing of the van that had been affected—'but as it is I've patched it up. Structurally, the van is in good nick.'

'And the engine?'

'The engine is in first-class order. For fifteen hundred you're getting a fine piece of merchandise, believe me, Mrs Hunter. I know you will never buy a car from me, but I wouldn't deceive you.'

Lois smiled.

'Why might I never buy a car from you?'

'Oh, *Mrs Hunter*,' Clifford turned and surveyed the pieces of twisted metal that made up his scrap yard. 'Ask yourself, now: is it likely?'

'I'll go and have a word with Oliver.' Lois suddenly felt as though a great weight had been lifted from her mind. 'How soon can you have the van ready?'

'You can drive it away today ... Well, perhaps tomorrow. Fill it up with petrol, pay the road tax and insurance, and you're ready to go.'

'Oh, there's that too, of course!' Lois gnawed at a fingernail. 'So, we're looking at a lot more than fifteen hundred, as we know Oliver has no money.'

'To be honest with you, Mrs Hunter,' Clifford removed a grubby baseball cap and scratched his head, 'a lot of travelling people don't bother with things like insurance and road tax, especially insurance. But it is best to be careful and, as you're concerned about Oliver, it would be a very nice gesture to be sure that he had a roadworthy vehicle that was fully insured.'

'Oh, I wouldn't dream of him going on the road without . . .'

'That's what I thought you'd say, Mrs Hunter,' Clifford nodded approvingly and rubbed the shiny surface of the blue van with the sleeve of his jumper. 'Well, once the money is paid—and I'd prefer cash, if that's all right with you—and the papers are in order, the van will be ready to be driven away.' Clifford paused as if he was about to produce a rabbit from his sweaty baseball cap. 'There's three months left on the MOT, so he'll have no trouble getting to Liverpool, or wherever it is he comes from.'

*   *   *

The die was cast. As she drove along the road

61

leading from the scrap yard to Stinsbury, Lois was aware of a glow of satisfaction at the prospect of a job well done. What was more, she decided she would say no more about the matter to Ken. They each had their own bank accounts and never questioned each other's financial arrangements. If he asked about Oliver—and she suspected it was a topic he would prefer to avoid—then she would say she didn't know what had happened to him, which, in a sense, would be the truth.

Hopefully, Oliver would soon be out of their lives for good. And there and then she made up her mind that if he returned again she would have no more to do with him. She would make that clear before she handed over the keys for the van.

Lois drove confidently into the car park and put her car in a bay at the far end, opposite the supermarket, alighting to get her parking ticket and stick it firmly on to the windscreen. She had spent quite a lot of time with Clifford and it was getting dark. She hoped she hadn't missed Oliver, who might well be on his way back to the yard.

Being late on a Monday it was quiet and there were few cars or people about, but in the distance she could see Oliver in his usual spot, apparently engaged in conversation with one of the passers-by. There seemed to be some sort of heated exchange and Lois wondered if it was the store manager complaining about him, perhaps asking him to move on; from the far side of the car park it was hard to tell. Deciding it was better to let the incident pass rather than get involved, Lois halted her steps and stood where she was, watching.

Suddenly the person to whom Oliver was talking began to kick him and, from the shadows of a pillar, emerged two other men, one of whom stood there, apparently keeping watch, while the other began to go rapidly through Oliver's pockets, practically ripping off his jacket as he did. A young man passing stopped to observe the commotion and then, quickening his steps, hastened away.

Lois, spurred on by indignation, sprang forward just as the terrified dog ran out from behind Oliver almost into the path of a passing car. The driver stopped, swore, drove round the dog, and hurriedly left the car park. Lois managed to grab the dog by its collar and held on to it while she shouted for help. Two people passed, looked at her, at Oliver, and then turned on their heels. Lois dragged the struggling dog to the safety of her car, bundled it into the back, and then raced the length of the car park, arms flailing, calling for help.

No one took the slightest notice of her. One or two people paused by their cars, looked at her as if she were a mad woman, then climbed in and quickly drove away. When she reached the pillar, Lois saw that Oliver was now lying on his face while the man who had started the attack leaned over him, still kicking viciously and shouting something Lois couldn't hear but which seemed to consist entirely of obscenities. The lookout by the pillar tried to grab her jacket, but she flung herself on to Oliver's assailant and, almost without knowing what she was doing, began to throw punches at him.

'Leave him alone!' she cried. 'Get off. Get away.'

The third man, who had been going through Oliver's pockets, giving him the odd kick as he did, looked up with an expression of fright, crammed something in his own pocket, and started to run away.

'Someone *help* us!' Lois pleaded as Oliver's main attacker turned round and, with an expression of fury on his face, struck her hard on the chest, trying to push her away. The lookout went over to help him by wrapping his arms round Lois's waist and trying to drag her away while, with both hands, she held on for dear life to the coat of the man who had hit her. He responded by beating her about the head. She was aware of an ugly puddle of blood forming beside Oliver's left ear as he lay motionless on the pavement.

At that moment two men appeared from inside the supermarket and ran over. One burly man seized the coat of the main attacker while the other tried to grab the man with his arms round Lois. Suddenly he let Lois go and, tugging at his companion, started to run away. Lois, however, still clung on to his coat and, although almost paralysed with fear, in pain and nearly exhausted, would not let go until she knew that the burly man had her—and Oliver's—attacker firmly by the arm. Then she relinquished her grip and sank breathlessly on to the pavement beside Oliver, whose arm was twisted at an ugly angle under his body.

Urgently Lois turned to him and put a finger on the pulse in his neck. It was rapid but strong. Oliver, though obviously badly injured, still lived.

*   *   *

Lois must have dozed, because Ken had come into the room without her being aware of it. When she opened her one unbandaged eye he was sitting by the bed reading the paper. For a few moments she looked at him, eye half-closed, so that he didn't realize she was awake. The whole dreadful business was now going to come right out into the open and she dreaded what Ken would say.

Ken lowered the paper and looked at her.

'Are you awake?' he whispered. Lois nodded, so he went on: 'How do you feel?'

Gingerly she put a hand to her head; but she couldn't feel anything because of the bandage that was wound right round it and over half her face.

'I feel a bit groggy,' she murmured.

'You were a very silly girl,' he said, moving his chair nearer to her bed. 'You could have been killed.'

'You can't just leave someone to be attacked.' She paused, hardly daring to voice the next question. 'How . . . how is Oliver?'

'Oh, he'll pull through.' Ken sounded offhand. 'He has a broken arm, a collapsed lung, but he looks at the moment better than you do.'

'You went to see him?'

'I just looked in. He, too, is rather groggy. I think he thought I was a doctor.' Ken leaned over her, his hand gently on her arm. 'You gave me a terrible fright, Lois.'

'I gave myself a terrible fright. I mean, really, Ken, there was nothing else I could do. I couldn't just *leave* him.'

'Apparently, everyone else did.' Ken showed her the headlines of the evening paper.

GOOD SAMARITAN COMES TO THE AID OF A
BEGGAR

Then he read on:

Mrs Lois Hunter, a Stinsbury magistrate, went to the aid of a beggar who was being attacked outside a supermarket in the town centre. The object of the vicious attack was thought to be theft, or maybe a personal

66

vendetta among vagrants. Although there were other people in the area at the time, no one else went to help the beggar or Mrs Hunter until the manager of the supermarket and his deputy were alerted and immediately intervened.

Mrs Hunter, 36, is the wife of Kenneth J. Hunter, Chair of the Stinsbury Rotarians and a prominent London banker. The couple have twin teenage sons at boarding school in Wiltshire.

Interviewed at his home, Mr Hunter said he was appalled by what had happened, and although he thought his wife had been foolish, he was also proud of her. It is especially ironic that his wife is a local magistrate who has a particular interest in the welfare of the disadvantaged. He said it was disgraceful that law-abiding citizens cannot walk safely on the streets of a small market town like Stinsbury, but he thought that the existence of thugs of the kind involved in the attack posed a special problem to the community.

The name of the beggar, who remains under sedation with a broken arm and internal injuries, is not known. One of the attackers was taken into custody and the two who escaped are being sought by police, who would welcome co-operation from the public, especially eye-witnesses.

When Ken finished reading, Lois had her good eye closed again. She was reliving those dreadful moments when she honestly feared for her life. She could picture Oliver lying there, surrounded by the three men; herself looking wildly around her for someone else to help as she dashed towards him.

'There were grown men who took no notice,' she murmured after a while.

'Darling,'—Ken put the paper down—'people are afraid of these types. There's no way of knowing whether they're carrying knives. You were very, very foolish. To do all that . . . for *him!*'

'He's a person too,' Lois replied quietly. 'I saw the man who gave him the first kick. Then another moved in. I couldn't stand it. Were they really after his money? I wouldn't have thought he had much. What's this about a vendetta?'

'The police thought Oliver might be part of a gang.'

'He is most certainly not part of a gang!' Lois raised her voice indignantly.

'You don't know that, Lois, do you? You don't know anything about him and yet he might have cost you your life. For what?'

'For the sake of humanity,' Lois said quietly. 'I couldn't see someone attacked and behave as though nothing was happening—as everyone else.' Her voice began to rise again. 'You know, Ken, although the car park wasn't busy there were several people around including big strong men, and no one wanted to know. I find that shocking.'

'You could have gone into the supermarket and got help.'

'So could *they*, but they did nothing. They just got into their cars and went home. I can't help asking myself how they feel now.'

'Probably relieved.' Ken's answer was terse. 'I don't think that Oliver's life is worth yours. Supposing something had happened?' His voice began to break. 'The boys, me—what would we have done?'

To her astonishment Ken began to weep, a phenomenon she never recalled seeing in the whole of their married life. Strong men, however, don't cry and as soon as the tears appeared he quickly corrected himself, blew his nose and raised a tear-stained face towards her. She realized then how much she loved him, how much she depended on him, and she held out her arms to draw him close to her.

For this moment it was almost worth the ordeal of the day before. He leaned against her and she alternately stroked his head and kissed it, aware of a feeling of togetherness, mutual dependency and need such as they had seldom experienced, even in their most intense moments of making love.

'Darling,' she whispered, 'I am *so* sorry.'

'You must *never* do anything like that again,' he said. 'I've been to hell and back, Lois, ever

69

since I had the call in the office. To hell and back.'

'Did you tell the boys?' She let go of his head and gazed at him anxiously.

'I telephoned the school last night as soon as I knew you were all right. They wanted to come and see you; but I told them you couldn't have visitors . . .'

'The dog!' Lois said suddenly. 'I put Oliver's dog in the car. Oh, Ken, do go and see . . .'

'The dog is all right,' Ken said wearily. 'In fact, he's at home.'

'Our home?' Lois looked surprised.

'What else could I do with it? I guessed immediately whose dog it was. The police didn't want it, and I don't expect your friend can afford kennel fees. Don't worry, the dog is having the time of its life. Never known such luxury.'

'I bet.' The pain began to throb again behind Lois's eye. 'Ken, I think I'll have another snooze. Maybe you'd ask the nurse if I could have a painkiller? My head is hurting a bit.'

Ken got up looking concerned. 'Darling, I hope they haven't missed anything?'

'No, I had it X-rayed this morning.'

'They think you'll be able to come home tomorrow.'

Lois held out her hand, took Ken's and squeezed it.

'What are we going to do about Oliver?'

'What are *we* going to do about Oliver? Why, nothing. You have practically given your life for him. Don't you think that's enough? At least he's alive, thanks to you. Let the social services look after Oliver, the police ... anyone. Please, Lois, I beg of you. Don't give another thought to what will happen to that man.'

But she knew she would. The events of yesterday had forged a bond between them that would be even harder to break than anything that had happened previously.

CHAPTER FOUR

Oliver was alone in the four-bed ward. The other beds were empty. He sat in a chair by his bed looking out of the large plate-glass window over the town or, rather, over the beautiful valley that stretched for miles from the bottom of the steep hill. He had one arm in a sling and the hand of the other was still bandaged. He didn't seem to hear Lois come in, and she gently laid a bunch of flowers on his bed and stood for a while looking at him, his eyes fixed on the far horizon.

He looked different from when she'd last seen him. Cleaner, leaner, more fragile. He'd lost a lot of weight, though he wasn't ever what you'd call a big man. About five feet ten or eleven in height, but well-built, muscular. He had black hair that sprang up from his brow and swept across his head without parting. It was springy, wiry hair that had obviously recently had the attentions of a barber. He was clean-shaven whereas before there had always been a dark stubble. She knew he had striking blue eyes, though these were now turned away from her. Blue eyes were unusual in a dark person and made her think of Italy or Greece. There was in fact something Mediterranean about Oliver's appearance and she wondered if one or both parents was foreign.

He wore a blue shirt, sleeves rolled up. His arms were covered with fine black hairs. He had on blue jeans and his legs were propped up on a chair.

She moved round the side of the bed and he turned abruptly, as though he were half afraid, like a jumpy cat.

'Sorry,' Lois said, perching on the side of the bed. 'Did I startle you?'

Oliver relaxed and attempted a smile, not a very convincing one.

'I was miles away.' He lowered his feet and tried to get up, but she put out a hand.

'Please, stay where you are. How are you?'

'They say I'm much better. I feel much better.'

'I'm terribly sorry I didn't come to see you before I was discharged.'

'It's quite all right. I understand.'

'I was taken home in an ambulance. I just wanted to be at home. You know how it is.'

He smiled again, but this time it was more like a grimace and Lois thought what a tactless remark she'd made.

'I wish . . .' he said.

'I'm sorry. That was a stupid thing to say.'

'I wouldn't have been surprised if I never saw you again,' he said, 'after what I put you through.'

'You didn't put me through anything,' she protested. 'You didn't know what was going to happen . . . and neither did I.'

'It all happened so quickly. But you could have run and got help. You might have been killed. Imagine how I'd have felt then.'

There was reproach in his voice which somehow she resented.

'You could have been killed too. Anyway, it's all over now.'

'It's not over.' Oliver's tone was sullen. 'They want me to bring charges, and I won't.'

'But you must bring charges. You were attacked.'

'I shan't bring charges, and if the police do prosecute I shall refuse to give evidence.'

'Why? Did you know them?'

'Of course I didn't know them. Oh, I see,' his voice became contemptuous, 'you think it was a "quarrel between vagrants", as it said in the papers. A fall-out among thieves.'

'I don't think anything of the sort. I never did.'

'You see, when you're a disadvantaged member of society, people think they can say what they like about you and get away with it.' He sighed and drew a cigarette out of a packet he produced from his pocket. 'The point is, they can.'

He lit his cigarette, regardless of the NO SMOKING notices clearly visible in the ward and indeed all over the hospital.

'Oliver, what are you going to do now?'

Lois sat down in the chair opposite him, the one on which he had rested his feet. 'I believe they're ready to discharge you.'

Oliver took another deep drag on his cigarette.

'They're going to try and send me back to Manchester. Apparently I really should be in the care of the social services there.'

'Well . . .' Lois put her hands in her lap. 'That might be the best thing. They will look after you and re-house you.'

'I don't want to be re-housed.'

'But, Oliver, you can't spend your life in a van.'

His gaze when he looked at her was hard and unfriendly. 'Why can't I?'

There was really no answer to that. One of the saints of ancient times had chosen to spend his life on top of a pole. Some people preferred to live in caves, deserts, forests.

74

Living in a van of some description was the modern way of non-conforming, dropping out.

'Oliver, don't you want to tell me a little about your life so that maybe I can help you?'

'Not really.' He gave a weak smile. 'Thanks, Mrs Hunter, but you've done enough for me already. You've been very kind. Clifford came to see me; there's a possibility he'll let me stay at his place until I can drive. I mean, I can still sleep in my old van. Then he'll try and fix me up with another.'

'He showed me the blue van.'

'I think that went.'

Lois thought for a few moments and then said carefully:

'Oliver, I'm still prepared to buy something to help you get home. I won't renege on that promise.'

'Clifford said you were ready to pay fifteen hundred plus for the blue van.' Oliver savagely stubbed out the butt of his cigarette in one of the hospital saucers. 'I really can't have you paying that kind of money. I can't accept charity like that. I was embarrassed when Clifford told me, and I guess that was why you were on your way to Stinsbury the day it happened?'

Lois nodded but didn't quite know how to reply. You can't tell a beggar that fifteen hundred pounds was quite a trivial sum of money to someone in her position. If you did they would lose what little self-respect remained. Either that, or they would despise you even more. In a way, that was how she suspected Oliver, for all his politeness, felt about her. There was something unknowable about him; a distance she felt he would always keep.

Lois looked helplessly around. She began to get up.

'In that case, I don't think there's anything more I can do.'

'How's the dog?' he asked abruptly.

'The dog's fine.' She sat down again, clasping her handbag in her lap. She wore blue slacks, a white shirt and a navy jacket. The day before, her hairdresser had come to the house to do her hair. She felt almost her old self again, except that Ken had insisted she have Beverley or someone drive her until she got the all-clear at her next check-up. Beverley had dropped her at the hospital and then gone into town to do some shopping. 'But I think he misses you. I tell you what . . .' she paused and then went on quickly, words tumbling out one after the other, 'if it's all right with the sister in charge, why don't you come home with me now to see the dog? You'd like that, wouldn't you, Oliver? Have some tea and we'll bring you back.'

'Well . . .' Oliver looked hesitant, thoughtful. 'OK, if it isn't too much trouble. Then maybe you could run me up to Clifford's yard and I'll have a look at the van.'

Beverley was waiting in the Range Rover outside the hospital when she saw Lois appear on the steps accompanied by a man. Behind them was a nurse who seemed to be helping the man down the steps. She carried a walking stick and had one arm under his elbow, supporting him.

Once on level ground he took the stick from her, whereupon Lois assumed the supportive role of the nurse and took his arm as they walked slowly towards the car.

Beverley knew immediately who he was. Her first reaction was one of shock, then surprise. He wasn't at all what she expected; not some dishevelled, disgusting-looking tramp—though it was logical to suppose that the hospital would have cleaned him up—but a personable, really quite attractive man of about her own age, thirty or thereabouts.

Intrigued, she hopped from the driver's seat and waited for them.

'Beverley, this is Oliver,' Lois said without further explanation, though she had never mentioned Oliver's name to her before.

'Hello, Oliver.' Beverley gave a cheery smile and gently grasped the bandaged stub of hand he held out to her.

'Oliver's coming to say "hello" to the dog. Bev's been looking after him. By the way, what's his name?' Lois looked at Oliver.

'Chump.'

'I've been calling him Scamp,' Beverley said. 'Would you rather sit in the front or the back, Oliver?'

'I'll sit in the back.' Lois began to climb aboard while Beverley led Oliver round to the passenger seat and opened the door for him. 'Beverley has taken quite a shine to Scamp—Chump,' she corrected herself.

Oliver looked back at her mournfully, as if this gave him a fresh stab of guilt. 'I didn't thank you for rescuing him. I not only owe you my life but the dog's life too. He could have been run over.'

'I think we should call a moratorium on thanks,' Lois said as Beverley manoeuvred the large vehicle out of the hospital car park. 'Let's wipe the slate clean.'

'Sounds like a good idea.' Beverley, glancing sideways at Oliver, couldn't quite get over the spectacle of this well-behaved, decently dressed, nice-looking man who smelt pleasantly of aftershave sitting calmly beside her looking interestedly around him.

She couldn't help wondering if there was more to this 'rescue' than met the eye.

*   *   *

Chump ran hysterically towards his master when he got out of the car in front of the house and had to be restrained by Neal, who was working in the garden, in case he knocked him over. Lois saw tears in Oliver's eyes as he greeted the dog, and she, Beverley and Neal turned away for a few seconds while master and pet had an emotional reunion.

Neal was a keen gardener, and he was turning over the ground, much of which at the moment was covered with early daffodils, in preparation for bedding plants later on.

Neal and Beverley Driver and their two children, Kathy and Francis, lived in a pleasant house a short distance from the Hall. At one time it had been the farmhouse, before the farm had been merged with the Higham estate. It was a low, rambling thatched building covered with roses, clematis and wisteria, which gave it an air of enchantment in spring and early summer.

The stables were behind the house and the horses were out grazing in the paddock while ducks and hens scratched and clucked about in the yard between the stables and the house.

The reunion over, Neal was introduced to Oliver and there was some general chat about the weather, the prospects for the spring. Then Beverley said she had to pick up the children from school, and Neal turned to resume his gardening, throwing the weeds and dead plants into a barrow.

'Do you feel like walking?' Lois turned to Oliver. 'Or shall Beverley drop us off at the top of the lane?'

'How far is it?' Oliver looked along the drive that wound ahead of them.

'Not far. A quarter of a mile?'

'I think I can manage that. It will do me good.'

'Neal will run you back to the hospital,' Beverley said as she took the wheel of the Range Rover again. 'Just give us a bell when you're ready.'

* * *

Feeling rather exhausted after his walk up the drive, Oliver sat in one of the comfortable chairs in the drawing room, head back, eyes shut. Chump sat attentively by his side. Not only the relatively short walk but the scale of the place overwhelmed him; the number of rooms, the size of the garden, the swimming pool. Everywhere there were signs of an affluence that was completely foreign to him; the sort of thing that featured in the pages of magazines he occasionally glanced at when they were left lying around in public places. People with a gracious lifestyle you knew you could never hope to emulate unless you won the lottery, and he couldn't afford the price of a ticket.

He found Lois extremely sympathetic and down to earth as a person, but her lifestyle was daunting. It had to be.

He felt he wanted to be gone from this place.

He opened his eyes as Lois came in with a tray, tea things carefully balanced on it. He got to his feet to help her, but she shook her head and, feeling helpless as well as hopeless, he sank back into his chair.

He had expected the tea to be brought in by a maid, and it was reassuring to know that the woman who lived in all this wealth behaved like an ordinary person.

'Milk and sugar?' Lois asked, looking across at him.

'Yes, please.'

'I'm sure you'd like a cake.' She came over with a plate and he gazed at the tempting selection before taking one awkwardly in the bandaged hand. 'Did you make them?'

'Not exactly.' Lois took one too and, with teacup in the other hand, sat down. 'Beverley is a great cook and she helps me out.'

'Is she your housekeeper?'

'Again, not exactly; but we have a farm which her husband Neal manages and she does a lot for us.'

Oliver bit carefully into the soft sponge. It was delicious. He finished the cake then he looked thoughtfully over at Lois.

'Why are you so nice to me?'

'What do you mean?'

'Well ... a man you found begging in the street. From the beginning you were nice to me, to say nothing of saving my life.'

'I wish you'd forget about the "saving life" bit.'

'But it's true. I could have been kicked to death.'

'Oh, I don't think so. Someone would have come and they'd have run off.'

'No one came until you called out. They just stared and walked away. You know that, Mrs Hunter. Why did you do it?'

Lois lowered her eyes.

'When you're in my situation, you realize how fortunate you are. Frankly, I think it was the pups who won my sympathy to begin with. I love animals.' She reached her hand out to fondle the ears of Sally, her golden Labrador who had accompanied her into the room. Her two well-behaved golden Labradors, Sally and her daughter Lucy, tolerated Chump in a slightly disdainful way, keeping their distance from him.

'I can tell that. You saved Chump as well.'

'What happened to the other pup?'

'I left him with a friend.'

'It must have been a wrench.'

'It was.'

'A friend in Cornwall?'

'Yes.'

She knew she would get no more out of him. He was simply not prepared to discuss with her any aspect of his personal life. But he was keen to know more about her.

'Have you always been like this?'

'Like what?' Lois got up to pour fresh tea and, pot in hand, stood gazing down at him.

'Going out of your way to be kind to the underdog?'

'No, I haven't really. I'm a magistrate so I am concerned with people's problems, and if I see someone who needs money I give it to them.'

'Do you buy them vans?'

Lois blushed.

'I don't feel I can accept any more of your hospitality, Mrs Hunter.'

'Why not?'

'I just don't feel comfortable here.' He looked around. 'I've never been in a place like this in my life. You must be very wealthy . . .'

'What can I say?' Lois swallowed her tea and replaced the cup on the table. 'I can't deny we have money, but I don't think we're ostentatious. We don't live a flamboyant lifestyle. We're not particularly extravagant.' She paused and then hurried on. 'Look, Oliver, at least let me . . . let me help you with the van and see you on your way.'

She gazed at him and saw how hostile and yet at the same time defenceless he was. He appeared at a loss for words.

She caught hold of his good arm. 'Let's go over to the yard and talk to Clifford. See if he can come up with any more bargains.'

'Well . . .'

'Oliver, you're in no condition to bargain,' she said severely. 'You cannot use either hand or arm properly. You can't drive or walk any distance. I know you want your independence, and I want to give it to you. Then, once you're on your way, we need never see each other again.'

*   *   *

Clifford had a red van, slightly larger than the blue, which he said was a real snip at two thousand pounds. Oliver gasped when he heard the sum and said it was out of the question. Neal, who had driven them to the yard and knew a thing or two about cars, opened the bonnet to inspect the engine and then got on his back to look underneath.

The upholstery was in good condition and there was even a fitted stereo, though a very old model. The only thing about the van—the really off-putting thing as far as Lois was concerned—was a pervasive smell of fish. It transpired that the van had once belonged to a fishmonger who plied his trade in the Dorset countryside.

'The smell will go,' Clifford assured them, 'in time.'

'I don't mind the smell at all,' Oliver said. 'And Chump will love it.' For once there was a note of humour in his voice. He had said a sad farewell to Chump, and once again Lois had seen him close to tears. He was clearly in a vulnerable state. Lois thought that really there was something quite childlike about Oliver, for all his pretence at being a tough, grown man; hard-bitten and streetwise.

'Clifford, if we buy the van, is there any chance you will let Oliver stay here for a while?'

'Not a chance, Mrs Hunter.' Clifford shook his head with such emphasis that Lois knew he would not retract. 'I have my business to think of. If I let Oliver stay, I'd have every tramp in Dorset wending his or her way here. I think you can understand my position.'

'But you *said* . . .' Oliver began.

'I know what I said, but I changed my mind because of the effect it would have on my business.'

Also the chance to make a sale, Lois thought, but said nothing, watching Oliver try and control his anger.

Neal was standing back, hands in his pockets, gazing at the van. 'I don't see why we can't have it at our place, Lois. There's lots of room. I mean, that's if you don't object. I certainly don't, and I know Beverley wouldn't mind. She's very fond of Chump. She'll be sad to lose him.'

'That's a splendid idea,' Lois said with enthusiasm. 'Oliver, what do you say?'

Oliver dug his feet into the ground, his expression mulish.

85

'I don't feel I can accept that sort of money, you buying me a van that costs over two thousand pounds. It's kind of you, but . . .'

'Well, if you feel like that'—Neal folded his arms and leaned against the side of the van— 'and I respect your point of view, why don't you pay for it yourself?'

'I couldn't possibly. How can I pay for it?'

'By earning your keep. There's lots to do on the farm for a man even partially fit, and a young man like you will soon be better. We would pay you so much an hour, by agreement—only we wouldn't. I mean, you wouldn't get any money, but you would be paying off your debt. What do you think of that?'

'It sounds a good compromise to me,' Clifford said enthusiastically. 'Oliver, I don't know if you ever heard the saying, but beggars can't be choosers. You've been pretty low and you can't get lower, in my opinion. What I say is, unless you want to go back to your life of vagrancy—and I don't think you'd be able to cope with your dog if you did, in your present state of health—you don't have much choice. No fucking choice at all.' Then, with a quick glance at Lois: 'If you'll pardon the language, Mrs Hunter.'

*　　*　　*

Wendy stood behind the famous author as she

signed her two-hundredth book that morning. Two hundred in three hours, well, getting on for four: a book a minute, and often the famous author didn't just sign her name but added a word or two, or took time for a brief chat with the customer. After all, her precious readers had made her such a famous name, her books selling almost in the numbers of the leading brand of detergent. In fact, her novels were frequently used as inducements in promotional campaigns: send off the coupon on the packet of detergent or jar of coffee and claim your free copy. All this had helped to make the author enormously rich. And yet she worked. God, how she worked. Up at dawn to pen her latest masterpiece—or rather, commit it to the word processor. Long dedicated hours to produce ... what? This particular famous author was no Kafka. It was doubtful whether her countless volumes of purple prose would be read in a hundred years' time, or even fifty.

But people might have said that once upon a time about George Eliot.

With a practised smile, Wendy swept another book from the author's hand and gave it to the happy purchaser. The author looked up.

'Tired?' Wendy asked sympathetically. 'Only ten more minutes.'

The author smiled obediently and bent her head to the next book placed before her.

Ten more minutes. Ten more books. Then

she would leap into a taxi, drop the author off at her hotel and return to the office to check up on anything else that had happened during the day, attend a series of meetings, and then a reception for a new book launch, the author not quite so famous as the one sitting in front of her now; but up and coming, and definitely young.

Every day was like this, more or less. Sometimes Wendy toured the country with an author. Some authors she liked more than others. Some she didn't like at all. Some were vain and egocentric. Others were painfully self-effacing, insecure, nervous of their new-found fame, afraid it wouldn't last. Some were thrusting and aggressive. They adored the fuss, the limelight. Often these were not writers at all but 'personalities', people who had become famous in other fields, often politics or the stage. She sometimes wondered why on earth they also wanted to achieve eminence in the field of authorship, particularly as most of them couldn't write.

Wendy enjoyed her work and was good at it. She was attractive and popular, patient and forbearing. She encouraged the timid and gave them confidence, she tolerated the rude and brash. Everyone liked her, almost. There were always exceptions. Wendy was thirty-four, an age when many women had husbands and families, some of them nearly grown-up. Her sister Lois had married when she was twenty-one and her twin sons were almost young men. Wendy adored her sister, to whom she had always been close, but she had never envied Lois. Indeed, at times she felt sorry for her, living deep in the sticks, following country pursuits: the women's institute, the guild of ladies who did the flowers at church on Sundays, the harvest suppers, the flower shows, the bring-and-buys and car boot sales, the numerous good causes, the hunting.

Wendy loved London and London life, parties and opera, theatre and dinners with friends . . . and yet. There were times when it palled. When it seemed too stale and familiar, terribly tiring. She was perpetually exhausted, always dashing about, never an evening at home, so that to go down to Lois and Ken for the weekend and slop about in wellies was bliss.

The last pile of books had almost disappeared, only a few dozen copies remaining. The bookshop asked the celebrity to sign those and, with much bowing and scraping, the manager saw them to the door of the shop and hailed a cab.

'Do you mind if I go on?' Wendy asked as they neared the hotel, glancing at her watch. 'I've got three meetings this afternoon and a book launch this evening.'

'You go, dear,' the famous author said, putting a hand on her arm. 'I shall just flake out on my bed.'

Oh, if only she could do that too. The cab stopped at Brown's Hotel; the two women embraced. They had known each other for some time. Wendy had handled all her books and they were fond of each other. Wendy promised to call her first thing the next morning with the schedule for the nationwide tour. Back to the office, time to grab a sandwich and a coffee from a plastic cup and then on to the first scheduled meeting, which was an all-important one on book jackets. Time to call Tim and her mother—hadn't spoken to her for two weeks—then another meeting, then change for the reception . . .

Rush, rush, rush.

Wendy eventually got home at about nine, threw her bag and briefcase down, went into the kitchen and inspected the contents of the fridge. The reception had been so crowded that when she got there all the food had gone. She had managed to get one drink and a handful of crisps. Now she was starving.

She got out a Marks and Spencer's Chicken Cacciatore, put it in the oven, poured herself a glass of white wine from the bottle in the fridge and went into the sitting room to play the messages waiting on her answering machine.

Several calls. Tim, whom she hadn't been able to contact that afternoon because he was in the auction room, several friends, and Lois, who wondered if they were coming for the

90

weekend and could she let her know soon?

Wendy picked up the phone and dialled Lois. She had been anxious about her sister ever since the accident. What a crazy thing to do, going to the rescue of a beggar. She could have been killed.

Wendy stood and listened to the phone ring, imagining the large empty house. She often wondered if Lois was really happy there on her own for most of the week. It was a funny arrangement, really, except that Lois and Ken seemed to have a very happy marriage, which was unusual in these days. Maybe that was why it was happy: they didn't see too much of each other.

She was about to replace the receiver when Lois came on the line and said breathlessly: 'Hello?'

'Hi, Lois!' Wendy sank down on the sofa and put her feet up.

'Oh, Wendy! How are you, darling?'

'Absolutely flat out. Exhausted.'

'And Tim?'

'About the same. I've hardly spoken to him all week.'

'But everything is all right?' Lois sounded anxious.

'Everything is fine, except that when we do talk we seem to spend our time arguing about the wedding.'

'Oh, not *still*?'

'His mother will be very upset if we don't

have it in London.'

'Well, it's hardly his mother's business, is it?'

'That's what I think. But she said all our friends are here, and she does have a point.'

'Neither of you are churchgoers, though. You don't have a church in London.'

'That's what I said.'

'Whereas the vicar here is very keen.'

Usually if Ken and Lois went to church on Sunday, Wendy and Tim went with them. It was another of those nice, country things to do.

'I really think we should have it with you.' Suddenly Wendy felt more enthusiastic. She could go down and stay with Lois a few days before and her sister would help her dress, and, yes, it could be a lot of fun.

Up to now, the prospect of the wedding hadn't been such fun because, frankly, up to now Wendy hadn't been too enthusiastic about the marriage. She loved Tim, no doubt about it, but she was really marrying because she felt it was time she got married.

It was true, all that business about being on the shelf was old hat. There were lots of women to whom careers were very important—she was one of them—and people lived together and didn't even bother getting married. But at heart she was a conventional woman and wanted to be a conventional bride.

'Wendy, are you really *sure*?' Lois said as the longish pause continued. 'Because if you're not . . .'

'Of course I'm sure. By the way, how are you?'

'Fine. I had another check-up and the doctor said I'm one hundred per cent. Oh, there's one other thing . . . I don't quite know how you'll take this, but you might as well be told because you'll see him at the weekend . . .'

'Who's that?'

'Oliver, the beggar, is living with us.'

'He's *what*?'

'Not in the house but in his van. It's parked in the field behind Neal and Beverley. It's only temporary, until he's better. Once he gets the use of his arm he'll drive off and that'll be the last we'll see of him.'

There was another long pause. 'Wendy?' Lois's tone was anxious. 'Are you still there?'

Wendy swallowed her wine so quickly that it nearly made her choke. 'I think that is the most ridiculous thing I have ever heard,' she burst out.

'He's got nowhere to go.'

'Darling, he's not your responsibility.'

'I think he is.'

'But why? I can't understand you, Lois.'

'I can't really understand it either,' Lois said in a voice so subdued Wendy could hardly hear her. 'I just feel I ought to do all I can for Oliver. I really can't tell you why.'

CHAPTER FIVE

Wendy was intrigued by the sight of the red van half-hidden behind the outbuildings of the Drivers' pretty farmhouse, as if it didn't want to be noticed.

Little had been said about Oliver since she and Tim had arrived late the previous evening, as though it was a taboo subject, as she suspected it was. There was a tension between Ken and Lois that Wendy hadn't noticed before. Lois looked pale, but that could be attributed to her ordeal. Ken was justifiably angry about that too. He could have lost his wife and, as often happens, anger rather than relief had followed anxiety, the way a mother smacks her child when it is found safe after being lost.

Wendy never had breakfast. After a tiring week she preferred to sleep in, so when she got downstairs no one was about. Lois had gone to church to do the flowers for the following day. Ken and Tim had gone riding. Wendy made herself coffee and toast, and sat outside eating it, enjoying the early spring sunshine. Then she took herself off for a wander round. Yes, there was a lot to be said for living in the country. It had an appeal after a week in which the traffic in the city seemed to have increased, the noise had got louder, smog denser, people's tempers more volatile and one's own nerves more fragile.

The wedding, which should have been a pleasure, was a never-ending source of friction. Tim wanted the wedding in September. Wendy thought they should wait until the following spring. Every time they talked on the phone there was a little argument and they had quarrelled all the way down about it. In a way, it would have been nice to have spent the weekend apart, which was perhaps a somewhat curious reaction for an engaged woman who saw little enough of her fiancé as, due to cramped conditions, they didn't share a flat but spent nights together when they felt like it. Vaguely too they had been house hunting but, again, there was so little time for that.

The van had a curiously empty look about it and as she got closer Wendy decided there was no one in. She wondered what Oliver did when he wasn't in his van. Lois had said he was paying for it by doing jobs on the farm. He was very particular about maintaining his independence.

Wendy realized she was quite curious about what sort of person this mysterious Oliver was.

She approached the van in the manner of a hunter stalking its prey: head forward, eyes alert for any movement that might spell danger. Hands deep in the pockets of her jacket, she stopped in front of the van and peered in through one of the side windows.

'Can I help you?' a voice said behind her. Completely taken by surprise, she spun round, shamefaced, as though she'd been caught snooping.

A man with his arm in a sling, dressed comfortably in T-shirt and jeans, stood staring at her. By his side was an engaging-looking mongrel dog furiously wagging its tail.

'I'm terribly sorry,' she said. 'I must seem terribly rude. I'm Wendy, Lois's sister.' She put out a hand and then saw that it was his right hand which was in a sling. However, he grasped her hand awkwardly with his left and nodded as if her curiosity didn't need any explanation.

'Just looking over the van, I suppose?'

'Oh, I didn't look inside.'

'Help yourself.' He threw open the door, which was unlocked, an expression of defiance in his eyes. 'Go on,' he said as she hesitated, 'have a look in.' There was in his tone the suggestion of a command.

Obediently, she peered in and then, removing her head:

'There's nothing to see. I mean, it's just a van.'

'Exactly.' Oliver shut the door again, with a certain ferocity. 'Like to see in the back?'

'No, it's quite all right. Look, I didn't mean to be offensive. I was simply curious. I was taking a walk, and . . .'

96

'You don't have to explain. I suppose it's natural that I'm an object of curiosity.'

'Well, that *is* understandable. After all, the whole story is extraordinary. But you shouldn't take it too personally.'

'Beggar taken up by Lady Bountiful.' There was a derisive note in Oliver's voice which made Wendy bridle.

'You don't sound grateful. But for her you might be dead.'

Oliver slumped against the side of the van and reached down to fondle the dog's ears. 'You're right,' he said, raising his head, 'but, honestly, I'm not ungrateful. Mrs Hunter has been good to me. She gives all the time and never asks questions. I think her very goodness embarrasses me. I would prefer to be independent—that's why I embarked on this way of life. Yet now I find myself in a state of abject dependency.'

He was articulate. His vocabulary was good. He was not an ignorant jerk, but might well have had a good education, maybe even university. She felt he was under a lot of pressure; there was an almost palpable feeling of self-restraint, of suppression, of reining in. The last few days must have been terrible for him. Lois had told her he didn't like to talk about himself, so she decided not to ask any questions. She reached over and patted the dog's head.

'Lois would be upset if she thought you felt

like that. She's a genuinely good person.'

'And her husband?' Oliver looked at her, head on one side.

'Ken goes along with Lois.'

'But he can't like me much.'

'I haven't talked to him so I don't know, but Ken would go along with Lois and support her. No one blames you for being attacked. They only think Lois was a bit foolish not to try and get help from elsewhere before rushing to your aid.'

'I just find this whole situation extraordinary.' Oliver gestured round. 'I can't get over people being so nice.'

'Weren't people nice to you before?'

Wendy joined him leaning against the van, arms folded. The dog sat companionably between them, wanting first one to pat him and then the other.

'Not really. I was brought up in care. I never knew my parents.'

'I'm so sorry.'

'I don't want pity. Please believe that. I'm just trying to explain why it is hard for me to understand kindness. Let alone accept it for what it is. I know Mrs Hunter must think I'm rude, ungrateful.'

'I'm sure she doesn't. I think she realizes that you want to be left alone; but I know she'd like to try and help.'

'Why, though? That's what I can't understand.'

'Perhaps that's because no one has ever tried to help you before. Or maybe they have and you've rebuffed them. Maybe it's because you're so terribly, almost frighteningly, self-contained. Did you know anything about your parents?'

'No. Except my mother was unmarried and left me in a home; but she wouldn't let me be adopted. It seems she hoped she'd be able to have me back one day. Eventually I was fostered, but I could never settle. I was difficult, a problem child and then a problem youth. So I was in and out of foster homes, in and out of the orphanage.'

'It must have been an awful life.'. Wendy sank to the ground, arms hugging her knees, and Oliver crouched down beside her. The dog settled happily at their feet.

'I don't know why I'm telling you all this.' Oliver looked across at her. 'I've never told anyone else. Never told your sister.'

'Maybe you just felt you needed to tell somebody. Why is it you're so anxious to go back if you haven't got a home?'

'It's where I belong. I've got friends there.'

'In Manchester?'

'Somewhere near there.'

'Did you ever work?'

'I'm a trained carpenter and cabinet maker. I'm fixing a few things for Neal in the house and about the farm.' He pointed towards the farm and then held out his injured arm. 'As much as I can.'

'Why don't you go and live with them in the house? That's what I find so strange.'

'It's something to do with the van being my home. It's really cosy inside. Come and have a look.'

Sensing a new mood—his whole demeanour was much more friendly, his tone of voice warm and confiding—Wendy got to her feet and followed him to the back of the van. When he opened the door she saw that it was indeed quite cosy, with more room than she'd expected. The back of the van was slightly taller than the cab, so it was possible for them to stand. On one side was a bed neatly made up, and on the other a chest, on top of which was a stove operated by bottled gas.

'I've lots to do,' Oliver said with an air of boyish excitement. 'I'm going to put a light up so that I can use the battery of the van, and the Drivers have a small armchair they don't want which would be ideal.'

'I'm getting married soon,' Wendy said, climbing into the back of the van after him.

'Oh, are you?' He looked surprised. 'What made you tell me that?'

'It's just that you seem more excited about furnishing your van than I am about buying and furnishing a house.'

'Are you sure you want to get married?' Oliver looked at her keenly.

'Well, I've known him a long time. His

name's Tim. He's awfully nice.'

'And he's definitely the right one?'

'Yes.'

'You don't seem too sure to me.'

'I am sure; but I couldn't help comparing your attitude towards the van to my outlook on nestbuilding. It's got nothing to do with my love for Tim.'

'And you'll have a whole house?'

'Quite.' Wendy looked at him and laughed. She thought what an extraordinary turn-up for the books it was that she felt so inexplicably at ease in the company of a man she instinctively disapproved of, whom she had been so ready to condemn and dislike.

*　　　*　　　*

'Of course, darling. I'm all right,' Lois repeated for, she was sure, about the tenth time. First Tony and then Peter had been on the phone from school anxious about her.

The voice at the other end of the line spoke for some time and Lois listened, nodding, a smile of exasperation on her face. 'Absolutely all right, Peter, darling. No ill effects at all. I've had another check-up and the doctor says I'm one hundred per cent.' Again she stopped to listen.

'Yes, he's fine. He was hurt much more than I was, of course. Actually . . .' pause, 'we've let him keep his van on our land until he's better.

Poor man, he had nowhere to go—' She was interrupted by an exclamation, then once more resumed her patient listening. 'Yes, I thought you'd approve. Dad's not so keen, but he'll come round. Yes, you know Dad . . .' Again a pause for laughter at the other end. Then more talk as Tony once more took over from Peter and voiced his satisfaction that Oliver was camping on their land. Lois nodded several times, trying to interrupt.

'No, he doesn't *want* to live with us. Apart from the fact that Dad would go potty, Oliver prefers his independence. He insists on it, I can assure you.' More comment, then, 'Yes I agree. The Government has done nothing for people on the streets . . . Hmm, I don't know that getting rid of them at the election is the answer—' she was interrupted by another explosion. Nervous laughter on her part.

'OK, let's agree to disagree, as usual. Anyway, Auntie Wendy is here . . . Yes, Tim's with her. They'll all be back any minute for lunch. Yes, darling . . . kisses to you too. Both of you.' She blew several kisses into the receiver and finally put down the phone. Wiping her hands on her apron, she returned to her work bench and preparations for lunch.

The twins were darlings. So thoughtful. They had been so anxious about her even though they'd had the weekend off after she came home from hospital to see her. She missed them. Speaking to them always gave her a twinge, and no one wrote letters any more. They were the complete antithesis of the problem teenager, kind and caring. Of course, like their aunt, they were strong supporters of New Labour, and politics was a subject to be avoided, especially with their father present, when they were at home. But teenagers did have such strong opinions and, secretly, she was glad that hers were always so firmly on the side of the underdog.

Lois looked at the clock, aware of a mounting sense of agitation. Tim and Ken had gone riding and Wendy, who had risen late and gone off on her own, had been due back to help her prepare lunch. Not that she really needed help, but she would like to have chatted with her sister. There was a lot to talk about. The wedding, and what to do about Oliver.

Suddenly, life's horizon which, hitherto, had been so serene, seemed to have been obscured by a dark cloud. Or perhaps not so much a dark cloud, she mused, throwing a cloth over the table, as a mist. Doubts and uncertainties had taken the place of that self-assurance and self-confidence that had instinctively governed her life ever since she could remember.

Of course, life was never problem-free entirely, but Lois had always considered herself to be amazingly blessed in having escaped most of the anxieties which plagued other people: money, their children, the state of their marriage, sometimes all three.

Take Oliver. What a contrast there was between her lifestyle and his. Goodness knows how many problems he had left behind or refused to face. And maybe that was her strength. She was a realist; she was good at facing up to things.

The kitchen door opened and Wendy popped her head round. 'Sorry,' she said apologetically. 'I promised I'd come back to help you.'

'That's OK.' Lois got the knives and forks from the drawer and began laying the table. 'I thought we'd eat in the kitchen. Tim won't mind, will he?'

'Tim? Not at all. By the way, I tried to ask Oliver to join us, but he wouldn't.'

'Oliver?' Lois looked at her in amazement. 'You've been talking to Oliver?'

'Nothing wrong, is there?'

'Of course not.' Lois went over to the kitchen bench and began sorting through the lettuce leaves for the salad, chucking the old tired ones into the bin and the fresh young ones into a colander to be washed. She turned to look at Wendy. 'I'm just a bit surprised. I thought you were going for a walk.'

'I was, but I saw his van and got ever so curious.'

'And he was there?' There was a strange, hard note in Lois's voice and Wendy wondered if her sister was just a little too possessive about her protégé.

'No. I think he was over at the farm and saw me. Wondered who I was, what I wanted. We had quite a long chat. Surprisingly, we got along famously.'

'I'm glad.'

'Well, it was nice to communicate, wasn't it? I knew you'd be pleased about that.'

'Of course.'

'One feels kind of protective towards him, and the dog is adorable.'

'You should have seen it when it was a puppy.'

'What happened to the other one? You said there were two.'

'He went to Cornwall and left one of them there.'

'Who with?'

'I've no idea.'

'I think he's rather dishy,' Wendy said after a pause.

'Dishy?' Lois stared at her. 'What a strange word.'

'You know—sexy. Don't you think he's sexy?'

'Not at all.' Lois sounded disapproving. 'I never thought of it, actually.'

'*You* wouldn't, being happily married.'

'And aren't you happily engaged?' Lois glanced slyly at her.

'Yes, but I can still find men sexy, and I do. That's not to say that I don't want to marry

Tim, who I think is sexy too.'

'You seem spoilt for choice.' Lois's tone was now one of ironic amusement. All her life Wendy had come out with strange remarks, but somehow one never got used to it and kept on being surprised by her, taken aback. She had the power to shock—and enjoyed it.

'You said he was secretive.' Wendy decided it was time to change the subject.

'He is. Extremely.'

'Why is he so secretive?'

'Well . . .' Lois shrugged. 'He's that sort of person.'

'Has he got something to hide?'

Lois didn't reply.

'Hasn't everyone got something to hide?' Wendy prompted her, curious about her sister's lack of response. Oliver had opened up to her in a way he obviously never had for Lois. Maybe he found Lois formidable, whereas she was unthreatening. She knew Lois would be most indignant, and perhaps hurt, if she told her about their conversation, so she decided to keep it to herself.

'I've got nothing to hide.' Lois gave her a sharp look and began to toss the salad. 'Do you mind sticking the rolls in the oven?' She glanced at her watch. 'The men should be here soon. By the way, is there any more news about the wedding?'

'Tim wants it to be this September. I say next spring. Oh, and I do think here. In the country.'

*   *   *

Oliver watched Wendy walk slowly back into the house and then he turned, got into the van, and lay down on the mattress, arms folded behind his head. Chump settled down by his side, his head resting on Oliver's lap.

It was strange the way he felt he could talk to her. He had almost surprised himself in the manner he'd let go. He didn't feel that way at all about Lois. To him she was, and would always be, Mrs Hunter; but Wendy ... the name came easily.

She was so fresh and unstuffy. Not that Mrs Hunter was stuffy. On the contrary, she was incredibly kind, but ... could a person be too kind so that there was about it, inevitably, an air of condescension? Mrs Hunter was way up there; Wendy seemed more earthy, someone like him. And yet she wasn't. She came from the same moneyed, upper-class background as her sister. But he thought he detected a core of unhappiness in her which found a counterpart in his own deep malaise.

There was also Mr Hunter, who Oliver had yet to meet. He was a little afraid of Mr Hunter. He gathered Mr Hunter didn't really approve of him, and rightly so. He had nearly caused the death of his wife. And then what did Mr Hunter think of her buying Oliver a

107

van and parking it in the grounds of the ancestral home? He had dreaded the first meeting with Mr Hunter and had hoped that it would be indefinitely postponed—postponed perhaps until his arm was better and he could clear off. Obviously, Mr Hunter wasn't too keen to meet him, which was a bonus.

* * *

'I just came to say goodbye,' Wendy said the following afternoon. 'By the way, this is Tim, my fiancé.'

Tim, broad grin on his pleasant face, stretched out a hand.

'Hi, Oliver!'

'Hi!' Oliver replied awkwardly, taking Tim's hand with his left.

'Interesting place you've got here.'

Wendy giggled. 'Perhaps we can get one like it? Think of the saving in housework.'

Not seeing the joke, Oliver stared at her. She saw the expression on his face and corrected hers. 'Sorry. Tactless and tasteless remark.' She could see he had no sense of humour. Some people hadn't; it didn't necessarily make them less likeable. 'Could Tim just take a peek inside?'

Oliver stared at them mulishly and Wendy realized she had been mistaken to bring Tim. She should have come and said goodbye on her own. Or maybe not bothered.

'I'm sure it's not convenient,' Tim said hurriedly.

'It doesn't matter.'

'Well, goodbye.' Wendy felt awkward, humiliated. She could see that Oliver felt patronized and, in a way, they had patronized him. She was ashamed of herself and tugged at Tim's sleeve.

'Better go, or we'll be late,' she said. 'Bye, Oliver. We'll see you next week.'

He looked up. 'Back so soon?'

'We're going to have the wedding here, probably in September, so there's a lot to do.'

Oliver turned and walked round the van without a word. Tim and Wendy, hand in hand, walked slowly back to the house.

'What a rum bloke,' Tim said. 'A man of few words.'

'He felt patronized. He was right.'

'I didn't mean to patronize him.'

'Nor did I, but my remark about the van was stupid.'

'I must say, he made me feel uncomfortable. There's something strange about him. Odd bloke. Did he tell you anything about himself?'

'No, nothing. Frankly, I think we'll all be happier when he's gone.'

*   *   *

Lois tapped on the back door of the van, first hesitantly then more sharply. There was no reply. Neal and Beverley hadn't seen Oliver that morning. They had been expecting him. Maybe it was an off day.

Lois was about to go back to the house when she saw Oliver walking in the distance, Chump at his heels. The first thing she noticed was that his sling had been changed; then she saw the plaster cast was off his arm. Oliver was walking with a decided spring in his step and, as he saw her, hailed her.

She went towards him, smiling.

'The cast's off?'

'Yes.' He rubbed the arm. It looked pale and withered, not like the other, which was lean and muscular.

'That's great. But listen, how did you get to the hospital?'

'Part walking, part hitching a lift.'

'You should have asked . . .'

'Mrs Hunter'—Oliver put his head on one side, his attitude one of mild exasperation—'you know I don't like favours. I enjoy the exercise and I'm used to it. It's the way of life I like.'

'I should know that by now.' Lois paused. 'Does that mean you're going to leave us soon?'

'I can't drive yet. I'm forbidden to drive. The arm isn't strong enough. I have to go to the hospital for physiotherapy.'

'I hope that from time to time you'll let me give you a lift.'

Oliver smiled his mysterious smile. 'We'll see.'

'Oh, by the way, a policeman is here.'

The change in Oliver's expression was remarkable. From that of a carefree man it suddenly took on a hunted look.

'There's nothing to worry about,' Lois hastened to reassure him. 'It's nothing to do with the van or anything—that's perfectly safe here. It's about the attack. They want you to press charges.'

'I told them I won't press charges and I refuse to give evidence.'

'But why?' Suddenly Lois felt angry. 'Why won't you?'

'Because I don't know anything about those men. Why did they do what they did?'

'Because they were greedy thugs.' Lois's sense of indignation grew. 'They wanted your money and they didn't care what they had to do to get it.'

'But they must have known I had very little. They might have been even more desperate than me.'

'You almost sound as though you were sorry for them.'

'Maybe I am.' The mulish expression she knew so well came into his eyes again, and with it came a defiant stiffening of the body.

'Then what a thing to do for a few pounds.'

'I don't want to see the police.' Oliver turned aside and began to make his way round

111

the van. 'They can't force me.'

'Oliver . . .' There was a pleading note in Lois's voice, 'Please don't be difficult. You see, you make it hard for me. Apparently the police want me to bring charges and Ken . . . he wants me to as well. It just makes everything so difficult if you won't co-operate.'

'Good. I want to make it difficult.' He paused and looked at her.

'But the police say—' she began.

'You can tell the police to fuck off,' Oliver retorted before she had time to finish and, opening the back of the van, he first encouraged Chump to leap inside then, jumping in himself, closed the door firmly behind him.

* * *

'I'm terribly sorry,' Lois said with a deprecating smile. 'I think he's still in shock. He just can't face seeing you. More coffee, Sergeant?'

She turned to the policeman, whom she knew from the magistrates' court. He held out his cup, helped himself to sugar and stirred it thoughtfully.

'Is he trying to hide anything, do you think, madam?'

'Like what?' Lois felt a rush of indignation.

'Maybe he has a criminal past.'

'Oh, I don't think so.'

'Why not, Mrs Hunter?' Sergeant Barnes looked at her curiously.

'Oliver's the sort of person you instinctively trust.'

'Some of the best con artists in history have been men people trusted,' the sergeant said grimly and produced a notebook from his pocket. 'What age is he, madam?'

'I really don't know. I would guess about thirty.'

'Thirty,' the police officer noted, 'or thereabouts.' He looked up. 'And his full name?'

'This may sound silly, but I don't know, I'm afraid.'

'You don't know his name?' Sergeant Barnes looked incredulous.

'Other than his Christian name. No.'

'Did you ask for it?'

'Yes. Yes I did.'

'And what did he say?'

'He just said he preferred to be known by his Christian name. He never replies to any personal questions.'

'Didn't that strike you as funny, Mrs Hunter?'

'No, I respect a person's right to privacy, if it is what they wish, and he obviously wished it.'

'And yet you bought him a van, madam. Didn't you see the documents?'

'No.' Lois, beginning to feel foolish as well as thoroughly confused, shook her head. 'I gave him the money. I mean, he had his pride . . .'

'Did very nicely out of his pride, if you ask me, Mrs Hunter.'

'Maybe the hospital has his name?'

'Maybe it has. That's a good point.'

'I'm sorry. I must sound foolish.'

The policeman stood up.

'Mrs Hunter, I think you are a very nice woman. A good woman, but if I may say so, madam, yes, a little foolish, a little impulsive. You know nothing about someone you nearly gave your life for. You buy him a new van . . .'

'Not new,' Lois said hastily, 'it only cost two thousand pounds.'

'That's a lot of money to someone who earns a living from the streets.'

'Maybe it is.' She lowered her head. 'The licensing authorities will have his name, surely? I know he has licensed the van and insured it.'

'I believe that has been done in your name.'

'Oh, I didn't know that.' Lois put a hand to her mouth. 'I'll have to ask him about it. Sergeant Barnes, don't think too harshly of me. What I did was a bit unwise, but it was done from the best of motives, I assure you. You see, I am firmly of the opinion that people have a right to privacy, to do what they want with their lives, as long as what they do is not criminal—and Oliver isn't a criminal, I'm sure of it. I don't think I'm easily taken in—as my court record will prove, if you care to examine it. If I think people deserve punishment, I see they are punished. There are a lot of bad hats around, of that I am fully aware.

'But there is something about Oliver that makes him different.' She looked up at the officer with a sweet, appealing smile. 'I should be most surprised if I were proved wrong.'

* * *

Oliver sat on the edge of his chair as if at any moment he intended to leap off and make a bolt for the door. His nervousness made Lois feel nervous too and her hand shook slightly as she poured the coffee from the tall silver pot into two fine porcelain cups. There was also a plate of fine *langue du chat* biscuits.

He had refused her invitation to supper, as usual, but had agreed to come for coffee. She'd felt almost elated at his acceptance of an invitation frequently made but always refused. She'd changed from jeans into a dress and high heels, taken extra care with the make-up, her hair. Couldn't explain it to herself, but somehow wanted to look her best for Oliver.

And Oliver, as always, looked nice, wholesome, but in better condition than when she'd first met him. His hair was close-cropped, he was clean-shaven, and he wore a white T-shirt under a check shirt, jeans and trainers. The understanding when he first took

115

up residence was that she would make him an allowance, just enough to get by until he could regulate things with the authorities. Something told her, however, that Oliver didn't like having much to do with anyone in authority, which was probably why he had taken to the streets in the first place. A strange man, Oliver. Unfathomable. This was largely why, she felt, she was so drawn to him. He shattered one's illusions of what respectability should be. He was a challenge.

'It seems ridiculous to have you living on the premises and us hardly knowing each other,' she said with a breezy smile as she passed him his cup, offered him a biscuit.

'Hardly living on the premises, Mrs Hunter.' He smiled politely and shook his head both at the offer of sugar and a biscuit. 'I'm only here on a temporary basis.'

'Still, I do want you to feel at home. You're not here on sufferance, Oliver, but as a welcome guest. You are to get well.' She looked critically at his arm still in a sling. 'There is no time limit. Please believe that.'

Oliver looked around, at his feet half-hidden in deep-pile carpet, at the brocade-covered chairs, the antique furniture—and he knew quite a lot about furniture—the paintings on the walls, surely the work of good if little-known old masters? Scattered around were tasteful *objets d'art*, either family heirlooms or things purchased over the years and with care from the salerooms. He could imagine the Hunters taking a fancy to some little statue or ornament costing many hundreds, maybe thousands of pounds, and thinking how nice it would look in the drawing room. And it did. Nothing was obtrusive, out of place, garish or vulgar. Yet it was all rich, moneyed, stylish. 'At home.' Some home, Oliver thought to himself, putting his cup to his mouth. He wished he hadn't come, but she was so persistent, so nice, so good to him that it seemed churlish always to be refusing. He told her he had a thing about eating with people, so he escaped the ordeal of a meal, but now he had agreed to coffee. Anyway, after the visit of the police he was curious.

'So, how did the visit go?' He finished his coffee and put the cup down on one of the highly polished side tables. 'The visit from the police, I mean?' he added, seeing the expression on her face. The visit had been a few days ago and he hadn't seen her since.

'I told them you were still in shock and didn't want to answer questions. More coffee?' She rose and he took up the empty cup and held it out. 'I also told them', she said, carefully replacing the pot on its tray, 'that I thought people had a right to their privacy. As far as I'm concerned, you've done nothing wrong. But something wrong has been done to you and you don't wish to take it further.'

'I have done nothing wrong,' he said. 'But I

117

don't like the fuzz ... the police. That's why I don't want to take it any further. I don't want anything to do with them. They have a habit of twisting things. That's a side of them I don't expect you've seen, Mrs Hunter. They're nice and respectful to people like you, but not nearly so friendly to people who live on the road. They'd like us all to be out of sight or behind bars. We've all got to be categorized, compartmentalized, accounted for. There's no place in the mind of your average copper for individuality.'

Lois felt at a loss for words. Oliver obviously had a thing about the police, some people did; an irrational fear. Or maybe there was a solid reason for his aversion. The police had suggested he might have a criminal past. Yet she believed him when he said he had done nothing wrong. She tried to choose her words carefully.

'The police suggested you might have reasons for not talking to them . . .'

'Such as?' Oliver tilted his chin aggressively at her.

'They didn't specify.'

'There, that's just what I told you, Mrs Hunter.' Oliver angrily banged the arm of his chair nearly upsetting his cup. 'Just because I don't conform . . .'

'They said you'd licensed the van in my name.'

'Is that a criminal offence?'

118

Lois lowered her eyes. 'I wondered why, too.'

'Because it's *your* van, Mrs Hunter. You bought it and you let me drive it. You can have it back any time.'

'No, no, of course I don't want it back. Oh, Oliver, I *do* wish you'd call me Lois.'

Oliver shook his head and, to her dismay, rose from his chair and brought his by now empty cup over to the table. 'I can't explain why, but I can't get the hang of it. It's something ...' he scratched his head. 'I suppose it's because you are a person in authority, a magistrate and that. Also you're loaded. You've been good to me, and I owe you such a lot. Believe me I'm very grateful.' He shook his head again and went to the door. 'I'd better let Chump out and take him for a walk. Thanks for the coffee.'

Lois smiled, but said nothing as she followed him out of the room. When they reached the front door, he stood back for her to undo the latch.

'Thanks, Mrs Hunter,' he said again, pausing beside her. 'It was great. I hope you understand. I *am* so grateful to you. I can't understand why anyone should be so *nice*.'

'I don't want it to be a barrier between us, Oliver,' Lois said gently, letting a hand rest lightly on his injured arm. 'I have the means and you don't. I have an advantaged life and yours is disadvantaged. I don't want this to be a burden to you. When you want to and are able to go, please feel free, without any debt or obligation. And, look, do pop in whenever you like, Oliver, you're always welcome.'

She was aware that now her tone was hostessy, maybe sounded superficial, but she couldn't help it. Couldn't defuse a tense and artificial situation. 'Good night,' she added. 'Sleep well.'

'You too,' he said, and she watched as he walked slowly down the path, hand in his pocket. Now that he was out of the house, his gait seemed jauntier, more relaxed, like a coil unsprung.

Oliver had been uneasy in her company and she had been uneasy in his.

Yet she so wished it wasn't like that. She wished she could talk to him, gain his confidence and trust, be a friend, get him to unwind with her as he so obviously could with her sister. Why could Wendy, who hardly knew him, who hadn't saved his life or given him somewhere to live, or helped to support him, find a way to communicate with him when she couldn't? She got on well with other people, men and women; with anyone else she could be normal and relaxed. So why not with Oliver?

Because he thought of her as Lady Bountiful, that's why. He was obligated to her and couldn't think of her simply as a friend.

Well, she'd have another go. She wouldn't

simply give up. When he was out of sight she shut the front door, bolted it and leaned against it for a few moments, thinking. She wandered back to the living room and turned on the TV to watch the news. She felt suddenly desolate and lonely. Slightly useless, if the truth be told.

It was only nine o'clock and there seemed such a lot of the night left in front of her.

She doubted if Oliver's visit had lasted more than twenty minutes.

CHAPTER SIX

Ken had avoided a meeting with Oliver because he knew it would inevitably lead to a row with Lois. He liked to pretend that Oliver wasn't there. But Oliver had been there for nearly a month, and now it appeared he would be there for much longer as his arm, which had been broken in several places, was slow in healing.

The general election on 1 May was drawing near and Ken was out every weekend, and sometimes midweek in London, canvassing for the Conservative Party. There were ominous signs nationwide that the Tories were on their way out. As far as Ken was concerned, the Tory Party represented all that he held dear about the British way of life, despite the sleaze, the general bickering among MPs, and doubts about leadership that had bedevilled it. Labour was even threatening to do away with the hunt, that bastion of country life.

Ken was not a bigoted, prejudiced man of the kind that some stereotypes of the typical Tory portrayed: a sort of modern Colonel Blimp. He was as good as his wife was good, and as long as people tried to do their best he was compassionate towards the needy and the poor.

But he did have a thing against beggars. He thought there was no need for them; that the Welfare State was sufficient to take care of them. He strongly objected to their attempts to waylay him, and others like him, on the streets of our cities and towns.

Lois and Ken were happily married in every sense. Ken adored his wife, but this streak of irrationality on her part as regards the question of Oliver left him bemused. He knew that she was good and kind and compassionate towards those less fortunate than herself, as was he. Giving a beggar a couple of quid and some tins of dog meat was one thing—though he would not even have done that—but taking them to your home and hearth was another. Lois had gone out of her way to befriend Oliver, yet as far as Ken could see Oliver wasn't all that grateful. It was true that he didn't abuse the hospitality Lois and the Drivers had given him. He was self-effacing, undemanding; but he was there, and every time Ken rounded the bend in the drive on his way home and saw that wretched red van tucked behind the Drivers' house he fumed. This weekend he decided the time had come to have it out with the unwelcome lodger. On the Saturday morning, saying nothing to Lois, he stopped by the Drivers' house on his way out to canvass and went into their kitchen where Beverley and Neal were having a cup of coffee.

They immediately offered him one, but Ken shook his head saying he'd already had one with Lois.

'I was actually looking for Oliver,' he said. 'Have you seen him?'

'He's usually about.' Beverley looked around as though expecting Oliver to step through a door, one of the many doors from all parts of the house that led into the large farmhouse kitchen. Beverley, knowing the tension that Oliver's presence caused between Lois and Ken, the difference in mood at the weekends ever since Oliver had been there, felt a *frisson* of alarm. 'Is there something you wanted, Ken?'

'I'd like to know when that young man is going to take himself off,' Ken said. 'It's time he was on his way.'

Beverley thought it might be in order to ask what was bugging Ken, as Oliver was quiet, inoffensive, almost invisible. However, she

123

knew better. Although there was a show of equality between the Drivers and the Hunters, there was no doubt in the minds of the former as to who were the bosses, where the money lay—and the power to deprive them of their homes and jobs if they so wished. You were nice to your employers, even if you liked them, which they did, because it didn't do to be otherwise.

'I'll go and look for him,' Neal said, getting up from his chair, empty coffee mug plonked on the table.

'Don't worry,' Ken put out a hand. 'Will he be in his van?'

'He might be.' Neal scratched his head. 'I haven't seen him for a couple of days, actually. Bev?'

Beverley shook her head. 'He may be away.'

'How do you mean "away"?' Ken looked indignant. 'I thought he was immobile? That he had a broken arm and that's why he couldn't drive.'

'But he can walk. He seems to enjoy walking. He goes off with the dog. He has treatment at the hospital, and I think he stays somewhere in the area. Oliver is a law unto himself.'

'So it seems,' Ken said disapprovingly. He looked around. 'Been useful in the house, has he?'

'Well . . .' Neal, who seldom did anything in a hurry, appeared to consider the question.

'He's a trained carpenter, but with only one good arm ... not much he could do really. Odd jobs here and there ...'

'He's quiet. No trouble at all. He's been awfully useful baby-sitting,' Beverley butted in. 'For the first time in ages Neal and I have been able to have evenings out.'

'He's willing and amiable,' Neal conceded.

'In other words, you approve of him?'

'Like I say, he's no trouble.'

'He's no trouble to me either,' Ken said somewhat disconcertingly, 'except that for some reason his presence annoys me.'

He then turned and walked out of the door that led to the yard and, through the back window, they could see him stomping off across the field towards the van.

Neal, arms akimbo, watched him. 'Whatever has got into Ken?' He turned to his wife, who was rinsing mugs in the sink.

'He just doesn't like the way Lois took Oliver in.'

'You mean, he thinks there may be something between them?' Neal sounded incredulous.

'I don't know what he thinks, to tell you the truth.' Beverley went up and put an arm round her husband's waist. 'But I do think it's a bit odd myself.' She looked up at him. 'And you must too, dear, surely?'

'I didn't really give it much thought, except that it was a kindness on Lois's part—and it *is* kind . . . They don't spend much time together do they?'

'Oh, no. Days pass and they don't see each other. At least, I don't *think* so; but you never know, do you?'

'Bev, are you serious?' Neal gazed at her with rounded eyes.

'I don't know what they do. For all I know, or you for that matter, he may be over there every evening having it off with her. After all, he's an attractive man. Why else did she do it?'

'Well, I never,' Neal said. 'I am absolutely flabbergasted. You amaze me.'

'I'm not saying it is that, mind you. I have no proof; but all I know is that Lois isn't herself and nor is Ken. Something or someone has come between them.'

*   *   *

As Ken approached the van he saw a movement behind it, and stopped. He wasn't quite sure what he was going to say to Oliver. He'd just been seized by an impulse as he passed the farmhouse and saw that red blob behind the barn that always aggravated him. He had so far desisted from confrontation with Oliver because he knew that's just what it would be: a confrontation. It would upset Lois, and he felt their relationship was strained enough without that. That was why he wanted Oliver out: his presence was interfering with

126

their hitherto happy marriage. A wife who behaved as irrationally as Lois had over a beggar was a problem, and each time he came home Ken hoped that Oliver would simply have gone so that no more need be said.

But Oliver was obviously one of those people who knew a good thing when they saw it: he hung on.

He walked round to the back of the van and there, peering in at the back window, was Lois. She was rubbing the window with her hand and cupping her eyes, trying to see in.

'Anyone there?' she called.

Then, conscious of a movement at her side, she turned and a look of astonishment took the place of curiosity on her face when she saw Ken.

'Ken! What on earth?'

'I could say the same about you.'

'But I thought you were going canvassing?' She had a plastic carrier bag in her hand and looked flustered. There had been something furtive about her movement and Ken thought she had been trying to hide the carrier behind her back, but realized it was too late.

'Just some things for him,' she said lamely. 'A couple of tins of food for the dog. A piece of cheese.'

'No wonder he doesn't want to go if you feed him.'

'Ken, don't be so horrible.' Lois pushed a piece of hair away from her eyes. 'He's got absolutely nothing, you know.'

'Except you,' Ken retorted. 'If it wasn't for you he'd be on his way by now.'

'I don't know how you can be so unkind.'

'I don't know how you can be so silly, Lois. After all this man has done. I really consider your behaviour, your attitude, verging on the abnormal.'

'That is an *awful* thing to say. Being kind to someone in need is not abnormal.'

'It's taking charity too far. I believe in helping people who help themselves. Frankly, I came to tell this young man that it's time he took himself off.'

'What harm has he done you?'

'I just don't *like* him here, Lois. I don't like him here hanging about when I'm away.'

The blood rushed to her face.

'I hope you're not suggesting . . .'

'I'm not suggesting anything.'

'I wouldn't dream—'

'I'm sure you wouldn't.'

'And I deeply resent the implication . . . that there's anything going on.'

'Well?' Ken looked at her, but she didn't flinch.

'Most certainly not.'

'You're here alone every night. I can't blame you for being lonely; but I won't alter the situation, Lois, unless you want to come to London with me.'

'And I am *not* having an affair with Oliver.

The idea is preposterous.'

'Wendy said she thought he was attractive. That's why I want to see the fellow.'

'So, *that's* what it is.' Illumination dawned. 'Just because Wendy said she found him attractive.' She smiled. 'You're *jealous*, darling! Don't tell me you're jealous?'

'I would be jealous if you were carrying on with him.'

'Well, I'm not. I can assure you of that.' She tried to put an arm through Ken's but he was unresponsive. She could sense how prickly he was. In a way it was good to make your husband jealous. Sometimes it did feel as though you were being taken for granted. She was never lonely and she didn't feel neglected. She led such a busy social life that the rare nights she was at home on her own she rather enjoyed, never more than one or two a week. Nice to have a tray in front of the telly, put your feet up in preparation for the otherwise busy life they led, the hectic times they had at the weekend.

Occasionally Oliver came in for a coffee after supper, still invariably refusing her offer of a meal, never staying long. It was as if he did it out of a sense of duty and not because he wanted to. They would chat about this and that, matters of no consequence, always avoiding personal issues. Things were easier between them, more natural, but she remained 'Mrs Hunter' and, hard as she tried, it was difficult to establish a real sense of rapport, of the confidence she so wished for—for his sake as well as hers. She thought he was a lonely man. Bev, with whom he sometimes would have a snack lunch, said he was a solitary, an oddball, if you like.

There was still the matter of the attack. Ken was as anxious as ever to press charges, but Lois thought the longer they left it the less likely the matter would be to end in court. If neither she nor Oliver pressed charges the police wouldn't have a case. The injuries were not really serious and all the witnesses had vanished. Besides, the thought of the publicity was hideous.

Ken considered this wrong, a denial of common justice against the felons who could have inflicted grave injury upon his wife. It was letting criminals escape justice, and that was just what the Tories were against.

Lois put the bag down near the rear of the van and then, once again, tried to take Ken's arm.

'Don't be so silly,' she said in a wheedling tone. 'Actually, I'm enjoying being the subject of jealousy. It shows you care.'

'Of course I care.' He looked down at her and this time did not try to remove his arm. Impulsively he leaned forward to kiss her cheek. 'I care a great deal.'

They started towards the house when there was a movement through the trees and Chump bounded ahead of Oliver who soon appeared trotting along behind him.

'Oh, look,' a note of false jollity entered Lois's voice, 'here's Oliver.'

The smile vanished from Oliver's face as he saw Lois and Ken, arms linked, standing together watching him. He slowed down and Chump, racing ahead, got to them before he did and jumped up in an effort to lick Lois's cheek. She leaned down and fondled the dog's ears.

'Ken, this is Chump and,' she looked up, 'this is Oliver. Oliver, you haven't met my husband, Ken.'

'How do you do, Mr Hunter?' Gravely Oliver stuck out his good hand.

'How do you do?' Ken said stiffly.

'Ken was just looking at the van. I brought a few things over for you.' Lois indicated the carrier bag on the ground. 'A couple of tins, some ham, cheese—the usual things.'

Oliver stooped and inspected the contents of the carrier then slowly he righted himself. 'It's very good of you, Mrs Hunter. However, I feel I should tell you that I don't eat ham. I'm a vegetarian.'

'But I've given it to you before!' There was a look of consternation on Lois's face.

'I know, I should have said something, but I didn't like to. You've been so kind. It was silly of me, but now I don't want to put you to any more expense.'

131

'Then ... what did you do with it?' Ham had always been a staple item in any food packages.

Oliver indicated the dog. 'Chump's not a vegetarian.'

'When do you think you'll be moving on?' Ken enquired with deceptive casualness.

'I hope very soon, sir.' Oliver held up his arm still in a sling. 'Unfortunately, my arm isn't quite better. They had to break it again and reset it. The first time it didn't take.'

As Lois winced, Ken nodded his head.

'I see. Presumably one can get a report from the hospital?'

'Of course ...'

Oliver looked nonplussed as Lois said quickly, 'Ken, why ever say a thing like that?'

'Because I would like a report, that's all. Here we have a young, fit man. Why does a broken arm take such a long time to heal?'

'He told you. It didn't set properly.'

'Ring the hospital, by all means,' Oliver said offhandedly, pointedly putting the key in the door of the van. Then he turned and stared at Ken, his expression every bit as unfriendly as his reluctant host's. 'Believe me, Mr Hunter, I shan't stay a moment longer in this place than necessary. Your wife has been goodness and kindness itself. Beverley and Neal have been great; but I want to be off, not hanging around taking charity, however well-meaning.'

With that, ushering Chump before him,

Oliver stepped inside the van and, with a polite smile at Lois but ignoring Ken, shut the door in their faces.

Ken looked about to make some riposte, moved towards the door, and Lois held on to him.

'Cheeky beggar!' Ken exploded.

'You were being most unpleasant.'

'He's a cheeky, insolent little twerp.' Ken stopped and, looking at his wife, raised a finger towards her. 'Look, Lois, if he isn't gone by this time next week I can't answer for the consequences.'

'And what do you mean by that?'

'I shall call the police and have him forcibly removed.'

*   *   *

When Lois got back to the house she was fighting to keep the tears from her eyes. In the kitchen, Wendy, looking somewhat dishevelled and still in her dressing gown, was filling the kettle.

'Sorry, we're hideously late this morning.' She rubbed the sleep from her eyes and, although it was nearly noon, had obviously just woken.

'It doesn't matter. You can sleep in as long as you like.'

Lois slumped wearily into a chair by the kitchen table. Wendy plugged in the kettle and then looked sharply across at her sister.

'Something the matter? You look all in.'

'There's just been a scene between Ken and Oliver.' Lois put her head in her hands. 'A horrible scene. And then he and I fell out— Ken and I, that is.'

'But I didn't think Ken had met Oliver. You said he always avoided him.'

'Well, today he wanted to confront him, for some reason. He's been in a peculiar mood. I do believe he's jealous of Oliver just because you said he was dishy.'

'Oh, that was a silly thing to say!' Wendy looked embarrassed. 'I mean, I do think he's quite dishy, but . . .'

'I know how you meant it. As you said, you can find someone attractive without falling in love with them. As a matter of fact, I don't find Oliver all that attractive, sexually. I know he's not much younger than I am, but I almost regard him as a sort of elder son. I feel protective towards him. I always have.' Her features twisted into a rueful smile. 'He's so sweet and considerate. I just found out today he's a vegetarian. Doesn't eat meat, which is probably why he would never accept an invitation to supper.'

'You invited him to supper?'

'Once or twice when Ken is away. Usually I'm so busy; but he'd come for coffee. Never stays long. Does it out of politeness. I often put him some ham and a few cans of dog meat in a carrier bag and today he said I shouldn't go to the trouble as he's a vegetarian. Didn't like to tell me before. Silly, but sweet, really. He's such a well-meaning person. Really nice. I wish Ken would see that side of him. He's so . . . *prejudiced*. And the thing is that Ken's usually such a nice, rational guy too. I can't understand what's got into him.'

'Maybe you should have tried to bring Oliver and Ken together sooner?'

'I did. It just didn't happen. Ken had made up his mind about him, even without seeing him.'

'In that case, perhaps Oliver should go,' Wendy said firmly and, getting up as the kettle boiled, put two spoonfuls of instant coffee into the two mugs she had on the bench and filled them with water. 'He has been here a month.'

'But he can't *drive*.'

'Well,' Wendy shrugged and balanced the mugs in both hands, 'I must take this up to Tim. We were awake half the night arguing. That's why I'm so tired.'

'What about?'

'What do you think?'

'Not the wedding again?'

Wendy nodded. 'We can't decide on how many people to ask, or on the hotel. It might be easier . . .' she paused and looked earnestly at Lois. 'We wondered if we could have a marquee in the grounds here? It will save the expense of a big hotel. You see, now that we're inviting so many people, nowhere is really big enough. We'd pay all the expenses, obviously. Do you think Ken would mind?' She gave her sister a pitiful look. 'It would save such a lot of trouble between me and Tim. It's all Tim's fault, this notion of a big wedding. We should have just bummed off to the register office as I said in the first place. If I'd known that getting married was such a hassle, I think I'd have had second thoughts.' She pulled down her mouth. 'Perhaps Tim would, too.'

'Maybe it's not too late,' Lois remarked sourly behind her back, but Wendy had already gone through the door.

*   *   *

Lois had a solitary lunch, just a snack as she wasn't really hungry. Ken had said he would not be back before dinner, which they were having with the Andersons, the local doctor and his pushy wife who thought her husband should have been a consultant, as a result of which she was permanently discontented and consequently rude to patients who dreaded her voice on the phone. They were both, of course, extremely nice to the Hunters and in addition Sonia Anderson was an excellent cook. Tim and Wendy were invited too, and doubtless Sonia's opinion would be canvassed on who to get to cater for the wedding—that is, if it was to be a marquee on the lawn at

136

Higham Hall, though there was plenty of time for a change in plan about that.

Lois felt extremely tired and depressed. In a way, she too was beginning to wish that Oliver would go. There was nothing one could blame him for and it would be most unfair to do so, but his presence had caused a lot of trouble between herself and Ken, unnecessarily so. However, the fact that Ken might be jealous of a younger man gave her a clue to his unease and, at the same time, she was pervaded by a glow of satisfaction at the idea that, in her mid-thirties and with two teenage sons, she was still capable of inspiring jealousy.

Thus a little cheered, Lois finished her frugal lunch and prepared to set off for her flower arranging in the church. Usually she only did one weekend in three, but because there was a hunt next week which coincided with her turn, she had swapped round with Madge, who was always ready to oblige a friend.

On her way out, Lois met Wendy and Tim coming down the stairs, Tim in riding clothes. Wendy, who looked pale and wan, was in jeans and sweater.

'Going riding?' Lois called.

'Just Tim,' Wendy answered as they reached the bottom of the staircase. 'I've got a headache.'

'I told her a blow would do her good,' Tim said, his manner rather agitated.

'But I don't *feel* like it, darling. Don't always be trying to force me to do something I don't want to do.'

'I am *not* trying to force you . . .'

Lois left the lovers glaring at each other and, with a wave, ran down the steps and walked rapidly in the direction of the garages to get her car.

Wendy stood at the top of the steps watching her go. 'She'll think we're always quarrelling,' she said, turning to Tim as he came out behind her.

'It does seem that way these days.'

Wendy went down the steps ahead of Tim, who followed her slowly, tapping his flank lightly with his riding crop. 'It's the tension of the wedding.' Tim caught up with her and his arm encircled her waist. 'Maybe we *should* have had it in a register office.'

Wendy stopped and glared at him.

'*Now* he tells me!'

'Well?' He looked at her. 'I don't mind, if it's what you want.'

'Oh, for heaven's sake, Tim!' she said crossly. 'People will think we're crazy, always changing our minds. Now we've asked Ken and Lois—'

'All right, all right . . . If that's what you want.'

'It *is* what I want . . . now.' She held out her hand and they walked together towards the stables where Tim's horse was already saddled and waiting for him, Ted holding on to the bridle.

'Good afternoon, Mr Gardener. Nice day for a ride. Miss Cartwright?' He looked at Wendy, who shook her head.

'Not today, Ted. I'm not feeling all that bright. I thought I'd go for a walk instead. What time will you be back, Tim?'

'Five-ish.' Tim looked at his watch.

'I'll see you for a drink in the drawing room. We're having dinner tonight with the Andersons. I think I'll have a nap after my walk.'

'Good idea.' Tim leaned forward to kiss her before mounting his horse, managing to whisper in her ear: 'I *do* love you.' Wendy nodded, smiled and stepped back to wave as he trotted out of the yard and made his way along the drive towards the gate.

'You don't really like horse riding, do you, miss?' Ted asked conversationally.

'I do quite. I just don't like hunting.'

'But hunting is a great sport.'

'I think it's horrible.'

'You'll have to get used to it if you're going to live in these parts, miss.'

'But I'm not going to live in these parts. Whatever gave you that idea?' Wendy looked at Ted in surprise.

'Oh, I thought you were, after you were married. Mrs Hunter said something about it.'

'We're having the wedding and our

139

reception here, probably, but we're not living here. We both have our work in London.'

'I'm sorry, miss. I misunderstood.' Ted turned to go back into the stables and Wendy wandered slowly around the side of the building where she found herself looking at Oliver's van parked in the field just behind.

There was no sign of life. He really was a man of mystery. She wondered what he did with his time. Life in a van must be awfully boring. She walked up to the van and peered inside, rather as Lois had done earlier in the day. This time, though, a face grinned out at her and the door swung open.

'Hello!' Oliver said cheerily. 'Come for a visit?'

'I was just seeing Tim off. He's gone riding.'

'Don't you like riding?' As Oliver got out of the van Chump jumped out after him.

'I quite like riding, but I hate hunting. They're going hunting next week.'

'Oh, good. I mean, I hate hunting too.' Oliver paused and looked intensely at her. 'Somehow I thought you would hate hunting.'

Wendy stopped and tossed back her hair. 'Why?'

'I just thought you would.'

'My sister's terribly keen on it.'

'I know. I think sometimes that's why I can't really gel with her, for all that she's so nice. I think blood sports are awful. They change a person. Must do. Ripping animals apart. It's

140

horrible, isn't it?'

'Horrible,' Wendy agreed. 'I say, do you want to walk for a bit? I was just going to stretch my legs.'

'I was about to do the same.' Oliver smiled and, as Chump bounded about, turned to lock the door of the van.

'Do you always do that?' Wendy asked watching him.

'Do what?'

'Lock the door.'

'Always.'

'But why? Here? Don't you trust people?'

'I do trust them; but I have to be careful.'

'But you don't have anything much to steal, do you?'

'It's not that. I just don't want my privacy to be invaded. Also, I don't want anyone to steal the van as Mrs Hunter has been kind enough to buy it for me.' By now, walking fairly briskly, Chump leading the way, they were well clear of the van and heading towards the woods at the back of the farm. 'Did you hear about this morning?'

'Yes.'

'Mr Hunter hates me. I seldom saw such hatred in someone's eyes. It was most unpleasant.'

'I don't think he *hates* you. He just doesn't know you. Actually, he doesn't like me much either.'

'Doesn't he? That's a good sign.'

141

'Why is it a good sign?'

'Work it out. He doesn't like you and he doesn't like me.' Oliver plodded steadily on. 'And he doesn't *want* to know me. He's anxious for me to be gone. I'm anxious to go, too.'

Wendy noticed now that Oliver wasn't wearing his sling.

'It won't be long will it? With the arm?'

'It *is* very stiff.' Oliver held it out before him and slightly twisted it. 'I have so little movement in it. They say it would be dangerous to drive. I wondered if Mrs Hunter knew anywhere else I could leave my van?'

'I'm sure she does; but I think she would be upset if you did.'

'Mr Hunter told her he'd have me forcibly removed if I didn't leave. I heard him tell her that after I got into the van.'

'Oh, I think his temper just got the better of him. He didn't really mean it. Lois is awfully sorry about it. I think she's going to talk to him and try and calm him down.'

They reached the wood and the sunlight seemed to follow them as they wandered through the trees, stopping now and then to admire the fresh undergrowth peeping through. It was a lovely afternoon and Wendy experienced a sense of freedom, almost of exhilaration, as she picked her way through the woods with this strange man, tall and robust beside her, the dog sniffing about in the undergrowth. She glanced sideways at him and

142

saw that he was thoughtful too, his eyes scanning the ground.

'Are you really happy?' she asked and he paused and looked long at her.

'Really happy? Is there such a thing?'

'You seem happy. I mean, you have a most peculiar life by ordinary standards, living in a cramped van, no money. No visible means of support. I've never met anybody quite like you.'

'I'm sure you haven't.' Oliver smiled. 'But then, I've never met anyone quite like you. We come from completely different worlds, Wendy. Tell me, what's Tim like?' Oliver, who seemed to tire easily, perched on the trunk of a tree that had been blown down by the gales and never replaced. All sorts of interesting flora and fauna were shooting up beside it.

'Tim may be a bit conventional by your standards, but he is nice. He's an expert on eighteenth century art and works for a well-known firm of auctioneers.'

'How long have you known him?'

'About five years.'

'And do you love him?'

'Very much.'

'But you said you argued all the time.'

'That's only about the wedding. Once we're married it will be all sorted. Tim is actually a real sweetie, terribly easy going.'

'It seems strange,' Oliver murmured, looking up at the sky glimpsed between the trees.

'What does?'

'When you're here getting married in the autumn, I shall be hundreds of miles away. Long gone from your life.'

Oliver lowered his eyes and they stared at each other and, in that moment, the seeds of doubt in Wendy's mind that had hitherto been nascent seemed to sprout and grow like the infant saplings about them in the wood which, one day, would turn into tall trees.

CHAPTER SEVEN

The book was called *Dropping Out*. It was by a forty-five-year-old man who had abandoned a career in the City to live in a ramshackle shed in the north of Scotland while he practised self-sufficiency. He did this with some success; in addition to selling the book to Wendy's publishers, who had paid a substantial advance, he had sold the television rights to a production company who had plans for a mini series.

What this would do to the author would be to turn him again into a wealthy man. If anything, it would make him richer than he had been as a City banker. Already he was showing the trappings of fame and power, and drove to his shed in a newly purchased

144

Porsche.

He was meanwhile making out in a series of first-class hotels as he and Wendy toured the country to promote the book. Edinburgh was the last stop. After that the author, Charles Fraser, would head for his shack—although he had now exchanged its discomforts for a nearby country house hotel where he had a suite—and Wendy would head home.

Wendy had liked Charles. They got on well. He enjoyed good food and good living and she had tried hard to fathom why he had ever abandoned the life of ease, which he obviously preferred, in the first place. Was it to try and make even more money as, ironically enough, he was doing?

Not at all, he had assured her. His intentions had been completely idealistic. He had enjoyed his Spartan life and, indeed, he'd no idea that his book would turn into a bestseller. *Dropping Out* was now climbing up the charts and, although it would never be number one, it seemed destined to remain comfortably in the middle of the top one hundred, and would probably climb the charts when the paperback appeared to coincide with the TV series.

Yet Charles had confessed, over a bottle of Bollinger to go with the oysters they had consumed in an Edinburgh restaurant, that he was unlikely to return to the simple life. It had palled. It was hard. His skin had become leathery and he was beginning to suffer from rheumatism. He was now planning to build a house with all the creature comforts, still in the north of Scotland, which he loved, and possibly within sight of his shack. From now on he would devote his energies to writing, perhaps a novel.

The signing in a large bookshop on Princes Street over, Charles was being taken to lunch by the store manager. Wendy had a seat booked on the afternoon flight so she turned down the offer of lunch. She and Charles embraced warmly in the foyer of the hotel and promised to keep in touch. This was routine with all authors to whom one became genuinely attached, but only for a time, and it hardly ever turned out that way. Life was too short, and not only did they fail to keep in touch once their brief moment of fame was over—and it usually was—she soon forgot even their names.

Charles would probably never write another bestseller, however hard he tried, but would be able to live in comfort for the rest of his life, if he so wished, on the earnings of his one successful book.

Wendy sat gazing out of the aeroplane window as they flew south over the patchwork of fields, villages and woodland that was England. It was turning into a beautiful month as the election hotted up and politicians toured the country in their shirtsleeves, the opposition urging the populace to change its government; the government exhorting it to give it yet another term. The polls predicted a colossal Labour lead, but hardly anyone believed them.

Wendy fervently hoped Labour would win. It was true that her sister and brother-in-law derided her as a champagne socialist, and it was also true that she enjoyed life's little comforts, and some of its major ones as well. But she did care. She cared about the beggars in the street sleeping in makeshift boxes, something that one had never seen before the Tories came to power, but which had been a feature of her life as long as she could remember.

Their very existence made her feel guilty and uncomfortable. Her mind flew, as it had ever since their walk in the wood, to Oliver and the strange and unexpected rapport which had developed between them. She had found herself looking deeply into his eyes, so full of a strange wisdom belying his years, and she seemed to see herself reflected there: a rather tortured, anguished soul, not knowing what direction she should take. This endless argument about the wedding seemed to be a pointer that all was not well. Oliver thought this was the case. She had found herself talking to him as though he was as wise and as old as Merlin, and she had gone back that night in a reflective, disturbed mood.

She knew she worried Lois and irritated Ken, and it was with a feeling of relief that she had returned to London and immersed herself once more in the whirl of office life.

It was true that her lifestyle gave her little time to think. The week was taken up largely with work, even in the evenings, and the weekends were mostly spent in Dorset now that the venue had almost definitely been decided for the wedding.

Almost ... There was still the vexed question of who to invite. Tim had dozens of relations, she and Lois hardly any, and then one's friends. What sort of priority should one give to them? Who would be most likely to take offence if they weren't asked? Should they invite people who were important to their careers? Tim's boss? Her managing director? And then there was Ken's attitude, one of grudging acceptance, his niggling little enquiries not only about cost but which of his and Lois's friends, people whom neither Wendy nor Tim knew, should be invited. And what about people like the Andersons, whom they all knew but none of them really liked, yet who would undoubtedly feel slighted if they weren't invited? What about people like them?

Ken had grown steadily more sour over recent weeks and it had only just dawned on Wendy that this was not only on account of the wedding, but also because of Oliver. Indeed, it had come to a climax the previous weekend, with a blazing row on the Sunday when Lois taxed Ken over his ultimatum about Oliver. She had gone so far as to threaten that if Oliver left she would too, which was absurd, but it indicated to what depths the relationship between husband and wife had sunk.

The noise had woken the couple sleeping late, as usual, upstairs, and when they had finally crept down for brunch the house was deserted. Ken had gone riding and Lois had taken herself and her two dogs off to Madge for a bit of TLC—TLC which, really, Wendy should have been the one to provide. It made her feel guilty.

Wendy hadn't said goodbye to Oliver. Things had gone too far on the day of their walk. Oliver now made her feel uncomfortable. There had been that moment when their eyes had met, remaining fixed, entranced by each other. In the circumstances it had been unnerving, unsettling, almost frightening. She had revealed too much of herself to someone who, well, was almost a complete stranger.

*　　*　　*

Once again the meet assembled in the yard of Higham Hall. It was to be the last of the season. Horses would be laid up, except for exercise, and the hounds spent the summer in their kennels. A breeding programme would be started. All summer long preparations would continue for the resumption of hunting in the autumn. This year the end of the season was especially poignant because of the awful threat, not only of vast areas being prohibited by the National Trust, but of the sport itself being abolished by an incoming Labour Government.

Blood sports enthusiasts were busy mobilizing themselves to campaign on behalf of a new Conservative Government, which they hoped would be more enlightened and understanding—at least insofar as country pursuits were concerned.

For Lois, the only good thing about the end of the hunting season was that the anti-hunt campaigners would disperse, at least for another six months, and that awful knot that came into her tummy at the beginning of each meet would disappear. This time there seemed to be more of them than usual, perhaps emboldened by the fact that, with an election so near, the more they called attention to themselves the better.

Beverley came round to collect the stirrup cups and Lois placed hers on the tray with a smile of thanks. Tim was riding today. Wendy was nowhere to be seen, probably in bed, her head under the pillow, as she disapproved of the hunt so much. Tim was nervous about offending Wendy, but he was a country man and she'd known that he was fond of blood sports before she got engaged to him. Nonetheless they always had a row after a meet. It was *de rigueur* and Wendy sulked for the rest of the day.

Really they were quite an incongruous couple, Lois thought, not for the first time. And yet in a way they were well suited. It was a strange contrast. They were from the same class; they had a lot in common, and Lois knew they had a wonderful sex life because Wendy always told her as much—to Lois's embarrassment; she would never dream of divulging the secrets of her own marriage bed, even to someone to whom she was as close as her sister. She didn't know why. It was an inhibition she had, which was what made her different from Wendy.

Tim came up to her, followed by Ken. Then the master blew the horn and the hunt set off, the usual colourful display of black and hunting pink enhancing the fresh, verdant colours of spring, the signs of which were all about them. Tim flanked her on her left, Ken her right, and as they rode into the barricade of abuse both escorts seemed to close in protectively.

They were nearly clear of the gate when a woman stepped forward from the crowd and blew a blast on a horn, aiming it straight into the ear of Ken's horse, Napoleon. Startled, the horse whinnied and raised himself on his hind legs so that he was almost vertical, whereupon

Ken, who had been expecting nothing of the sort, fell off and landed on his back, narrowly to escape being trampled on by the rider immediately to his rear. There was a horrified gasp from the crowd and, looking up, Lois saw that, well to the back and trying hard now to get out of sight but unable to because of the banner they were carrying between them, stood Wendy and Oliver. The sight of them angered Lois so much that she nearly turned her horse into the crowd to get to them, but by now pandemonium had broken out.

The policeman was hastily summoning help and, possibly, an ambulance on his walkie-talkie and Tim had leapt off his horse and was kneeling beside Ken, who appeared to be unconscious.

At that moment, Ted, who had ridden on ahead, came cantering back and, taking Lois's reins, held Whisper steady while she dismounted and ran over to the supine form of her husband. Tim had his finger on the pulse in Ken's neck and looked up with a reassuring expression as Lois knelt beside him.

'He's OK. At least, his pulse is quite strong. Have they sent for an ambulance?'

'The policeman was talking into his radio.'

'Great! He'll be all right.'

By now a small crowd had gathered around Ken, who began to stir. Lois gently took his hand as his eyelids fluttered and a little colour seemed to be returning to his face.

She leant her cheek against his.

'Darling, are you all right? Ken, it's Lois.'

Ken opened his eyes and looked directly into hers. 'God, where am I?' he asked, looking up at the blue sky. 'Is this heaven?'

'You're still earthbound, darling.' Lois laughed shakily. 'You were thrown from your horse.'

Ken struggled to try and get up, but Lois placed a hand gently on his chest.

'Please, Ken, stay where you are. You might have broken something. An ambulance is on its way. Do you have any pain?'

'Slight pain in my leg,' Ken said. 'What on earth caused Napoleon to shy?'

'Some lunatic blew a horn into his ear.'

'The bastards,' Ken grimaced, looking round at the crowd, which was thinner now that most of the protesters had slunk away. Two exceptions were Oliver and Wendy, who, their banner crumpled between them, stood dejectedly a few feet away, looking on.

When she caught sight of them, Lois jumped up and, with an exclamation of rage, went over to them.

'How *could* you?' she hissed. 'How could you? Look what's happened to Ken.'

'*We* didn't do anything,' Wendy protested. 'We were right at the back.'

'We certainly didn't approve of what happened,' Oliver murmured but, nevertheless, he looked shamefaced.

'You were morally responsible,' Lois shouted, realizing that her whole body was shaking. 'You and others like you are responsible for the maniac who blew the horn into Napoleon's ear. Ken could have been killed. We don't yet know the extent of the damage.'

Behind her, Tim stood staring at his fiancée, his expression incredulous.

'You . . .' he spluttered, 'you told me you were going for a walk.'

'I was. I did, and I met Oliver on the way, struggling with his banner. He couldn't really manage it because of his wonky arm, so I said I'd help him. I thought it was all a bit of a lark.'

'A lark! The whole thing is beneath contempt,' Tim retorted. 'I'm really ashamed of you, Wendy!' And with that he turned and went back to Ken's side just as the sound of the ambulance could be heard coming up the drive.

*   *   *

Lois crept into the bedroom and, balancing a tray on one arm, stood by the half-open door before shutting it gently behind her. She tiptoed across the room and put the tray down carefully by the bed. Then she sat down in a chair by the side of the table and looked over at the sleeping form of her husband.

The sound of her movements had disturbed

154

Ken. He opened first one eye and then the other.

'Sleep well?' she asked, getting up and crossing to the bed.

Momentarily Ken appeared dazed, then ran his hands over his face, blinked twice, and nodded.

She stooped and kissed his forehead.

'I was so worried,' she said. 'Thank God you're all right.'

Miraculously, he was all right. Except for a few bruises, and a mild case of shock, he was completely unscathed from his fall, which could easily have broken his back.

The ambulance men had checked him over and, instead of taking him to hospital, had driven him the few yards home and put him tenderly to bed. The family doctor was then summoned; he gave Ken a thorough examination, told Lois to keep a careful eye on him and left a supply of pills to help him sleep.

'I've brought you a little breakfast,' Lois said. 'Tea and toast.'

'Great!' Ken struggled to sit up, still looking dazed. 'I think those pills knocked me out.'

'Otherwise OK?' Lois looked anxiously at him again.

'A bit bruised.' He rubbed his backside. 'Those bloody anarchists. That *sister* of yours . . .' he glared at Lois, who lowered her head.

'I wondered if you'd seen her.'

155

'*Seen* her? She had a great big banner which she was holding with some man. You could have seen them a mile off.'

'It was Oliver.' Lois raised her head, her expression abject. 'I've told him to go.' She put out a hand as Ken struggled to speak. 'Don't take on, darling. Don't upset yourself. It's not necessary. I've rung Madge and asked her if she'd let Oliver leave his van on her land and she said that she would. Wendy is going to drive it over for him this morning. Then she and Tim are going straight back to town.'

'I hope you've told them the wedding's off here, too.'

'I think she knows that.'

'What on earth possessed her? You, me, Tim, riding in the hunt and she joins forces with that reprobate—who has already caused enough trouble—to wave a banner of hatred and defiance against her hosts. I can't get over it.'

'Neither can I. It's deeply irresponsible. She said she saw Oliver struggling with the banner and only meant to help him.'

'And Oliver was a guest here, too.'

'Exactly. Inexcusable. He did apologize, but he is so much against blood sports he didn't think.'

'What a lot of trouble that creature has brought.'

'He has.' Lois lowered her head again. 'I realize that now. I can't say how sorry I am

156

that unwittingly I was the cause of all this. I'm sorry I was so stubborn. I'm sorry too that Wendy is my sister. I mean, I'm not sorry, because I love her, but all this business about the wedding has been too much.'

'They've been here every bloody weekend.'

'I know, and you've been terribly tolerant, Ken. All I can say is that it wasn't them who caused the accident. Oliver and Wendy were as horrified as Tim and I.'

'And if they find the chap who did it, *I* shan't hesitate to bring charges.'

Ken edged a piece of toast into his mouth and then swallowed his tea.

'It was a woman.'

'Huh . . . the female of the species, deadlier than the male. Does anyone know who she was?'

'Unfortunately she ran off in the scrum. We shall probably never find out who it was. But, certainly, she had nothing to do with Wendy and Oliver. They didn't know her. They didn't know anyone, in fact.'

Lois leaned down and put her head against Ken's.

'Darling, I am so terribly sorry. I really didn't think through the consequences of my actions when I took pity on Oliver. I was motivated by the best intentions.'

'Let that be a lesson to you,' Ken said gruffly, but she saw that at last he was smiling.

*   *   *

As they left the drive and paused at the main road Oliver looked back and gave a deep sigh.

'I'm really sorry I couldn't say goodbye to Lois and thank her.'

'She'll understand; but I think it wouldn't have been wise. She can't get over what happened to Ken.' Wendy looked both ways and then drove the van in the direction of the town. 'Except that *we* didn't do it. I mean, *we* had nothing to do with his accident. Nothing at all. We were nowhere near him.'

'We were *there*. It's the principle of the thing.'

'I suppose I can see her point of view. It was a bit much, Oliver, demonstrating against the people who were giving you shelter. At the time I thought it was just a lark. Especially with Tim there too; it seemed so funny. I thought it would amuse them, but now I can see how stupid I was. Even if nothing had happened to Ken, to them there's nothing remotely funny about demonstrating against the hunt. It was silly, especially as Ken had taken such a pronounced dislike to you. I should have discouraged you, instead of regarding it as a bit of a prank.'

Wendy drove along the road looking to right and left for the turning that led off to Madge's farm.

'Do you know where you're going?' Oliver

158

asked.

'I think so.'

'It's good of you to help me.'

'I don't think I could do otherwise, especially now that we're partners in crime.' Wendy chortled and looked at him. Then her expression became more serious and she pulled over to the side of the road. 'Oliver, I don't think you're going to get anywhere in this old crate.'

The van had started with difficulty and then rattled and bumped along, never reaching more than twenty miles an hour whatever the speedometer indicated.

'I suppose I'll get over to Miss Cooper's and decide what to do then.'

Wendy tried restarting the van. It spluttered ominously and then stopped. She sat for a moment and then tried again, letting out the choke and putting it in again sharply. It worked. The van shuddered and began to move slowly along the road as cars coming up behind them hooted and then tore past them, horns blaring angrily.

'I doubt this thing is even legal,' Wendy said.

'I'll get on to Clifford. The trouble is it's been standing idle in the field for such a long time.'

'I don't think it's roadworthy, Oliver, I really don't. It will cost a fortune to put right.'

'The MOT has a month to go,' Oliver said stubbornly.

'It will never pass another and, Oliver,' she looked sideways at his arm, 'you still can't drive.'

Wendy had arrived after Lois's interview with Oliver and offered to take him over to Madge, an offer he had gratefully accepted. The Drivers had given him a wide berth ever since the incident, as if they too felt he was partly to blame for what had happened. Certainly they held him guilty of demonstrating against people who, after all, had been kind to him. But his point was that he hadn't been demonstrating against them but against the principle of the hunt; the savagery of killing animals for sport. He felt passionately about that and he still did, not caring who he offended in the process.

Madge was expecting them and stood at the farm gate holding it open as Wendy, calling a cheery greeting from the cab, drove through. She stopped in front of the farm and, jumping down, shook Madge's outstretched hand.

'This is awfully sweet of you, Madge.' She turned as Oliver came slowly round the front of the van followed by Chump, keen to make a new friend. 'This is Oliver. Oliver, Madge Cooper.'

Oliver offered his good hand. His right was once again in a sling to prevent him using it.

'It's very kind of you, Miss Cooper.'

'This is Chump,' Wendy indicated the dog frenziedly wagging its tail. 'Ken and Lois are

160

rather upset about what happened yesterday.'

'I'm doing this merely to oblige my friend,' Madge said, swinging the gate shut before stooping to fondle Chump's ears. 'I can't say I approve of what happened either.'

'But we didn't have anything to do with the actual incident,' Wendy protested.

'I understood you were waving a banner against so-called cruel sports. Well, I'll have you know that I hunt too and I am an animal lover. I do *not* consider it cruel, but humane. Now, I thought you could park it there—' she indicated a field which was again behind a barn, rather as the geography had been at Higham Hall. She studied the van for a moment, her expression censorious. 'It didn't sound too healthy to me as you drove up. Where did you say you're going?'

'I really just want to get out of here,' Oliver said, 'away from Stinsbury, as quickly as I can. Believe me, Miss Cooper, I shan't stay a moment longer than necessary.'

*   *   *

Wendy got to the office early on Monday and rapidly began to go through her diary for the week. She hardly had a free moment until Friday. There were numerous interdepartmental meetings, two book launches and a short author tour in the north of England that would take her away for two nights.

At the weekend she and Tim were due to go to Paris for the wedding of an English friend of theirs to a French girl. Thank God there had been no plan to go to Dorset. She suspected that Dorset would be off the itinerary for some time now.

The office was still empty. Only the doorman had been at his desk when she arrived shortly after eight, leaving her car in the basement car park. He had made some joke about her not being able to sleep, which she acknowledged with a smile. Then she'd made her way through the empty corridors to her desk in publicity, swamped as usual with jacket proofs, fax messages, memos from this person and that, and a pile of as yet unread books she was supposed to promote.

Wendy loved her job, or had done. She felt she would still love it were there not so many complicating factors, and she realized that Oliver was one of these.

Wendy went across to the coffee machine in the corridor and filled a plastic mug with black coffee. Then she took it back to her desk and, slumping in her chair, sat gazing out of the window at the morning rush-hour traffic, bumper to bumper, forcing its way slowly along the busy Westway into the West End. The office was a large purpose-built block in that amorphous part of London not far from the BBC Television Centre. It was a hell of a place to get to from Hampstead and the morning and evening rush hours were ghastly.

Rush, rush, rush. It was totally different from Oliver's lifestyle, yet his at the moment was scarcely easy or enviable.

She realized she was becoming as protective towards Oliver as her sister had been, and she wondered what it was about this strange man that had so affected them both.

Strange. That was the word for Oliver. Not strange as in odd, but strange as in unusual, mysterious, enigmatic. Maybe charismatic was the word to use; some strange power of attraction; but whereas Lois had been adamant that Oliver's attraction for her wasn't sexual, Wendy wasn't so sure.

She felt she was quite seriously attracted to Oliver, that the events of the weekend had merely brought her feelings to a head.

*   *   *

Her boss, Simon Kemp, head of marketing, was someone with whom she had always got on well. It was thanks to him that she had been promoted over men and women every bit as capable, equally ambitious. She felt she owed Simon, and now she was going to let him down. She knocked nervously at his door a few minutes after he got in. She thought she'd give him time to settle, look at the post. She felt so nervous she desperately wanted a cigarette,

163

and she'd given up months before. She would go out after the interview and buy a pack, that was for sure.

Simon called 'Come in' and Wendy slid round the door as he looked up.

'Wendy! God you're pale!' he exclaimed, rising from his seat, his expression one of concern. 'Are you OK?'

'I'm OK, but I need help.' Wendy sank on to a seat opposite Simon. 'And I'm afraid what you're going to hear, you won't like.'

'You're leaving?' Simon gazed at the blotter on his desk and began doodling.

'I would like a leave of absence. I don't want to go permanently, unless you want me to.'

'Of course I don't want you to.' He looked up. 'Something wrong? Having a baby?'

Wendy couldn't help smiling. 'I haven't got myself in "trouble", if that's what you mean. Women don't bother about that sort of thing these days, Simon.'

'I suppose you're right.' Simon smiled. 'But something is wrong . . . Tim?'

'It's kind of Tim, kind of something else. Kind of some*one* else really. I just need to take time off and think about it. I have to help someone. I have to go away. I need about three months, Simon, to sort it all out. It will be unpaid, naturally . . .' she looked appealingly up at him, 'if you say "yes" I would be terribly grateful if you told no one about our conversation, or the reason for my going.

If, on the other hand, you say "no" then, regretfully, I shall have to hand in my notice with immediate effect.'

Later, when Wendy walked to her car, she felt as though a great grey cloud had lifted and, in the heavens, the sun was shining.

PART 2

. . . And Took Care of Him: Wendy

CHAPTER EIGHT

'A new dawn has broken, and it is wonderful.'

The newly elected Prime Minister, addressing his supporters after his tremendous victory, seemed almost to choke on his words, and Wendy felt herself choking too, blinking back tears. Around them burly men paused in the act of demolishing their colossal breakfasts and clapped. One or two booed derisively but, on the whole, not surprisingly, the inhabitants of the transport café near Salisbury seemed to be in favour of the new Labour Government which had just been returned with a huge majority.

It was six a.m. and the café was full, all eyes on the large television screen suspended from the ceiling relaying the latest results, pictures of Blair and his wife returning to London, footage that kept on being played over and over again. Wendy had voted before leaving London and now here were the results to prove that most of the country, the affluent as well as the dispossessed, felt as she had. There was an air of euphoria all round.

Wendy and Oliver had spent an uncomfortable night in the van parked in the forecourt of the garage to which the transport café was attached. They'd only just made it to this haven before it finally conked out.

Another result was announced, another Labour gain, to fresh cheers from the roomful of supporters. It was a hot, cheerful place; the delicious smell of fried bacon had wafted over to them before dawn and Wendy had been eager for a hot cup of tea and nourishment.

She'd arrived the day before without warning, without letting Lois know that she was going to Madge's. She went by train and took a taxi to the farm, carrying only an overnight bag. She had surprised herself by her own action; it felt as if she were taking part in some kind of film, now being played back in slow motion.

Everything seemed to work out as though it had been carefully planned, which it hadn't. None of it was planned. By chance, Madge was not in, so there was no way yet that Lois and Ken could know what she'd done. And that's how she wanted it to remain for the time being.

She was taking off, dropping out, doing a bunk.

Of course, one didn't want to worry anybody. She had written brief letters to Tim and her family which she would post in a day or two. In the meantime, Tim would assume she was on an author tour; their relationship had been strained anyway since the weekend. That weekend which now seemed years away, instead of a few days.

As luck had Madge away it also had Oliver

fiddling with the van in the yard. As he emerged from underneath, wiping his good hand on a greasy rag, he looked as though he was pleased to see her.

'Any luck?' she'd asked and he'd shaken his head.

'Well, we're taking off today, this moment, as soon as we can make it.'

'Taking off?' he exclaimed, surprised.

'That's what you want, isn't it?'

'Yes, but . . .'

'Don't ask questions,' she said, throwing her case into the back of the van. 'Let's see if we can get out of here before Madge comes back.'

It was like escaping, running away from school. In a way she couldn't help feeling it was a bit of a lark, rather as she had felt the previous Saturday when she and Oliver had raised the banner above their heads condemning the bloodthirsty murderers. Black heads of foxes alternating with gigantic drops of fake blood.

Luck had held and the van had bumped and rattled along until, just before Salisbury, it packed up. By stopping and starting they managed to make it into a garage, which was closed, as was the transport café beside it. It had been nearly nine.

They had then left the van and walked up the road to a pub they had passed on the way in. It was too late to order cooked food, but an obliging landlord agreed to make sandwiches

171

to accompany a bottle of wine.

Now this breakfast tasted as good as any gourmet meal Wendy had ever eaten and, with a Labour victory in the bag, and her future uncertain, she felt euphoric. Suddenly the adventure, instead of being a risky thing to do, took on a whole new dimension; above all, it was going to be *fun*.

Impulsively she leaned across the table and clutched Oliver's hand.

'Great, isn't it? Isn't it *great*?'

Oliver seemed less euphoric. He leaned back in his chair, eyes on the screen, breakfast finished, knife and fork neatly side by side on the clean plate in front of him. 'Aren't you pleased?' she asked, her expression slightly puzzled.

'Pleased?' Oliver shrugged. 'Do you think it will make any difference? They're all wankers, these politicians.'

'Oliver! I'm surprised at you.'

'Look, Wendy, you can hardly call yourself a Socialist, can you?' He looked askance at her.

'Yes, I can. I believe in equality.'

'Do you believe in common ownership of the means of production?'

'That's old hat. Old Labour. We believe in a mixed economy.'

'So do the Tories.'

'No, they don't! Don't tell me you're a *Tory*, Oliver.'

'I'm not anything. I've never voted in my

172

life. Don't suppose I ever shall.'

'That's opting out.'

'But I *have* opted out.' He gave a bleak smile. 'Didn't you realize?'

'You mean, you like the way of life you lead?'

'Yes. Nobody forced me into it. Nobody shook a finger at me and said, "Oliver, you must live in a van." I *like* living in a van.'

'For ever?'

'Perhaps. Certainly for the time being.' There was another roar and more cheers as yet another Labour victory was announced, and the rest of what he said was drowned.

Oliver jerked his head towards the door. 'There seems to be some activity in the garage. We'd better explain to them what we're doing here.'

*   *   *

The head of the mechanic appeared from under the bonnet of the van.

'I'll give you ten pounds for scrap,' he said, attempting to close the bonnet, which stubbornly failed to yield to pressure.

'Come off it,' Wendy said. 'We paid two thousand pounds for it only a few weeks ago.' She looked at Oliver, who nodded his head in confirmation.

'Then you were had,' the mechanic said. 'Someone gave it a coat of paint, but the works

173

are kaput.'

Without any warning the bonnet thundered down, nearly trapping his hand. 'See, nothing works,' he said, shaking his hand as if he'd had a narrow miss. 'Even the hinges have gone. This old pile has been on a junk heap for months. Someone's painted it over and sold you a pup.'

Oliver looked crestfallen.

'But I trusted the man who sold it to me.'

'Can we get a second opinion?' Wendy began to feel desperate. The adventure seemed in danger of being aborted before it had properly begun.

'Look, love, do me a favour.' There was a note of contempt in the mechanic's voice. 'We're not talking about Rolls-Royces here, you know, or even a half-decent vehicle. We're talking about a piece of scrap metal.'

'Then what can we do?'

'You'd better get something else, if that's what you want. Do you need a van? I may be able to help you out.'

Mystified he looked from one to the other—the well-heeled dame and ... hard to know what to call the bloke. It was so difficult to categorize social classes these days, but it was easier to tell with women than men. The woman definitely had class, the man ... perhaps not.

'Do you think we could leave it here while we decide what to do?' Wendy said in a wheedling tone. 'In the meantime, how do we get to Salisbury?'

'Try hitch-hiking or calling a cab, love. Maybe one of the men in there'—he jerked his head in the direction of the café—'would give you a lift.'

'I think we'll get a cab.' She turned to Oliver. 'Let's go and have a coffee and think about the van.'

'Look, if you're dumping this wreck on me and buying nothing in return, I need to know immediately,' the mechanic's tone hardened. 'For one thing, I'll charge you ten pounds a day to leave it here, and I want five days' payment in advance. If, on the other hand, you'll sell it for scrap, I'll give you twenty pounds.' He paused for a moment and looked speculatively at Wendy. 'How a lady like you came by a vehicle like this, I do not know.'

'It's mine,' Oliver said. 'She was helping me out.'

'That figures . . .'

'Don't be rude . . .' Wendy began heatedly, but the mechanic held up his hand.

'I'm sorry, I didn't mean to be offensive, but I do have other work to do.' He indicated the cars in the forecourt and in the garage workshop awaiting repair.

'We'll take the money,' Oliver said, and then to Wendy: 'No sense in hanging around.'

'I'll make it twenty-five,' the mechanic turned towards the garage, 'and that's generous.'

*   *   *

Chastened, they returned to the café, minus a van but richer by twenty-five pounds. It was only an hour or so since they'd had breakfast, but they ordered coffee. Most of the early breakfast eaters had left and only a scattering remained. The waitress who'd served the breakfast brought over their coffees, her expression a compound of sympathy and curiosity.

'Trouble?' she asked conversationally.

'Yes, trouble of a sort.' Wendy took the coffee and helped herself to sugar. 'Our van's a write-off and we're stranded.'

'Nowhere to go?' The woman's eyes widened.

'I'm not homeless, if that's what you're asking; but it is inconvenient.'

The waitress's eyes wandered over to the window where the van could clearly be seen outside the garage, and then back to Wendy as if she too were asking herself how come a lady like this had an old crate like that. She thought they made an odd couple.

'You want to be careful with Martin out there—' She jerked her head in the direction of the garage. 'He's a mean old sod.'

'You don't need to tell us,' Wendy retorted. 'We just found that out for ourselves.' She

176

looked ruefully up at the waitress. 'Do you think you could call us a cab in about . . .'—she looked at her watch—'ten, fifteen minutes?'

'Where d'you want to go?' the waitress asked.

'Salisbury.'

'What are we going to do in Salisbury?' Oliver leaned over the table in order to lower his voice as the waitress went back to the counter and began dispensing breakfast to some overnight travellers.

'What do *you* want to do, Oliver?'

'I don't know.' Oliver shook his head. 'I feel absolutely trapped.'

'But you're not.' Wendy instinctively put her hand over his again.

'I am.'

'You've got me.'

'I scarcely know you.'

'It doesn't matter. You've got me.'

'I just can't understand what's happened.' Oliver slowly shook his head. 'This whole thing is unreal. Do you know there are moments when I'm sorry I ever met Lois or . . .' he paused as his gaze fell to the table.

'Me,' she finished for him.

'Well, one led to the other. I don't regret meeting you, but this whole thing has been a mess.'

'You might still have been kicked to death if Lois hadn't intervened. Let's put it like this . . .' Wendy paused to light a cigarette

177

from the pack she now carried permanently in her pocket. 'You would have come back to Stinsbury, right? From wherever it was you went—Cornwall, was it?' Oliver nodded.

'That had nothing whatever to do with Lois?'

He agreed.

'Whatever happened you would have had to come back?' She looked at him again.

'Right.'

'So, whatever happened you would have been attacked. I mean, that had absolutely nothing to do with Lois?'

'Right,' he added again.

'So, you might have been killed. Look . . .' Wendy drew her chair closer to the table. 'I have an idea, or two ideas. See which one you like.'

Oliver leaned forward, listening attentively.

'The first is that we go back to my place in London. I can get fresh clothes, you can take a bath. We then set out to look for another means of transportation, or,' she looked quickly up at him again, 'I can give you the fare to the north and home you go. Finished. Out of our lives for ever.'

*   *   *

Oliver lay in the dark, hands behind his back, unused to the feel of soft springs beneath, even though he was sleeping on the sofa and

178

not a proper bed.

The events of the last few days, the last few weeks, had been incredible, and unsettling to a man who only wanted to live the simple life, preferably on his own. He had been taken over by two women and his life had changed.

Chump lay at his feet and—as if unused to the luxury: the centrally heated flat, the vague air of opulence and the good life—seemed to be having difficulty in sleeping too. Wendy couldn't sleep either. From her bedroom off the sitting room where he lay he could smell cigarette smoke. Himself, he occasionally smoked a joint when he could afford it, but was making a determined attempt to give up tobacco. Far too expensive a habit for a man of the road.

Oliver was not used to relationships. He was a man who liked solitude; the company of the birds, his dog. He loved the countryside and was unhappy in the town, maybe because he'd mostly lived in town during those difficult years of growing up, either in small ugly terraced houses where he'd been fostered, or in the handsome former stately home set in parkland on the edge of the city which was the orphanage.

However much you wanted to try and adapt after a life such as he'd lived, to become part of normal society was almost an impossibility.

And now there was Wendy. He was attracted to her as he felt she was to him. They scarcely knew each other, had been acquainted such a short time, yet it seemed they belonged together. He hadn't been the least surprised to see her turn up at the farm to drive him away, as if he knew instinctively that she would come and rescue him.

And yet he felt that Wendy was offering him charity rather as her sister had and, although he didn't particularly want to work and lead what others would consider a normal life, he didn't want to be a kept man either, in bondage to a woman.

He wondered what it was about him that had appealed to these two women, so alike and yet in other ways so dissimilar.

The door leading into Wendy's bedroom opened and he could see the glow of light beside her bed. The smell of smoke was stronger. Chump growled and then got off the couch. Oliver could feel his tail thrashing about with pleasure as he greeted Wendy.

'Hi!' Wendy, cigarette in hand, sat beside him on the couch.

'Hi!' He felt an immediate arousal and slid an arm round her buttocks.

'I couldn't sleep,' she said, stubbing out her cigarette.

'Nor could I.'

His grasp tightened, and her yielding, pliant mouth, smelling strongly of tobacco, bore down on his.

Hand in hand they stood inside the camper van as the salesman outlined its merits. It was brand new, and upholstered in cream and blue. To an habitual van dweller, it was indeed the last word in luxurious living.

'And this is the central-heating unit,' the salesman opened a door with a flourish. 'At the press of a button—' and he pressed it. The van filled with heat.

'This is where you cook. The same principle.' The salesman pressed another button and a hatch flew open revealing a gas stove with four jets. 'Fuelled with butane,' he said. 'You keep your spare canister under here—' and he flung open a door under the stove. 'Eureka.'

As for the bed . . . the salesman gave them a knowing smile as he demonstrated how it filled the rear space of the van; a full-sized double bed.

'You'll never want to get up,' he promised and the lovers exchanged glances.

It was in excess of twenty-four thousand pounds on the road, and a snip—if the salesman was to be believed.

'And could it be used immediately?' Wendy asked.

If their finances and paperwork could be settled, it was ready to be driven away. He paused. Would there be any difficulty in financing? There were hire-purchase schemes available. A year at nought per cent interest, or five at ... They would pay cash, Wendy said. Oliver swallowed. Or rather, Wendy corrected herself, a cheque, a certified cheque if she could ring the bank?

The salesman pointed to the telephone on his desk. Everyone appeared delighted.

*   *   *

Afterwards they walked down Baker Street and then into Regent's Park. The sun still shone on the new Labour Government. They walked across the bridge and along by the side of the lake. People were even sitting in deck chairs.

They reached the Inner Circle and went into the restaurant. It was afternoon and they hadn't eaten. They'd got up late and made coffee. Poor Chump had been dying to go out so Wendy had taken him into the street in her dressing gown. He was now in her car which she'd parked in the Outer Circle having seen the van advertised in the *Ham & High*. After their snack they'd let him out and take him for a walk in the park.

They got sandwiches and coffee, and chose a seat by the window looking on to the rose garden.

'Well!' Wendy bit into her sandwich and gazed across at Oliver.

182

'I still can't believe it's real,' he said, appearing to inspect the sandwich. She knew he was talking not only about them but about what had happened over the past weeks.

'From rags to riches,' he went on in a mocking tone with an attempt at a smile.

'I shan't do it if you don't want to. The offer is still there. The fare home . . .'

'Home,' he grunted and bit into his sandwich.

He finished the sandwich, swallowed his coffee and wiped his mouth on the paper napkin.

'I feel I'm taking charity from you as I took it from your sister.'

His words made Wendy freeze.

'It is not *charity*. It's for me too.'

'You're not really giving up anything. Twenty-four thousand quid . . . Whew!' He wiped a hand across his brow.

She ignored the last remark. 'I don't have to give up anything. I'm not making any sacrifices, if that's what you mean. I was tired of my job, tired of Tim and all those ghastly plans for the wedding which kept changing by the hour. If you like, I'm using you.' She leaned across the table and her hand rested on his. Her touch was carnal and his fingers curled around her palm in a gesture reminiscent of their lovemaking during the night. Their bodies had a harmony that seemed extraordinary for the first time. It was as though they'd been loving each other for years.

'Was it like that with Tim?' he asked, and she knew what he meant.

'Never!' She shook her head. 'So you see, I'm using you. I'm being totally unscrupulous. I couldn't just bunk off on my own. I couldn't take off. I'd have nowhere to go, wouldn't know what to do. With you ... it's different. You need a partner, you see, to play truant.'

He seemed intrigued. 'When did this notion occur to you?'

'On the way back from Edinburgh. Then, after that ghastly weekend, I went to see my boss to ask for a sabbatical. I've got three months.'

'And after that?' Oliver looked at her.

'We'll see.'

'It won't be easy,' he said. 'I'm not easy.'

'Neither am I.'

Oliver seemed to drift into deep thought and Wendy, watching him, would have given a lot to read his mind. She couldn't get over what had happened either. This was the sort of thing you read in corny novels.

'There's just one final thing,' he said at last.

'And that is?'

'I don't want anyone to know where we are.'

'That's all the more exciting,' she said. 'Agreed,' and leaned right across the table, stretching herself to kiss him.

'It was terribly rude, leaving like that without a word.' Madge tossed Wendy's letter on to the kitchen table. Lois picked it up and read through it again:

Darling old Sis,

I'm doing a bunk. Things have got on top of me and I'm taking some time off. I am terribly sorry about the hunt. Please don't worry about me. Much much love, Wendy.

PS. Don't be surprised if you don't hear from me for a while.

'Old Sis' was the term she used when she wanted to ingratiate herself with Lois. It was a way of emphasizing the difference, although slight, in their ages. Lois was the elder sister, she the protected younger one. In a way, it was asking her sister not to condemn her childish behaviour.

'Tim had a letter just like it,' Lois said, 'only differently worded.'

'Did she call off the engagement?'

Madge, summoned in a hurry to give her counsel and support, picked up her coffee mug from the kitchen table. Behind her Beverley leaned against the dresser.

'No, she just said that she hoped Tim would understand. All the terrible rows had got her down. As far as I can see, they were mostly

185

originated by her. Tim agreed with everything she wanted.'

'Is he terribly cut up?'

'Hard to tell. He's a man who keeps his emotions under tight control. But I think he must be. Don't you?'

'I would have thought so. Have you talked to her boss?'

'He said she asked for long leave last Monday—right after the weekend, and you know what happened then. He was reluctant to discuss the matter as he seemed to think Wendy was old enough to make up her own mind. It's not as if she's a child,' Lois sighed deeply, 'though I often think she behaves like one.'

'I'm quite convinced she's the woman who was seen with Oliver.'

Madge leaned back in her chair as Beverley drew out a chair joined them at the table. She and Neal had been as distressed as anyone by the week's disastrous events.

'It seems like that to me, too.' A passer-by, a friend of Madge's, had reported seeing the van leave Madge's yard with a blonde woman at the wheel. The couple had been laughing.

'Do you think they planned it at the weekend?'

Lois shrugged. 'Seems like it.'

'I wish I'd been there!' Madge struck the table with her fist.

'You couldn't have stopped them.'

'At least we'd have known it was Wendy and you wouldn't have had all this worry.'

'We do know it's Wendy.' Lois, looking pale and tired, brushed her hair away from her face. 'Who else could it have been? He couldn't drive. She's fair. They were in cahoots at the weekend. I'm convinced it was Wendy. He couldn't stay here and he didn't feel comfortable with you.'

Madge coloured. 'I didn't set out to make him uncomfortable.'

'I didn't mean it in a nasty way,' Lois protested, 'but he knew you were my friend. Naturally he'd feel awkward.'

Oh, Oliver ... she knew instinctively how he'd felt. She knew him so much better than he thought. If only he had been able to confide in her and not her sister. Lois sighed. She felt guilty and she felt afraid. She was afraid of her own emotions, her fear, her jealousy of Wendy. She, the good elder sister, the one who always did the right thing, would somehow like to have had the courage to have done what Wendy did.

'You poor dear ...' Madge looked sympathetically at her friend, unable to guess the source of the chaos in her mind. 'You're having the most awful time, and all because you did a kindness to a stranger.'

CHAPTER NINE

Margaret Cartwright had never worried much about her daughters. That is, she had worried about normal things like colds and minor childhood illnesses, but otherwise not. They had always been clever, obedient children, but not abnormally so, and self-possessed. As adults they had each done well in their respective spheres: Lois had married a man the family liked who was also wealthy and successful. She had a nice home and had given Margaret two grandsons on whom she doted. Wendy had seemed all set to be a career girl, a thirty-something success story who ran a large publicity department, drove a BMW, carried a mobile phone and dressed in power suits. But she had not eschewed love and marriage and had become engaged to Tim, whom the family also liked.

If anything, Margaret had worried about Wendy more than Lois simply because Wendy was just that bit more unpredictable, a little on the wild side. However her chief worry had been her husband Douglas to whom she had been devoted, yet whom she had also feared.

Margaret had been a ward sister in a large London hospital when Douglas was a houseman. She had helped him to the top of his profession, always subsuming her needs and wants to his. A brilliant surgeon, he had been a choleric and demanding man. His temperament and job had taken its toll of him; he had collapsed and died at the age of fifty-five. Everyone said what a loss he was to the medical profession.

But from then on Margaret blossomed. She found a host of hobbies and pastimes that she had hitherto, being second string to Douglas, had no time for. She had sold the large house in Mill Hill and bought a bungalow in Brighton, a town brimming with activities which she enjoyed to the full.

Never having played golf in her life, she joined the local club and rapidly became proficient. She eschewed clubs specially for older people and became a member of the Wine and Food Society, the Dramatic Society and the Bridge Club. She went frequently to London, or to first nights in the provinces, with the Theatre Club. She travelled abroad at least twice a year and made new friendships among both sexes. She even had time to read a lot.

She felt she had done her share of good in looking after Douglas for twenty-five years, so, unlike Lois, she tended to avoid good causes and voluntary work. She became selfish and she liked it. Enjoying her new-found freedom she had no desire to marry again. A neat, small woman with fading blonde hair and fine bone structure, whom her daughters resembled, she

189

was sixty-five and as self-possessed as she had taught them to be.

Margaret had also received a rather odd, short letter from Wendy—the first letter she had received from her younger daughter since her schooldays—which made it all the more curious. Why had not Wendy simply telephoned, as she normally did, and told her she was taking time off?

Time off for what? Margaret wondered, and soon after receiving the letter, she was on the telephone to Lois, who was wondering the same thing.

The matter-of-fact, well-behaved Cartwrights did not like mysteries and certainly did not expect one from a member of their own family. Secrets had always been shared. There was a sort of cabal-like resistance to surprises.

A week passed, during which no more was heard from Wendy, and then Lois broke the bombshell that it was thought she had gone off with a beggar they had befriended, whose van they had allowed to stay on their land. Oliver was mentioned by Lois to her mother for the first time on the telephone. She was, for once, worried enough to make a trip to Dorset to hear more.

It was quite an extraordinary story. A case of another daughter behaving untypically, as far as Margaret was concerned. How ridiculous for sensible Lois to become so involved with a beggar, to the extent of offering him a home—which was what letting him park on the Hunters' land amounted to. Telling it once more had reduced Lois to tears, and she now sat across from her mother, head in hands, a Kleenex pressed up close to her cheek.

'But you could have been killed!' was Margaret's first comment as Lois finished her story.

'I know,' Lois nodded, making a supreme effort to control herself. Cartwrights did not easily give themselves up to tears.

'What did Ken say?'

'He was terribly upset.'

'I should think he was, and then he has to get injured too by the same man.'

'No!' Lois shook her head. 'Oliver had absolutely nothing to do with Ken's fall.'

'But you said he was there, waving a banner?'

'It was one of those large banners that it takes two people to hold. That's why Wendy was there too. He had a gammy arm so she helped him carry it, and then hold it. She said it was all a bit of fun.'

'A bit of fun!' Margaret snorted. 'Deeply irresponsible. Quite cruel really. But then,' she added thoughtfully, 'there always was this streak in Wendy.'

'What do you mean, Mum?' Lois looked up.

'Something wild. You remember when she

was a girl ...' Yes, always a bit rebellious, nonconformist, sister Wendy.

'But no one could have foreseen this,' Lois said.

Margaret agreed. She then did another uncharacteristic thing. She rose and, crossing to her daughter, sat on the arm of her chair and pressed Lois's head close to her bosom. 'Poor love,' she crooned, 'you have had an awful time.'

'Mum!' Dissolving, finally, into real tears, Lois turned and embraced her mother and the two women sat there for some time hugging each other, Lois feeling like a little girl again.

A sharp tap on the door made them spring apart. The knock came again, and then Beverley put her head round.

'Sorry, am I disturbing ...'

'No, no, not at all.' Lois vigorously wiped her eyes.

'Tim is on the phone.'

'Is there any news?'

Beverley shook her head. 'Would you have a word?' She passed the cordless phone to Lois.

'Hi, Tim! How are you?'

Tim it seemed was fine, in the circumstances.

'Any news, Tim?'

Tim had none at all. In fact, he wondered if he could come down? He felt so upset. Couldn't concentrate on work. His boss had suggested he had a few days off.

'Certainly, darling,' Lois said. 'My mother's here. She's concerned too, of course. When can we expect you, Tim?' Lois nodded, then nodded again and looked across at her mother.

'Tonight? Great. No, not at all, there's plenty of room.' She passed the phone to Beverley, who had stood by listening. 'Could you see that the bedroom is all right? Clean towels, that sort of thing?'

Beverley nodded. 'I'll see to it now.'

'Poor Tim,' Lois said to her mother as Beverley left the room. 'And to think he was so nearly one of the family.'

Margaret, still sitting on the arm of Lois's chair, crossed and uncrossed her legs. 'You think, then, that it's all off?'

'What else can one think?' Lois, now dry-eyed, tucked her tissue in the sleeve of her cardigan. 'He'd hardly have her back if she's gone off with another man.'

*   *   *

Tim had taken it badly. Yet he blamed himself for being so censorious at the weekend.

'I can hardly believe it was only last week.' Tim helped himself to mustard and then looked round at the grave faces watching him. Lois, Ken and Margaret, as mystified, as shocked by what had happened as he was, nodded in agreement. They then all relapsed into silence while continuing with their meal.

It was just over a week since the election. The night that dismay in the Hunter household at the size of the Labour victory, or rather the magnitude of the Tory defeat, had been compounded by the disappearance of Wendy which, very soon, had been linked to the sudden departure of Oliver from Madge's farm. Somehow it seemed that life, which had hitherto been pleasant, normal, with no highs or lows, had become complex, uncertain, insecure. Who knew what Labour, with their ruinous spending plans, would do to the economy, education, the health service? The country might enjoy a brief boom, but, in Ken's opinion, everything would soon fall apart when the cracks began to show, when the much vaunted Labour Party discipline and cohesiveness, which had helped to win the election, collapsed.

Then there was the question of the Tory leader. Major might have led them to disaster, but who would replace him? Ken backed his namesake Kenneth Clarke; however, it was not up to the local parties but to the few remaining Tory MPs.

Ken's initial delight that 'the beggar', as he preferred to call Oliver, had gone, took a nose-dive when it transpired that his sister-in-law might have gone with him. How could you live this sort of thing down? It was sure to get around in the locality and the Hunters would be the object of spurious gestures of sympathy from people who would secretly find the whole tale titillating rather than shocking.

Of course this was not the nineteenth century and families were no longer ostracized because of misdemeanours on the part of their black sheep: but still, being the object of pity among one's neighbours was to be avoided, particularly if you were a prominent member of the hunt and the rotary club, and your wife was a Justice of the Peace.

By the time the cheeseboard was passed round spirits had revived, helped by a couple of bottles of Ken's best Burgundy. It was, after all, not the end of the world.

'We first have to be sure that Wendy *has* gone away with Oliver,' Ken said, tapping the table prosaically. 'Lois is convinced. I am not.'

'I'm sure she at least drove Oliver's van away from Madge's farm,' Lois said firmly. 'Who else could have done it?' She looked round as all shook their heads. 'A blonde, attractive woman, laughing. There are no other blonde, attractive women that we know of in Oliver's life.'

'But we don't know, that's the point,' Ken interjected. 'We know so little about the bugger . . .' He cast a glance at his mother-in-law. 'Sorry, Margaret. But you see, Oliver was a man of mystery. That's why I think he appealed to the women . . .'

'He did *not* appeal . . .' Lois began

indignantly.

'He did.' Ken's expression was a model of patient understanding. 'He did, darling. He was appealing to the women . . .'

'It was the dogs . . .'

'It was *not* the dogs.' Ken struck the table. 'What rubbish! You're deceiving yourself, Lois. Wendy called him "dishy". I remember being quite struck by the phrase.'

'Did she?' Tim murmured, his spirits scarcely rising at the news.

'Now, don't get all emotional,' Margaret said in an attempt to restore calm. 'There is absolutely no point, Ken, in losing your temper.'

'Time we had coffee, anyway,' Lois said, rising and checking her watch. 'And time for the news. I haven't seen it all day.'

'You haven't missed much,' Ken murmured gloomily. 'Blair, Blair, Blair.'

*　　*　　*

As Tim helped to pass the coffee Margaret did indeed feel a pang. Tim and Wendy had been together for five years and she was so fond of him. He was everything you could want in a son-in-law. Good looking, clever, kind, beautifully mannered. He had a nice family and he had money. Heavens above, what on earth had possessed Wendy?

'Thank you, dear,' she said, taking the cup

from Tim with a smile. 'You know, you mustn't despair . . .'

'I don't,' Tim said, taking a seat next to her on the sofa. 'But if Wendy has chosen another man . . .'

'She couldn't possibly *stay* with Oliver, even if she has gone off with him.' Lois, her expression indignant, looked at them from across the room where she had just turned on the television, keeping the volume low.

'Why not?' Tim looked at her with a strained smile. 'She's got enough money to keep him. She's not dependent on him. If he has gone off with Wendy, he's got it made. Hasn't he?' His expression bitter, he gazed across at Ken for confirmation.

'It was a moment of madness,' Lois insisted. 'Lust for adventure.'

'I tend to agree. I don't believe she'd stay with Oliver.' Ken had his eyes on the TV screen. 'She'll soon be back.'

'But would you have her . . . That is, if . . .' Margaret's voice trailed off and she looked enquiringly at Tim. 'Would you have Wendy back in those circumstances?'

'I don't know.' Tim leaned forward and clasped his hands, looking at no one in particular. 'No, I don't suppose I would. I mean, frankly, if she went off with him, she can't love me. Can . . . can she?'

No one answered.

They'd missed half the news, but settled

down to watch the rest. Ken and Tim had a brandy. The two women declined. The main news was followed by the local news for the West Country.

A picture of a dog filled the screen. Its tail wagging, it looked searchingly at the camera, wearing the pathetic expression of a lost dog looking for an owner. In the background the announcer's voice was grave.

'Lost dog clue to mystery of murdered woman,' he said, and the camera then panned to a house standing back from a narrow wooded lane, separated from it by a police ribbon and two policemen standing sentry by the gate, while assorted onlookers kept their distance.

'A dog which has been for several weeks at an animal shelter is believed to hold the key to the violent death of an unidentified woman whose battered body was found three days ago at a lonely spot near Falmouth. The body was badly decomposed and the woman is believed to have been dead for some time. A post mortem is due to take place tomorrow, and the police are appealing to the public for more information.

'The dog had been on the road for some days, if not weeks. It appeared lost and in poor condition when it was found and taken to the animal shelter.

'South West Water have once again . . .'

The voice droned on, but Lois didn't hear

198

any more. The dog . . .

The door of the lounge was abruptly pushed open and Beverley stood dramatically on the threshold, her face red with exertion.

'Did anyone see the dog?' she cried as they all looked up. 'It's the image of Chump.'

'It isn't Chump,' Lois shook her head as Ken got up to switch off the TV.

'It *is* Chump . . .' Beverley insisted. 'I'd know that hangdog expression anywhere. I've seen it often enough at the back door begging for tit-bits.'

'Oh, my God,' Margaret's hand flew to her mouth. 'Wendy.'

'It couldn't be Wendy,' Ken said robustly. 'The bloke said "badly decomposed body". Dead for weeks.'

'Let's phone the police.' Tim jumped up.

Ken flapped an arm in his direction. 'Don't let's get all excited. There must be lots of mongrel dogs that look like that . . .'

'I don't think it's Wendy,' Lois said slowly. 'I don't think it's Chump. But he *is* very like Chump, and Chump had a twin.' As everyone looked at her, she went on rapidly. 'When I first met Oliver he had two puppies. Then later he came back with only one, now grown up. That was Chump.'

'Where had he been in the meantime?' Margaret asked in a tone of voice that suggested she already knew the answer.

'Cornwall,' Lois said. 'He left the dog in

Cornwall.'

'That's it, then. It's the same dog.' Tim's manner was extremely agitated.

'Not necessarily,' Lois said. 'It might just look like Chump.'

'It *is* Chump, or his twin,' Beverley insisted. 'And Neal thinks so too.'

'Let's ring up the TV station and try to find out some more.'

'No, don't let's,' Lois said quickly. 'I don't see any need to panic. The dead woman isn't Wendy. It couldn't possibly be. This time last week she was alive and well. Even if the worst had happened,' she paused and swallowed, 'her body wouldn't, couldn't decompose in a week.'

'But it still may be something to do with Oliver,' Tim said. 'Didn't you say that he occasionally went off for long periods?'

'Oliver wouldn't kill anybody.' Lois sounded shocked.

'You're always defending Oliver,' Ken said testily. 'You make me mad.'

'That's your trouble,' Lois retorted. 'You're too impatient. If it hadn't been for your impatience, none of this would have happened.'

'I'd like to know what you mean?' Ken rose and stood over her, his manner threatening.

'Certainly.' Lois looked fearlessly up at him. 'Oliver would not have left our land— remember, you ordered him off—and Wendy

200

would not have gone off with him. She would still be here. She and Tim would still be engaged and we would not be worried sick, if you hadn't lost your temper and been so unreasonable.'

'I can't really see what we're getting ourselves in such a state about.' Tim, calmer now, helped himself to another brandy. 'We have established it can't be Wendy, even if it is the dog. But what if it is the dog's twin?'

'It's just possible Oliver knew this woman.'

'He left the dog with a friend,' Beverley said. 'He told us, didn't he, Lois?'

Lois nodded but didn't speak.

'He said he'd gone to Cornwall to see a friend,' Beverley went on. 'He stayed there six months.'

'You seem anxious to implicate Oliver,' Lois said tartly.

'I'm not implicating him. I just think you should follow up the matter of the dog. It seems logical to me. To put your minds at rest, if nothing else.'

*   *   *

Oliver liked to lie in but usually Wendy woke quite early, sometimes before dawn. She would listen for the sounds of birdsong to break, not as frenetic as in the mating season, but strong enough: a sound one also heard in London, strangely, at least at the short

201

distance she was from the Heath.

Chump seemed to sense her waking and grow restless. So she would slither out of bed and, covering her nakedness with a coat, venture out into the cold dawn.

The weather had taken a tumble since Labour's glorious victory, and May was a cold, changeable month.

She would walk round the van while Chump did his duty and then frisked about in the field, or wherever they happened to be. If it was a road she kept him on his lead and walked him along, pretty confident of being uninterrupted except for an early traveller or a milk lorry.

Since leaving London they had travelled west and now they meandered through the Welsh mountains, a territory unfamiliar to either of them and with which they had both fallen in love. They never went far in a day. After getting up, breakfast, ablutions, a longer walk with Chump, they would drive a few miles into the next valley and then find a suitable spot to camp.

They didn't feel the need for human companionship other than each other, and even then it was a curious sort of relationship. There was much sexual activity but little conversation. Oliver was a man of few words.

Wendy knew that one day she would have to return to the world and Oliver would move on.

At the moment, cocooned in the Welsh mountains and in the intensity of their physical relationship, it was idyllic. Wendy felt guilty about not contacting her family, but it never occurred to her that they would be worried. Her mother never showed much emotion, and Lois would be annoyed, no doubt, but she would be sustained by Ken who, doubtless, would have had quite a lot to say about his impossible sister-in-law.

In a way, giving them all a chance to settle down was a good thing and the longer she was away the better.

About Tim she preferred not to think. She had written him a second, longer letter, but she had not broken off the engagement, although she felt sure it was at an end. Because of her temperament she was able to put it out of her mind and not think about it.

Wendy whistled to Chump, who came galloping back from the field where he had been chasing rabbits. It was a grey, cold morning with a thick mist obscuring the towering hills around them, almost as though winter had returned. In the distance smoke began to curl upwards from a farmhouse from which they would shortly seek fresh milk, eggs and ham or bacon if it was available.

Food was simple, Oliver being a vegetarian. It was largely dairy-based with lots of fresh vegetables; but Wendy continued to eat meat and fish and Oliver didn't mind.

It was nice to get back indoors. She shut the door and, lighting the gas stove, put on the kettle. Then she gave Chump his breakfast and he ate hungrily. When the kettle had boiled she poured water over the teabag she'd put in a mug and turned towards the bed.

Oliver lay awake watching her.

'Tea?' she asked. 'It's a horrible cold day.'

Oliver shook his head. 'Come and get warm then.' He held back the duvet for her and she crept inside, putting the mug on the window ledge. They lay together, his arm encircling her, when suddenly he let out a brief cry, as if in pain, and tried to withdraw his arm.

'Oliver, what is it?' She sat up startled.

Oliver's face was momentarily contorted and one hand gripped his arm.

'Oliver, you've *got* to have something done about that arm,' she chided.

'It's nothing. Just a spasm.'

But there were a lot of spasms and they seemed to be getting more frequent.

'I think we'll have to stop somewhere and get a physio for you.'

'Don't be so silly.' His face relaxed and he settled down again. 'It's just when I move my arm in a clumsy way. There . . .'—he remained leaning on his good arm and began to stroke her breasts—'that's all the therapy I need.'

'Sexy beast,' Wendy said, arranging herself on the bed so that Oliver could settle into her comfortably.

They could go on like that for hours, the tea on the window ledge forgotten.

Later they went up to the farm. Wendy felt curiously elated and happy. More so than ever. It wasn't just sex, though the sex was good— the sex had also been good with Tim. There was something about Oliver she found perpetually intriguing. He was a difficult, moody man, but such people were always more interesting than those whose lives were an open book.

It was quite true to say that she knew little more about him than she had when they first went off together. She *knew* him better; but that was not the same as knowing about him. She knew nothing about him, except what little he had told her of his past at the beginning of their relationship.

But that morning after making love they talked. He told her he was happy—the first time he'd done that—and she'd replied that so was she. They continued to talk as they washed and dressed. Now, hand in hand, they tramped towards the farm, Chump ahead of them or lagging behind when he stopped to sniff out a good smell, a rabbit or a nice bit of cow dung.

She was trying to explain what 'escape' meant to her.

'I feel I always wanted to escape,' she said.

'But from what?' His hand clenched hers tightly.

'Maybe convention?' She paused and lifted her head taking in great gulps of fresh mountain air. 'My God, it's so beautiful,' she said. 'This is why I had to get away, Oliver. I knew there was more to life than ceaseless activity and a big pay cheque.'

'Didn't you want to get away before?'

'Never consciously. I suppose when Tim and I got engaged I thought that was a change. But I felt it might be more like captivity than escape. That's why we started to argue endlessly about the wedding. It was absurd.'

'I'm happy,' he said again. 'I didn't think I could be with someone else. I was always a loner. But somehow you fit in.' He leaned over and planted a kiss on her cheek. They stopped walking and momentarily clung to each other, not kissing, just hugging and holding.

'There must have been other women ...' Wendy ventured and then stopped. He had never mentioned anyone else. Maybe he'd been married?

'There were women,' he said briefly. 'Why talk about it? They didn't fit in. You do.'

'I'm extremely flattered that I fit in,' Wendy said at last. 'I feel quite privileged.'

He smiled as if he accepted this and didn't think it odd. He never thanked her for the van or the food that she bought, or the extra clothes, the wine. He knew she had money, but it made no difference to him whether he had these things or not. And he knew that she knew it; that he wasn't after her for what he could get out of her, and if she disappeared tomorrow he would survive. He would beg his way round the country as he had before and he wouldn't mind. He was self-sufficient. It didn't do to think about the future. They lived entirely in the present.

*　　*　　*

A cheerful farmer's wife came to the door and invited them in. It was an isolated spot and she seemed glad of the company. 'On holiday, are you?' she asked.

'Sort of.' Wendy blew into her cold hands and smiled. 'Actually, we're running away.'

'Running away?' The farmer's wife momentarily looked mystified. 'Ooh, I suppose I shouldn't ask. What people do is their own affair.'

'We're not running away from anybody,' Wendy went on while Oliver, as usual, remained silent. 'I mean, I haven't left a husband, or Oliver a wife. We just decided to opt out of life for a while.'

'Well, that sounds nice.' Her expression still mystified, the farmer's wife nevertheless managed to smile again.

'Going native, talking to the hills.'

'Making for anywhere, are you?' Her lilting Welsh accent was so easy on the ear.

'We adore it round here. Neither of us had

ever been to Wales before. It's so beautiful.'

'Come from London, do you?'

'I do.' Wendy turned to Oliver but he still said nothing, and Wendy thought that he disapproved of this chatter. She remembered him saying that he didn't want anyone to know where they were, as if he wanted to keep their adventure secret.

'Well, could we have a dozen eggs, some milk and butter, if you have it. We'd better be getting back.'

'Won't you have a coffee?'

Wendy looked at Oliver but he shook his head.

'Tempting, but no, thank you.'

'Pity, I'd be glad of the company. Did you say you'd like bacon too?'

*   *   *

As they went back down the hill, their purchases in two carrier bags, the farmer's wife stood at the kitchen door watching them. Odd couple, she thought. The man hadn't said a word. It was almost as if they had something to hide. She shut her door and thought no more about it.

*   *   *

'Why must you be so unfriendly?' Wendy asked when they were halfway down the hill.

'I'm not unfriendly.'

'You are. She was a nice lady and she wanted to chat and have a cup of coffee with us. There was no harm in that, but you were so uncooperative and unfriendly. Almost hostile. I felt embarrassed. I can't understand you sometimes.'

'Maybe next time you go and get things from the farm you should leave me behind.'

'Maybe I will.'

He strode rapidly ahead, leaving her to wander slowly after him. This was not his first temper tantrum. If Oliver didn't get his own way he was inclined to be sulky. There was a side of him that slightly frightened her. She felt there was a hint of violence in his make-up, but he kept his emotions under control. Certainly he had never been rough with her. He was a very tender lover.

When she got back to the van he was lying on the bed, his eyes closed. She unpacked their purchases and stowed them carefully away.

'How about an omelette for lunch?' she asked. He didn't reply. 'I'm a dab hand with omelettes.'

Still no reply.

Wendy went and sat on the bed and gazed at him. She sat there for about ten minutes saying nothing and eventually he opened his eyes.

'Sometimes you're like a spoilt little baby,' she said in a soft, gentle voice and reached out for his hand. 'I do understand, Oliver. I know you've been badly hurt in your past and it's hard to change. Sometimes I think you're like a crippled, wounded animal.'

'Communication is hard,' he said and she thought she detected the suspicion of tears in his eyes. 'I do try, but it's hard. I'm not used to talking, you see, Wendy . . .' He squeezed her hand, his expression softened by a suggestion of gratitude, almost devotion. 'I am grateful and, yes, I'd like an omelette. Very much.'

Wendy got up with a smile and, fastening her apron round her waist, broke the lovely new-laid eggs into a large plastic bowl and began to beat them.

But Oliver, watching her, felt sad. He had known that, inevitably, things would go wrong when he exchanged life in a broken-down van with only a dog for company for the luxury of a spanking new camper van with central heating, a double bed and four gas rings, and the company of a beautiful, glamorous, but, above all, successful woman whom he physically desired.

He knew they had nothing in common; they didn't really understand each other. He had never understood anyone else and no one had ever understood him. It was too much to ask. He was wounded and flawed by his origins, his childhood. He was an outsider; he couldn't and didn't belong.

Besides, he and Wendy were really hopelessly ill-suited, and their relationship would be punctuated by the niggling little arguments and quarrels and misunderstandings that had marred her relationship with Tim. Eventually, inevitably, the affair would end and they would go their separate ways.

The only thing he didn't know was when.

CHAPTER TEN

The police sergeant in Cornwall led Ken into a small room at the end of a long corridor. It was plainly furnished with table and chairs and a machine for tape recordings. Obviously some sort of interrogation room. Only Ken was not being interrogated—not as a suspect, anyway.

There were blown-up photographs arranged in some kind of sequence on the table and another policeman standing by them as if on guard.

'Do take a seat, Mr Hunter,' Sergeant Greaves said politely. As Ken nervously sat down, the sergeant took the seat alongside him. The policeman behind the table, whom the sergeant introduced as Constable Richards, remained standing. 'I'm afraid the photographs are not very pleasant, Mr Hunter. If you find it too much, please say so.'

'Go ahead,' Ken said, swallowing, trying to compose himself.

Constable Richards held up the first photograph, which was about five by seven and in colour. Ken looked at it, felt his stomach churning, and looked away.

'It's not my sister-in-law,' he said. 'Most definitely.'

'Are you sure, Mr Hunter?' The sergeant's voice was gentle, almost pleading. 'Could you just look at another one, sir?'

The woman was about Wendy's age, but she had dark hair. Her decomposed face had been hideously mutilated, the nose almost removed, one eye missing, but it was clearly not Wendy. She was quite a swarthy-looking woman. Thank God it was not Wendy.

He shook his head again.

'She was about five foot four, Mr Hunter.'

'Wendy is about five-five, five-six. She is fair-skinned and has fair hair and sculptured, fine-boned features. That is definitely not her, Sergeant.'

The sergeant looked at his colleague, who, with a rueful air, scooped the pictures up again and put them carefully in a large envelope.

'I'm glad it's not your sister-in-law, sir. But that doesn't solve your problem, does it? As to her whereabouts, that is.'

The sergeant produced a pad and drew a line under his scribbled notes at the top of the page. 'Can you tell me all you know about this man and about your sister-in-law? How and when did they meet? What is the link with the dog? This connection seems to be important. As much detail as you can, please, Mr Hunter.'

*   *   *

As Lois stooped towards it, the dog seemed to recognize her and pressed his nose against the wire mesh of his cage, tail wagging furiously.

Her first job was to ascertain its sex, and she saw immediately that it was a dog, not a bitch. Both Oliver's puppies had been male. She was at once relieved and depressed. She was relieved because, in a way, she knew the dog was a link with Oliver. Depressed for the same reason. She didn't want him to be a murderer or for there to be a connection with the murdered woman. Well, she knew he wasn't a murderer. Oliver couldn't possibly have harmed anyone. She knew that in her bones, whatever Ken or anyone said.

She looked up at the young kennel maid who had accompanied her. 'Do you think I could have him out? I'm pretty sure it's the right dog.'

'Of course.' The girl undid the latch of the cage and the dog paused hesitantly at the entrance, as if not quite sure what to do. On either side, imprisoned inmates yapped encouragingly.

An animal shelter was at once a happy and a sad place, Lois thought, putting out a hand for the dog to sniff. Since she'd last seen him he

213

must have been through many adventures, poor thing. Like Chump, he was still scarcely past puppyhood.

'It's the right age,' she said and the dog came up to her and licked her hand. She fondled its ears and looked into its eyes and, as it gazed back at her, she sensed recognition, although it seemed far-fetched, as if the dog could remember those far-off days when she had bought food for it in a supermarket.

'Is it the same dog?' the girl asked anxiously.

'It's not the *same* dog. I think it's the brother. I can't be sure until my friend has seen it.'

'Would you like me to get her?'

Beverley was waiting in an anteroom of the shelter.

'Look, could we take it into the yard and let it run round?'

The kennel maid clipped a lead on to the dog's collar and handed him over. 'Take all the time you want.'

The dog strained ahead as if anxious to be out of this place. Lois imagined he was watched with some envy by the other occupants of the spacious and well-constructed cages, but cages nevertheless. Small prisons.

Beverley got up with an exclamation as Lois and the dog came into the room. The dog went up to her, but it was quite obvious that it was merely a friendly, inquisitive gesture and not one of recognition.

'Chump?' Beverley asked, a question mark in her voice. The dog wagged its tail and nuzzled her hand with enthusiasm. It was obvious that he was prepared to love anyone who would take him away; but it was just as obvious he didn't know her.

'We're going to let him run in the yard,' Lois said as she and Beverley, followed by the kennel maid, headed for the door. 'But it's not Chump, is it?'

Beverley shook her head. 'I think it's his brother, though. Everything is similar, except that I would know Chump.'

'And Chump would know you.'

In the yard they took off the lead and let the dog scamper around sniffing in corners and relieving itself against a tree. Then it ran back to them and they both stooped and fondled it again.

'Well?' the girl asked.

'How did you find him?' Lois said as she got up.

'He was brought in by someone who had seen him hanging about near where the ... Where that woman's body was found. It's quite a remote area near Mylor Bridge. No one missed her because no one seemed to know her, or anything about her. It's unusual for a dog these days to be let run loose; then someone remembered, or thought they remembered, that it had come from this cottage, so they went to see if the dog did

215

belong to the person there and there was no answer. The place seemed deserted.

'They assumed that she'd moved on and, as some people do, left the dog behind, so they brought it here.

'A few weeks later the police found the body, and the woman who brought the dog in contacted the police. It was the only clue they had—not much to go on. Pity the dog can't talk.'

'It was just chance we saw it on TV,' Lois said. 'You see, someone we know had a dog just like it . . . but that's another story. Well,' she looked sadly at the dog, 'thank you very much.'

'What will you tell the police?' The kennel maid clipped the lead on to the dog's collar again.

'We shall say we think it is the brother of the missing dog. All this must seem very mysterious to you, but you see my sister has gone missing with a man who had a dog just like this. We know that there were two of them and one was left in Cornwall . . .'

'I do hope the dead woman wasn't your sister.'

Lois shook her head. 'No, no—thank God. My husband spent the morning with the police. He was so upset at what he saw it's given him a migraine and he's lying down in our hotel bedroom. I said I'd check on the dog with my friend here.'

'I don't suppose you'd like it?' the girl said and, as Lois and Beverley looked at her, she added shyly, 'You know, give it a home? Otherwise ... we don't want to—and it's not our policy—but we have so many animals at the moment we may have to have him put down.'

*   *   *

Tim and Simon Kemp had met quite often in the past. Wendy liked to entertain and was good at it, and Simon and his wife Natasha, a dark-eyed Russian beauty, were frequent guests and asked them back. It was the Chelsea/Hampstead set that the publishing business revolved around, and most of the people at the dinner parties were in some form of media or the arts.

Tim found Simon waiting for him in the Covent Garden restaurant he'd chosen for lunch. He apologized for being late and, seeing that Simon already had a drink, ordered one for himself.

'I've been in the country,' Tim said by way of explanation, 'with Wendy's sister, Lois.'

'Yes, tell me about all this.' Simon leaned over the table as the waiter brought them their menus, appearing interested rather than concerned, although his first thoughts at the moment seemed to be on food.

'Wendy has disappeared.'

'I think I'll have the seafood salad followed by chops.' Simon closed the menu and took up his drink. 'How do you mean, "disappeared"?'

'She's been gone a month.'

'Maybe she's just taking a break. That's what she told me.'

Simon felt a bit awkward in Tim's company in the circumstances and would have liked to refuse the invitation, except that Tim was so pressing. He said he would come to the office if Simon couldn't make lunch, as the matter was one of some urgency.

Being a practical man who liked his food, Simon felt he might as well get a meal out of Tim rather than sit listening to him in the office.

He wondered if Wendy had decided to disappear because things between her and Tim were not going too well? He suspected that this was the case.

'What exactly did she tell you?' Tim asked after giving their orders.

'She just said she wanted time off. She was tired. Had a lot of strain—which was true. Heavy work load. When she comes back, I intend getting her an assistant.'

'You think she will come back?'

'God, yes.' Simon looked with approval at the bottle of wine the sommelier had brought and was showing to Tim. 'Of course she'll come back. Any reason to think she won't?'

Tim watched the cork being drawn from the

wine and tasted the contents. Then he leaned his chin on clenched hands, wondering what he should tell him. He didn't want to alarm Simon too much—they'd all have egg on their faces if Wendy turned up unharmed—nor did he want to jeopardize Wendy's job. On the other hand, any clue was vital as to Wendy's whereabouts.

'We have every reason to think Wendy went off with a man she hardly knew.'

'Oh, dear,' Simon looked embarrassed. 'Tim, I'm so sorry . . .'

'No, it's not about me,' Tim said quietly. 'It's not just jealousy. It's a practical matter about Wendy and her safety. The man she's gone off with might be a murderer.' And as briefly as he could, he told Simon about Oliver and the strange hold he seemed to have on two sisters of such different temperaments.

'My God, it's like a novel,' Simon said when he'd finished. 'Except that I don't think I'd believe it—I'd tell the author it was too far-fetched. I thought you and Wendy . . .'

'September.' Tim looked at the table, then up at Simon.

'It's all over, even if she does come back?'

'Naturally. What else?'

Simon looked sympathetic. 'How can I help?'

'Any way you can contact Wendy? She left no clue as to where she was going?'

Simon shook his head.

'I thought abroad. I don't know why. I

imagined her taking time off in the sun. She said she needed a break. I didn't ask her to specify. Not my business really, though I asked if she might be pregnant.' Simon smiled at the memory, but Tim remained impassive. 'The last thing I imagined her doing was going off in a broken-down van with a penniless man. It seems bizarre.'

'Neither of the sisters could see anything wrong with him. It's as though they were mesmerized by him.' Tim warmed to his theme. 'At first Wendy was disapproving: "How *could* Lois?" That kind of thing. That was before she met him. Then she seemed to fall under his spell too. It was so sudden. I tell you, she hardly knew him, or anything about him. She didn't even know his name.'

'His *name*?' Simon looked startled.

'His surname. He would never tell anyone what it was. He kind of revelled in being mysterious. He and Wendy met three times, no more, and then she ran away with him.'

'And you're *sure* it was Wendy? Sounds most unlike her.'

'Everyone is sure. Now it's a police matter, I'm afraid. Ken said the woman in Cornwall had been raped and hideously mutilated. You can't imagine the state he and Lois were in when they got home.'

Simon, clearly shocked, listened to what other details Tim could tell him. Precious few.

In turn he could give hardly any help at all.

Just a promise to get in touch immediately, should Wendy telephone.

On his way back to the office, Simon thought it odd she hadn't done that already. After all, she was a professional who cared about her job, and she'd left in a hell of a hurry. One would have thought she'd have rung to make sure everything was all right.

Unless, perhaps, she couldn't.

*　　*　　*

The police didn't mind Lois taking the dog home with her. It couldn't tell them anything and they knew where it was if ever they wanted it. They couldn't expect the animal shelter to hang on to a stray for ever.

'It's obviously enjoying itself now, madam,' Sergeant Thompson of the Dorset Police observed as he stood beside Lois in the garden of Higham Hall, watching the dog run after a ball thrown by Margaret.

Lois nodded. 'He settled in immediately, despite the presence of our two dogs, who view him with some disdain. He's going to be looked after by our housekeeper, who was very fond of Chump.'

'But it's not the dog that Oliver had here?'

'Oh, no. Definitely not. Now, shall we go inside?'

'If that's all right.' The sergeant stood back to let her pass, taking in the size of the hall, the proportion of the rooms, the atmosphere of affluence that pervaded the place.

It was a rum story indeed, a lady with a place like this getting so involved with a beggar.

They made themselves comfortable on either side of the French windows opening on to the garden and, from time to time, the dog would run by and then disappear again.

'Your mother seems fond of the dog, Mrs Hunter.' Sergeant Thompson crossed his legs and got out his notepad, positioning it carefully on his knee.

'We all are.'

'Now, if I could have some details, madam. We are, as you know, co-operating with the Devon and Cornwall police acting on information supplied by you concerning the disappearance of your sister—which was, exactly when, madam?'

'It was the day of the election, the first of May. She was here the previous weekend, and so was he ...' and Lois repeated again the sequence of events that she already seemed to have told the police a dozen times.

'That makes it roughly five weeks ago,' he said when she'd finished.

'More or less.'

'And you've heard nothing from her since?'

'Nothing.'

'Doesn't that strike you as odd?' He raised his head and looked at Lois searchingly.

'Yes, it does. She was engaged to be married. Her fiance, Tim, is distraught.'

A frown appeared on the policeman's face.

'Do you think she was kidnapped?'

'No. I think she went voluntarily. She and Tim had been having quite a lot of arguments about their wedding: where to have it, who to ask. Silly little things, but they seemed to take control of the relationship, if you know what I mean. Then, of course, the hunt. Tim is also a keen hunter so he, as much as we were, was furious about what happened. I think that was the trigger. But she certainly wasn't kidnapped. Oliver couldn't drive; he had a broken arm which was slow to mend.'

'The arm he broke in the incident involving you?'

'Yes.'

'And have you recovered from that, Mrs Hunter?'

'Oh, yes. Quite.'

'But you never brought charges?'

'No.'

'Didn't you want to?'

'Oliver didn't. He wouldn't co-operate. It seemed pointless.'

'We wondered if there was any connection with the incident here and what happened in Cornwall.' The sergeant was still making notes in his book. 'But there doesn't appear to be. At least one of the men who attacked you came from London, and as we couldn't hold him he has gone back there. The other two appear to be local men, though one we never caught.'

'It never occurred to me that there might be a connection. I thought they were hooligans. Sergeant . . .' Lois paused and he looked up again.

'Yes, Mrs Hunter?'

Lois levelled her gaze at the policeman. 'I would like to tell you something, and it is this: contrary to what my husband and others may have said, I don't think Oliver is a danger to my sister. I don't think he murdered that woman.'

'But how can you be so sure, Mrs Hunter?'

'Because I knew him. He was, is, gentle, a vegetarian, an animal lover—incapable of violence, I'm sure.'

'Then why did you get in touch with us, madam?'

The policeman looked perplexed.

'Because when we saw the dog on TV, my husband insisted. It was so like Oliver's dog, Chump. I believe they're related. When I first met him, you see, he had two puppies and he told me he'd left one in Cornwall.'

'But he never told you anything about what he'd done in Cornwall?'

'No.'

'Or who he'd been with?'

'No.'

'Didn't you ask?'

'No.'

Weren't you curious, Mrs Hunter?'

'Well, I may have been curious, but Oliver was very secretive. He was secretive by nature. We knew so little about him.'

'Even his surname, I understand.' The policeman glanced at his pad.

'That's true, he never told us.'

'That would have made me suspicious, madam, all that secrecy.'

'I think he wanted to forget about the past. His origins, maybe. Basically he was a loner. I'd hoped to get him to confide in me, but he never did.' She gave a deep sigh. 'I think he may have confided in my sister.'

'But she didn't tell you anything?'

'No. I didn't ask her.'

'You seem a secretive person, yourself, madam.'

'No, I'm not.' There was a slight edge to Lois's voice. 'I simply respect people's privacy. As I like them to respect mine.'

*　　　*　　　*

'He seemed a nice man,' Margaret said as, with a wave, Sergeant Thompson got into his car and drove off.

'Yes, he was. Only it seems they think Oliver killed that woman, and I know he didn't.'

'But, darling, you can't be sure.' Margaret gripped her arm.

'I *am* sure, Mummy. He's a good man, a

kind man. If you'd known him, you'd agree. Ken said the injuries to the woman were too horrible to contemplate and it gave him nightmares for days afterwards. Oliver simply couldn't do a thing like that. I told the policeman that I didn't think Wendy was in any danger.'

'I wish I could be sure.' The new dog, who they'd christened Rusty because he was the colour of old iron, laid his ball at Margaret's feet and looked pleadingly up at her, begging her to throw it to him again. Rusty had now been joined by Sally and Lucy, who couldn't resist a game, and, as Margaret picked up the ball and hurled it with all her strength across the lawn, all three dogs pelted after it.

Margaret was in a dilemma. She had been with Lois for nearly a month, apart from the occasional brief visit to her bungalow in Brighton to be sure everything was all right, driving back to Stinsbury the same day. Ken didn't like Lois to be left alone. Margaret knew this was because he thought that Oliver, who he was convinced was a murderer, would come back and kill Lois, as he had killed her sister. It was a terrible burden for Margaret to bear; having never met Oliver, she could not share Lois's conviction of his innocence. As a result, she feared for her own safety, as well as Lois's. If this maniac did come back, what was to stop him murdering them both? But she was Lois's mother and she loved her and, because

Ken was convinced that Lois was on a fine edge, perhaps close to a breakdown, then her place was with her daughter.

Neal went round the house at night to check that everything was locked up, and an alarm had been rigged up between the house and the farm.

Lois knew nothing of Ken's deepest fears. She thought her mother stayed to keep her company. Now she turned to her and said, 'Mum, I know you want to go home. I'm sure I'll be OK now on my own.'

'No, I like being with you,' Margaret insisted.

'But, Mum, you've got your own life. It's not fair to expect that you should give it up. I'm a big girl, don't forget. Besides, I'm sure that any day we'll hear from Wendy and . . .'

'Darling, you can't be *sure* of that.'

'But I am sure.' Rusty came back again and, this time, it was Lois who threw the ball.

'I don't think Wendy would have worried us for all this time.'

Lois stopped and looked at her. 'Mummy, you don't . . . you can't think that Oliver . . .'

'Lois, I'm beginning to think, with Ken, that you've got some obsession about this man.'

'I have not,' Lois replied tartly.

'It's odd. You knew absolutely nothing about him. You took him on trust. If you ask me, he abused that trust terribly. If all was well, if all they wanted was to go off together, why on earth shouldn't they have got in touch? It simply doesn't make sense.'

*   *   *

Wendy lay on the sand, letting it run through her toes. In front of them the sea stretched to infinity. On either side were the cliffs that semicircled the bay. Next to her Oliver lay on his back, eyes closed. He slept a lot.

She was utterly, blissfully happy. All the tension and strain of her job, the rows and aggravation with Tim, had drained out of her during the past few weeks. Life was completely Sybaritic; undemanding, inconsequential. She now understood why people disappeared or took to the road, never to return to their former lives; why they forsook security and the trappings of normal life—home, mortgage, job, car, even their spouse and children.

Every day for her and Oliver was something new. From the moment they opened their eyes in the morning until they shut them at night, usually locked in each other's arms, they could do as they pleased. Nothing mattered. If they liked where they were they stayed there. If they wanted to walk they walked. If they wanted to stay in bed all day this is what they did, except to let the dog out, and get something to eat. Then they might wake up one morning and decide they wanted to move on, whether it be only a few miles or over the next mountain and beyond.

Finally they had come to the seaside in a remote part of a Welsh peninsular: two beautiful, protected beaches at the bottom of steep cliffs. The weather was unpredictable, but some days were good enough for them to go on the beach, like today, and they swam and sunned themselves and picnicked. At night they climbed the hill, cooked fresh fish bought that day for supper, or sometimes ate in a pub.

Nothing was allowed to intrude on this idyllic life: no newspapers, no radio, no TV. Oliver never seemed to have the slightest interest in what went on in the outside world, which was why he had been so apathetic about the election. Governments could come and go, regimes fall, earthquakes or natural disasters decimate huge areas of land. He didn't care. He didn't even know the name of the President of the United States.

Gradually, Wendy felt that she could be like him. She could become a traveller too. She had stopped buying papers. She had even lost interest in what the Labour Government, *her* Labour Government, was up to. She didn't care.

Oliver was the most utterly peaceful person one could ever wish to be with and his gift of worldly detachment, of disassociation, had seeped into her.

But it was unreal.

One day she knew it would all end. It would

229

have to end. Something would happen to make it end; but not yet.

When that day came, she would go back to her job, and Oliver . . . Oliver would move on.

She got a handful of sand and, playfully, let it trickle on to his midriff. He rubbed his stomach as if in sleep then scratched it. Finally he opened his eyes.

'I think we should send a postcard home,' Wendy said.

'Don't mention me,' Oliver said.

'Why shouldn't I mention you? I could send Lois your love,' she added slyly.

His expression remained deadpan.

'I'd rather you didn't.'

'Because you think you behaved shabbily to Lois?'

'Perhaps.'

'Do you think she was in love with you?'

Oliver lay for a while, eyes closed, and she thought he had fallen asleep again.

'Can't say,' he said at last.

'I think she was in love with you.'

'Didn't she love Ken?'

'Yes.' Wendy put her head on one side. 'But they've been married nearly sixteen years.'

'Do you think people don't go on loving?'

'I think it's difficult. Things change. They led such separate lives too, Ken in London all week. God knows what he gets up to there.'

'You think he had someone on the side?'

'Why not? Most men do. I don't regard men

230

as the most faithful of creatures. I think Lois was lonely without realizing it. Unfulfilled. Ken away all week, the boys at school. She's still a young woman and she didn't have enough to do.'

'What about being a magistrate, all those good causes she was into?'

'They're not *really* fulfilling, are they?'

'I thought she enjoyed it.' He paused and opened his eyes, shading them against the sun. 'She was good to me,' he added.

'Were you in love with her?'

'Not a bit.'

'Are you in love with me?'

He closed his eyes and didn't answer.

*   *   *

'If you send that card,' Oliver said as they climbed up the cliff at the end of the day, 'please don't say you're with me.'

'I might not send it.' Wendy paused, puffing. 'Anyway, for all they know, I might be in Thailand or New Zealand. Why spoil a good time?'

CHAPTER ELEVEN

Ken pushed open the door of the City wine bar and scanned the room for familiar faces. At

231

first he didn't see anyone that he recognized. As usual it was pretty full after a working day and he waited patiently for his turn at the bar. Then, from the corner of his eye, he saw the group from the bank who had momentarily been obscured by a party of people apparently celebrating a birthday with a great deal of noise and popping of Champagne corks.

As the revellers moved aside, a voice hailed Ken and, after collecting his pint, he went over to his colleagues who invariably forgathered there after work.

There were about half a dozen of them: Phil Stephens, David Major, Christopher Howard, Lorraine Grey, Archie Stewart and Miranda Kershaw, who was an economist and the only one not in his department. The others, like him, were in the overseas section of the bank, dealing with foreign investments. Miranda occasionally joined them because she seemed to be friendly with Lorraine Grey.

The hour spent in the bar at the end of the day was a great source of comfort, as well as relaxation, to Ken. He was not a heavy drinker and would only have a couple of beers or a glass or two of wine, so it was not the booze that was important but the company. In the past few weeks, this small circle of friends had been essential both in the work place and outside it.

They knew all about Wendy and Oliver; Ken had painted a very black picture of

Oliver—one blacker could not be imagined—and the whole office sided with him and waited almost as anxiously as he did for news of the police investigations. Like Ken, they were convinced that Wendy was in danger—if she was not dead already.

But no news was forthcoming. There was to be another local appeal and then the police would try to interest the national press, radio and TV; but with so much crime around it wasn't going to be easy to persuade the nationals to take it seriously.

It was a Wednesday, halfway through the week. Ken had spoken during the day to Lois, whose main concern was the boys, who were due home soon for the summer holiday. Normally the family went to France. They had a house in Lavandou which had been in Ken's family for generations. Ken usually spent two weeks, Lois and the boys stayed a month. Wendy and Tim had used to come, along with Margaret, and various younger friends for the boys, all for varying periods.

It seemed out of the question that this summer the normal happy family holiday could possibly take place, unless there was a dramatic about turn and Wendy showed up unharmed. Lois had suggested that Margaret might go with the boys, and when Ken protested she had said she was perfectly all right on her own.

'Problems, Ken?' Archie looked at him

sympathetically. 'You look more worried than usual.'

'A bit preoccupied.' Ken perched on one of the stools beside the bar and raised his glass at the sea of faces gazing at him. 'Cheers!' He drank from his glass.

'No worse news, I hope?' Christopher filled up the wine glasses of those nearest to him.

'It's only about our summer holidays. We usually go to France. But, this year . . .'

'You've a long time yet, surely?' Christopher put the empty bottle back on the bar.

'Not really. It will soon be the end of June. The boys will be breaking up.'

'But you might have some good news,' Lorraine said cheerfully. 'Wendy might come back.'

'You think so?' Ken grunted. 'I wish I shared your optimism.'

'You really think . . .'

'I don't know what to think.' Ken looked over at Miranda, who, while taking everything in, said little. Because she didn't work in his department, he barely knew her. But something about her appealed to him. She was small and dark-haired with a wistful expression, a tanned complexion and deep, unfathomable brown eyes. He always thought there was something Latin about her—Spanish or South American.

'Are you drinking, Miranda?' Ken asked her.

'I'm fine thanks, Ken.' She raised her empty glass. 'Oh, OK, then ... just a half. Lager, please.'

He ordered another half-pint of beer for himself and a lager for Miranda. He held it out to her and she wove her way over to him while the other members of the group, who had worked that day on some complex international deal, were huddled together discussing it.

'I was so sorry to hear about your domestic troubles,' Miranda said. 'Lorraine has only just brought me up to date. You must be worried out of your mind.'

'I am.' Ken passed a hand across his face. 'It's the fact that we don't know anything for sure.'

'But Lorraine seems to think ...' There was a movement in the corner and the group began to break up. Briefcases were picked up from the floor and umbrellas collected from a stand. Lorraine looked across at Miranda.

'Coming, Miranda?'

'I'll just finish my lager,' she said, holding up her glass.

'Actually, tonight I'm in a bit of a hurry. It's my evening class.' Lorraine sounded impatient.

'Don't wait for me, then,' Miranda said. 'I'm not in any rush.'

The others murmured their farewells as they made for the door, and Miranda and Ken found themselves alone.

'If you're not in any hurry, why don't you come and have a meal with me?' Ken looked across at Miranda, who was upending her glass. 'I could do with the company.'

'It's awfully kind of you, but . . .' Miranda appeared to hesitate.

'I'm sorry. I forgot you had a husband,' Ken said quickly. 'You'll want to be getting home.'

'Not at all. It's Joe's basketball practice this evening. He won't be in until late. I think, Ken, in the circumstances, I'll accept.'

They finished their drinks and Ken, feeling his spirits suddenly lift, thought how pleasant a prospect it was: an evening in the company of an attractive woman who was not his wife or sister-in-law. Pleasant and also novel. He was a faithful man. He loved Lois and it had never occurred to him to look outside his marriage for female companionship. He knew a lot of women, and enjoyed mixed company; but it had been a long time since he had invited a woman to dinner.

'I thought we'd go to the chop house,' he said as they made for the door. 'Do you like steak?'

'Love it.'

Her face seemed to flush with pleasure, and he enthusiastically took hold of her arm as they crossed the busy street.

*   *   *

There was, after all, quite a lot to talk about. Ken filled the first hour while they had their starter and main course with a detailed account of Oliver's entry into their lives and his disappearance with Wendy. As Miranda was not part of his team, she hadn't heard the whole story. At the end she said:

'You really do dislike that man . . .'

'Hate him,' Ken said.

'You think he's as evil as all that?'

'I think he wanted to seduce my wife and when she wouldn't play he got her sister instead. Wendy, being in a dodgy relationship, was much more vulnerable.'

'How awful.' Miranda, completely taken up with the story, gazed at Ken.

'That's why I'm worried about Lois's safety now.'

'You think he'd come back and *kill* her?'

'He might. I would like to get her out of the country, but she won't go in case her sister makes contact.'

'How awful for you, Ken,' Miranda said again. 'I *am* sorry,' and she briefly touched his hand in a gesture of sympathy.

'Oops, sorry,' she said, suddenly looking embarrassed. 'I didn't mean . . .'

'I understand.' He smiled easily at her. 'It's sweet of you. Really.'

'I just feel you've had such a tough time.'

'I have, and being up here all week isn't

237

easy, even though I have plenty to do.'

'Yes, what do you do?' She looked at him curiously, and he sensed that the balance of the relationship had subtly changed to one of intimacy. It was a pleasant feeling ... the low lights of the chop house, the smell of charcoal from the grill, the candles guttering on the table, their closeness pressed together in a small crowded space, somehow engendered an atmosphere of illicit sex or, at least, its possibility.

'Well ...' He thought for a while. 'I like music and I occasionally go to concerts in the Barbican and the Festival Hall.'

'Alone?'

'Oh, yes.' He looked surprised. 'Why not? Also, I like the cinema.' He smiled once more. 'Again, I go alone. I have a club I belong to and I eat there about once a week, and about once a week I either entertain friends of ours in a restaurant or someone invites me for dinner. I have the odd business dinner too.'

'And Friday you go home?'

'Yes, Friday night through to Monday morning, so only four nights of the week to fill in.'

'I suppose it makes for a happy marriage.' She sighed.

'How do you mean?'

'I don't honestly think it's good for couples to be together the *whole* time. Though there are limits.' Her tone seemed to harden and, on impulse, Ken said:

'Tell me about your husband.'

'Joe's a sportaholic, if there is such a thing.' Miranda gave a light, artificial laugh. 'Sport, sport, sport all the time with Joe.'

'What does he do?'

'He's an economist with World Trade International. Heard of it?' She paused as Ken nodded. 'We don't really see much of each other, probably less than you and Lois.'

'Lois and I see each other for two full days,' Ken said, but two full days out of seven didn't seem a lot, so he added, 'and sometimes three nights too.'

'Joe and I scarcely ever see each other. He has something every night. The gym, basketball, football and, in summer, cricket every weekend.'

'Are you interested in sport?'

'Not at all,' Miranda said firmly.

'I like hunting and golf,' Ken said rather lamely, as if trying to offer an excuse for Joe.

'But I'm sure you don't hunt and play golf every day?'

'No.'

'Or every weekend?'

'Well, Lois plays and hunts too,' he said virtuously. 'You've no children, I take it?'

Miranda shook her head. 'And I don't want any either.' She momentarily studied the table. 'Frankly, it's a lousy marriage, Ken. You don't know how lucky you are.'

She raised her eyes and looked at him, and he thought how appealing she was; how sexy and desirable. What sort of husband would be foolish enough to leave a woman like that to her own devices?

*   *   *

' . . . The couple are believed to be touring the country in a red van.'

Martin Henshaw, who had been half-asleep, his chin lolling on his chest, jerked himself awake and saw on the screen a picture of a small red van.

'What did they say?' he asked his wife, a keen knitter who was sitting watching the box, her needles clicking away.

'They say a couple have disappeared in a red van. The man is wanted for questioning about a murder.'

Martin scratched his head and memory came flooding back.

'That's odd,' he said. 'Did they say how long ago?'

'About six to eight weeks.'

'I had a couple whose van broke down and they left it with me.'

His wife nearly dropped a stitch, recovered herself and looked sharply at him.

'Have you still got it?'

'As a matter of fact, I have. It's in the yard. I've been meaning to do it up. It's in quite

240

good condition. They were an odd couple, come to think of it. I thought so at the time. The woman did all the talking. Bloke never said a word, as if the cat had got his tongue.'

'You should telephone the police, then.' His wife looked up at the screen. 'They said they'd give the number again at the end of the programme.'

*   *   *

Martin Henshaw was a man with many things on his mind. He was none too efficient and his business affairs were muddled. He was behind with his VAT and income tax, and he had a stack of unpaid bills stashed away in a drawer.

He was, however, a first-rate mechanic and a cunning one, always on the lookout for a good deal, never slow to give a misleading estimate when he thought he could get away with it, which was how he managed to keep the business going. Otherwise he would have been classed as an absolute failure.

He forgot about the broadcast on the local news the next day, and the day after; but the day after that he suddenly remembered and went to the back of his yard where the van, in worse shape than when he had acquired it, lay on its side, now missing two wheels which he had removed early on to fit on to a repair job he was doing.

Martin frequently bought wrecks or near

wrecks and then stripped them for parts. In that way he was able to make, if not a profit, at least enough to get by.

That night his wife asked him if he had telephoned the police. He admitted that he hadn't. Having thought it over, he'd decided it would be more trouble than it was worth. The last thing he needed was the police sniffing round, finding out things that weren't good for them.

But he'd done nothing wrong, his wife said. And what if that man was a murderer?

Martin told her he'd think about it, but, knowing him, his wife decided to take the matter into her own hands. She phoned the police for him.

Accordingly, the following afternoon while Martin was putting petrol into the tank of someone's car the police arrived. Seeing the van at the back of the yard, the two officers immediately went over to examine it. Eventually, after he'd taken the money for the petrol, Martin joined them.

One of the policemen was taking notes about the number and so forth, while the other walked round the van, inspecting it carefully.

'So this has been here for some six weeks, has it?'

'About that,' Martin mumbled. 'How did you know?'

'Your wife rang. Said you had it in the yard.'

'Oh, right. I asked her to do that,' he said

242

shiftily.

'What was wrong with it?'

'It needed doing up. I bought it for scrap and then thought I'd make a bit of money if I could get it on the road, but I've not got round to it yet. You know how it is.'

Martin, cursing his wife, smiled feebly.

'Who left it here?'

'A couple. Man and woman.'

'Can you remember anything about them?'

'The woman was ...' Martin paused and screwed up his eyes as if trying to visualize her. 'Well, she was quite classy.'

'Fair or dark?'

'Fair, I think. Yes, she was quite good-looking.'

'And the man?'

'He never said a word. She did all the talking. I had the impression that she was in charge. He was dark-haired. And, oh, he had his arm in a sling.'

'Did they just dump it here, or what?'

'They wanted it repaired and I said it would take time and cost a lot of money, and they said they didn't want to wait. They weren't from round here.'

'Do you know where they were from?'

Martin scratched his head again as if trying hard to turn over the little grey cells. 'I think they were from London. If my memory serves me, they were trying to get to Salisbury. I don't know anything more about them. They came from the café and then went back there after accepting my offer for the van. I suppose they got the waitress to call a cab.'

'Would she remember them?'

'I dunno. She might.'

The first policeman put his notebook into his pocket and then spoke into his walkie-talkie before looking at his partner. 'We're going to have to take this van away for examination,' he said to Martin. 'In the meantime, please don't touch it, or let anyone go near it.'

*   *   *

Peter looked hopefully up from his breakfast plate. 'Any more, Mum?'

'Really!' Lois said with a smile, getting up from the table. 'I don't know where you put it all.'

'Me too, please, Mum.' Tony pushed his plate across the table. Lois took up the plates and went over to the Aga where she ladled on more bacon, tomatoes and sausages. 'That should see you until you get to France,' she said, putting the plates down in front of them.

'Oh, Mum!' Tony pulled a face. 'No egg?'

'You want more eggs too?'

Really there was no end to the prodigious appetite of teenage boys. Lois cracked the eggs over the frying pan, a smile still on her lips. She would miss them. Only just home from school, they were going off to France with her mother, who was finishing her packing upstairs.

Rusty, who liked to divide his time when he could between the two households, sat hopefully by the side of the table strategically placed between the two boys in the hope of titbits. Occasionally he was rewarded with a piece of sausage or a bit of bacon. Lois pretended not to see. Sally and Lucy were far too well bred to beg, which was where Rusty betrayed his working-class origins.

'Mum, when are you going to come over?' Tony asked, not bothering to wait for his egg as he tackled the mound of food on his plate.

'As soon as we hear from Auntie Wendy that she's all right.'

There was a pregnant silence behind her—they scarcely ever stopped chattering—and when she turned to look at them she saw a pair of grave faces.

They were not identical twins, but they were very alike. Tall, blond and blue-eyed. They'd turned fourteen the previous term and she and Ken had gone to the school and taken them out for a celebration.

Sometimes she wished they hadn't gone to boarding school but to one of the good local schools instead. Ken, however, had been adamant. It was a Hunter tradition that the men went to the same school, and they'd gone.

She thought maybe now she wouldn't have

245

given in so easily, but five years ago, at the age of nine, to boarding school they'd gone.

'What do you mean, that Aunt Wendy's "all right"?' Peter asked as she tipped a fried egg on to his plate.

'We're a bit worried about her. She's been gone a long time.'

'With that bloke?' Tony poured tomato ketchup all over his food.

'We think so.'

'Dad said he committed a murder.'

'He *didn't* commit a murder,' Lois •said sharply. 'There is absolutely no proof. Personally, I think that they're all right. They've probably gone abroad. Tim went to see Simon, Wendy's boss, and he'd formed the impression it was her intention to go abroad. They're probably somewhere remote and can't get in touch. Also . . .' she poured herself fresh coffee and brought it back to the kitchen table, 'they found the van Wendy and . . . Oliver went off in. It was quite near, only in Salisbury. They left it at a garage, so that means they probably *did* go abroad.'

'But why wouldn't Aunt Wendy tell you, Mum?'

'She did.' Lois stirred her coffee, trying hard to conceal her anxiety from the boys, aware from their intense expressions that she had not quite succeeded. 'She wrote us a letter saying she was taking a long break. I guess they're somewhere like China or Russia. The post

246

takes ages from places like that.' Squaring her shoulders, she gave them a bright smile. 'I'm perfectly sure she's all right.'

'Then why not come to France with us now?'

'Because Daddy thinks we ought to stay here, just for the time being.'

'It *is* quite serious, Mum, isn't it?' Tony asked, wiping his plate carefully with his bread. 'Dad said the police are going to make an appeal on TV.'

'We just need to know where they are and what has happened, if they're in England. That would clear the air; but, personally, I think they're somewhere far away.' She sighed deeply. 'However, until we know something, here we stay.'

There was a tap at the kitchen door and, without waiting for a reply, Neal came in.

'Are we ready?'

'Goodness, is it as late as that?' Lois leapt up, looking at her watch.

'I thought we'd leave a bit of time in case the traffic's bad.' Neal smiled at the boys. 'Excited?' They both nodded and rapidly finished what was on their plates.

'They've got everything packed and in the hall, Neal,' Lois said. 'You can start putting the bags in the car if you like. Come on, boys, hurry up. Tony, go and wipe your face, it's covered with tomato sauce. And you'd both better spend pennies.' Then she went to the

247

door and called, 'Mum! Neal's here. He thinks you'd better leave a bit early to allow for the traffic.'

'Coming.' Margaret's voice could be heard from a long way off. 'Can someone come up for my case, please?'

'Right away,' Peter said, racing for the stairs.

Now that they were ready to go, Lois felt a pang. She'd hardly seen the boys because Ken had been anxious for them to go and get the French house open and aired. Someone kept an eye on it during the year, but there was always a lot to do. Lois wished she was going with them. She adored the South of France and the house really was a second home, full of lovely memories, including her and Ken's honeymoon.

Through the open front door, she saw Tony helping Neal to put the cases in the back of the Range Rover, then Peter hurried out with her mother's case. Neal would drive them to Heathrow, where they'd catch a flight to Nice. On arrival in France they'd pick up their hire car, and by tonight they'd be making beds and maybe going out to the local bistro for their first meal on French soil.

The dogs scampered up and down as if on the verge of an adventure. Each was embraced in turn by the boys, who now regarded Rusty as part of the family.

'I do envy you.' Lois first kissed the boys

hard and then flung her arms round her mother.

'Then come, darling. Come as soon as you can.' Her mother stood back and looked at her.

'I shall. The moment we hear something— and I'm sure we'll hear something soon.'

Her mother's expression was doubtful. 'You will let me know as soon as you do, Lois?'

'The very moment.'

'Anything—good or bad.'

'*Anything,*' Lois promised, and kissed her firmly on both cheeks, reluctant to let her go.

*   *   *

'Goodbye. Goodbye.' They were off. Arms flailing out of the car's windows, faces turned to look back at the house. Then round the bend in the drive, out of sight.

Lois felt depressed. She'd tried so hard to keep her concern from her mother and the boys; but somehow the fact that the red van had been found, and so near, seemed sinister. After all she had bought it on the understanding that it was as good as new, or at least good enough to get Oliver as far as he wanted to go.

The police were taking it extremely seriously, and had removed the van for forensic tests.

It was now established once and for all that

249

Oliver and Wendy were together, but where had they gone since then and where were they now?

Rusty, alone of the dogs, bounded along the drive as if in pursuit of the car but, halfway down, he halted, looked at Lois and rushed back. Because of his erratic wanderings as a puppy he would probably always know that awful sense of insecurity that adults who have endured similar situations in childhood feel. Also, who knew but that he might have witnessed a horrific murder? She knelt down to pat and soothe him. He licked her face gratefully and trotted obediently at her heels, the best-behaved dog in the world, rejoining Sally and Lucy as Lois drifted round the garden inspecting the herbaceous borders. She'd neglected the garden. Gardening was supposed to take your mind off things but lately she hadn't had the heart for it. She was restless, ill at ease, trying hard to keep up an appearance of *sang-froid* which she was far from feeling. Even she now thought that Wendy, however selfish, would not have left them without news for nearly two months!

Maybe Oliver *was* a murderer. Maybe Wendy *was* dead . . .

In the still of the night, at two or three o'clock in the morning when she lay awake alone and thinking, she went over all the dreadful possibilities in her mind.

The trouble was, she thought, looking at the

beautiful display of lupins which came up year after year, even if she did nothing the garden would still go on looking beautiful. It was tended by a full-time gardener who, at the moment, was mowing the lawn on his little petrol-driven buggy. He waved at her and she waved back. In the foreground, a sprinkler, going backwards and forwards, created an evanescent haze in the sunshine.

It was a warm, mellow English summer day and she wished that her spirits could be as sunny. If she were honest, she would like to put the clock back to the time before she met Oliver, committed that random act of kindness. Was it only nine months ago? He seemed to have dominated their lives for much longer. Now, despite the summer, the cloudless sky and tranquil, perfumed air, it was as if a great storm was waiting to gather. The police were launching a nationwide appeal for the missing couple, or anyone who had seen them, to come forward. The daily papers were being briefed.

Soon there would be no peace left for them, which was why Ken had been so anxious to get the children out of the way.

As she turned to go back into the house, she saw Beverley coming up the drive towards her.

'Hi!'

'Good morning,' Beverley said, shading her eyes. 'Glorious day.'

'Glorious,' Lois replied, bending to stroke

251

Rusty who had rushed to her side. 'I thought you might have gone to the airport with Neal for the drive?'

'No . . .' Beverley's pause seemed awkward. 'Actually, Lois, there's something I wanted to talk to you about.'

'Oh? You sound serious. Not bad news I hope?'

'It depends how you take it,' Beverley said.

'In that case, we'd better sit down.' Lois sighed. 'I really don't know that I can take any more bad news.'

'It's not as bad as that!' Beverley gave a nervous smile as they sank into the two canvas chairs that had been left out on the terrace since the previous day. Rusty sat contentedly on the stone between them, head resting on his paws. As the gardener drove away to the far end of the garden the hum of the engine grew more distant.

Immediately in front of them was an ornamental pond stocked with exotic fish. In the middle of it an antique fountain spewed out gentle jets of water, creating a mesmeric effect.

'Neal and I want to leave, Lois.'

'Oh, no . . .'

'I know it's not a good time to tell you, but when is? We've put it off as long as we can, hoping you'd hear from Wendy.'

'But we so *depend* on you.'

'I know.' Beverley twisted her hands in her

252

lap. 'That's why it's so hard to tell you.'

'And you've been here for such a long time.'

'That's it.'

'Your children were born here. You're part of our family.'

'Please don't make it worse,' Beverley besought her, eyes pleading.

'Have you had enough? Is it something . . .'

'It's got nothing to do with you or Ken, or the situation about Wendy. Nothing at all. We love living here and we shall miss it. Terribly. But we desperately want our own place and there's a small farm in Scotland we're interested in. If we don't take it, it may be a long time before we get another chance, something we can afford.'

'*Scotland*?' Lois gasped.

'Neal's family were originally from Edinburgh, and we both love Scotland. We've been looking for some time and what's brought it to a head now is that this smallholding near Aberdeen has just come on to the market. It's a hundred acres, mainly sheep, not too remote. Ideal for us. The elderly farmer died and his heirs want to get rid of it quickly. Hence it's very reasonable and includes stock. We have to make up our minds urgently.'

'You saw it when you had your week off?'

'Yes.'

A week earlier, the Drivers had returned from a short holiday. It seemed a bit sneaky of them not to have said anything then, but when was a good time to give bad news? And it was bad news. Neal and Bev had always been so rock solid, so dependable, so essential to the functioning of the estate, with Ken being away all week. However, they had their own lives to lead, and to want a place of their own was understandable. You couldn't condemn them.

'I shall miss you terribly.' Lois reached out and put her hand over Beverley's.

'And I shall miss you. We won't be moving for a few weeks—we'll give you time to get someone else. Plenty of people will be after a job like this, with a house.'

'But we'll be lucky if we get someone like you.'

'And I really *hate* leaving you with all this trouble about Wendy . . .'

'It will sort itself out soon,' Lois said briskly. 'By this time next year or maybe next month or, who knows, even next week, we'll have forgotten it ever happened. Ken and I will be off to France, and you'—she turned with a smile to Beverley—'will be planning your move. It's quite an adventure.'

Always the perfect optimist. Stiff upper lip. At least in public.

CHAPTER TWELVE

It had been a busy day at the magistrates' court. There was a morning session and one in the afternoon which went on late, and Lois felt more tired than usual as they retired to the magistrates' room to discuss the day's cases over a cup of tea. There had been the usual crowd of dropouts, petty thieves, drug addicts and ... beggars. Usually they proved to be drug addicts and thieves as well. No wonder people felt prejudiced against them.

Madge had been chairman of the bench and had a lot of paperwork to see to. A third, fairly new, magistrate was an acquaintance of Lois's and they chatted about this and that, nothing of any importance, while Madge signed papers for the clerk of court. Committing this person to custody, letting that one have bail, and so on.

As usual, Madge and Lois left together— their fellow juror was going in the opposite direction—and they wandered towards the centre of the town where they'd left their cars.

Madge paused in front of the supermarket.

'Anything you want today?' she asked, drawing a list from her own pocket.

Lois shook her head. These days she always felt peculiar when she went past the supermarket, and shopped there far less than

255

she used to. In her mind's eye, she always saw Oliver as he had been that first day lying on the pavement in front of the store, the puppies pressed close to his chest. She wondered whether it had been Chump or Rusty she'd seen first.

Today, suddenly and unexpectedly, she thought of something else and her hand flew to her mouth. Madge looked at her curiously.

'I just thought ... You know I had assumed that Wendy and ... Oliver'—she always paused before she said his name—'might be abroad, but Oliver wouldn't leave the dog, would he? He was devoted to it.'

Madge's expression was dubious. 'If he did that murder ...'

'Which he didn't!' Lois interjected sharply.

'Well, *if* he did—and let's suppose, for the sake of argument, he did—' she put out her hand in an attempt to stop Lois interrupting. 'He didn't treat Rusty too well, did he? Leaving him to roam all over the place and risk being starved or run over.'

'That's why I know Oliver didn't do it. He was devoted to animals.' Lois looked intensely at her friend. 'He was a kind man, Madge, a gentle man. That's what you don't seem to understand.'

'I just don't feel you know him as well as you think,' Madge said, realizing she was on dangerous ground. 'You have to know someone terribly well to say that about them.

256

You hardly knew him at all.'

'I knew him *instinctively*. We were on the same wavelength.'

'And did your sister know him instinctively too?'

'That's a catty thing to say, Madge.' Lois's tone was cool. 'I'm surprised at you.'

'Lois ...' Madge dropped her voice aware that people passing were looking at them. 'I am your friend, believe me. We know each other well, don't we?'

'I thought we did.'

'We do.'

'Except that you've made up your mind about Oliver. I know you have.'

'My dear, as a magistrate I go on the evidence. Whatever his merits or virtues, as you saw them, he didn't behave at all responsibly did he? He used you and he left me without so much as a "thank you", never mind a box of chocs or a bunch of flowers.'

'People like Oliver don't obey natural laws,' Lois said.

'Really! You're *always* making excuses for him.' Madge's voice began to rise, and Lois felt she had had enough.

'I'm sure,' Madge continued, 'even if you found out he had murdered your sister, you'd find an excuse for that!'

Lois began to shake with intemperate rage. 'What a perfectly *foul* thing to say,' she said. Then she turned her back on Madge and half-ran, half-walked towards the car.

Madge watched her go, uncertain whether to run after her or not. She'd gone too far. On the other hand, it was infuriating the way Lois always spoke up for Oliver, wouldn't hear a word said against him. It was unnatural, almost as though she'd been in love with the man.

Perhaps she had.

Deep in thought, Madge made her way into the supermarket, recalling, as she passed the doors, the beggar who used to lie outside and had left such havoc behind him.

She'd ring Lois in a day or two, apologize, try and make it up to her.

*   *   *

Somehow Lois knew that her friendship with Madge, such as it was, was over.

This was a time when you discovered who your true friends were. Sometimes she thought she had precious few. She knew everyone was against Oliver. The only person who would feel about him as she did was Wendy, and where was Wendy now?

She knew Beverley was equivocal about Oliver, and everyone knew how Ken felt. The boys seemed to be on the side of their father, and her mother, well, she just didn't know or didn't want to know. She certainly didn't want to think her daughter had gone off with a man who was a murderer.

If only Wendy would ring.

And what friends had one, Lois thought as she turned into the drive. You gave your life up to being married and then found you had no friends of your own, or no real ones. Your husband's friends were your friends, and vice versa. You met for dinners and at parties, at the hunt or other social occasions. Unless you kept in touch with old school friends, or had a lot of hobbies, or went out of your way to meet new people, you didn't.

So that when you wanted someone to turn to you hadn't anyone.

*　　　*　　　*

As Lois opened the front door the telephone was ringing, for how long she didn't know. She threw down her bag on the hall table and rushed to answer it, but just before she got to the phone it stopped ringing.

She was so convinced it was Wendy that she could have burst into tears. Maybe, impulsively, Wendy had rung and, with no answer . . . It didn't bear thinking about.

Then she remembered the call-back facility. You could use it to trace incoming calls. Her hands trembled with excitement as she thumbed through the phone book looking for the number: 1471. She threw herself at the telephone and dialled.

'Telephone number 0171 359 2645 called

today at 7.05 p.m. To return the call please press 3,' was the message.

The number was repeated and, feverishly, Lois wrote it on the pad at her side. Then she replaced the receiver and stared foolishly at the page, realizing that the number was familiar. It was that of the Barbican flat.

Ken. Disappointment, but never mind. Maybe Ken had heard something. She lifted the receiver again and pressed 3. She leaned against the hall table listening, imagining Ken hearing the phone, coming across to it, picking it up. But why, if he had just rung, was he taking so long? Maybe he'd got into the bath.

She visualized the inside of the Barbican flat, which was quite small: two bedrooms, a largish living room, kitchen and bathroom. She hadn't been there for ages. The stark concrete environment, the massive doors and iron gates which opened and then thudded closed behind you, the long dark corridors, all reminded her of a prison.

Never mind. He'd ring again. She was on the verge of replacing the receiver when a woman's voice at the other end spoke tentatively: 'Hello?'

Lois was about to say wrong number but instead she said, brusquely: 'Is Ken there?'

'Er . . .' The woman, clearly taken aback, hesitated.

'Who am I speaking to?' Lois still couldn't quite take in that a woman was answering

Ken's phone. 'This is his wife.'

'Oh, er, Mrs Hunter.' Flustered, clearly, but trying to take control. 'I'm a colleague of Ken's at the bank. Miranda Kershaw.'

'I see.' Long pause. 'Is Ken there, Miss Kershaw?'

'Well . . . I thought you might be him.'

'Forgive me, but I don't quite understand what you're doing there.' Crisp, headmistressy tones.

'Ken and I are working on a project. He asked me to meet him here. He gave me the keys.' Growing confidence in her voice. 'I thought you might be him. He's a bit late.'

'But someone just rang this number.'

'Yes, that was me. I wondered if Ken was still at home. It being Monday, I thought . . .'

'No, Ken left early this morning. I understood that today he was going to Norwich.'

'Ah!' Relief in her voice. 'That will be it.'

'I still find it strange that he gave you the keys.'

'I assure you there is nothing to worry about.' The hitherto diffident, placatory tone now assumed a chilly formality. 'Incidentally, it's *Mrs* Kershaw, Mrs Hunter.'

'Perhaps you'd tell Ken I rang,' Lois said, and put down the phone.

She stood for a long time looking at nothing in particular. Miranda Kershaw? She'd never heard of her. Yet what would a woman colleague be doing in Ken's flat, their flat, at— she glanced at the clock in the hall—just after seven in the evening?

Why would Ken work at home with a colleague, male or female? He hardly ever brought work home. He said he put in a long enough day in the office and didn't believe in homework.

She shook herself and bent to stroke Rusty, who was demanding her attention. She supposed he needed to be let out though Beverley had taken him for a walk in the afternoon. Golly, she'd miss Beverley.

She opened the front door again and out Rusty shot. Leaving it open, Lois wandered into the drawing room and poured herself a drink. Then she stood for a long time at the window watching Rusty scamper about on the lawn chasing imaginary rabbits. She took a sip of her drink. Everything in her world seemed to be collapsing: Wendy gone, Oliver gone, Beverley and Neal going, Mother and the children away in France, she and Madge not getting on . . .

And now, supposing . . . It had to be faced; other women's husbands did. Supposing Ken and this woman were having an affair?

What would be left in her life then, and who could one possibly trust?

*   *   *

Feeling like a criminal, Lois put her key into the door of the Barbican flat and let herself in. She had come up on an afternoon train and it was now just after seven. It was about this time that, forty-eight hours before, she had rung the flat and Mrs Kershaw had answered it. Since then she had not been able to get the other woman out of her mind.

At first she thought she'd wait until the weekend and have it out with Ken. But she couldn't. How would she start? Much better to confront him on his own ground, as it were, than that it should come out of the blue over breakfast or whatever. Besides, weekends were so busy. Next Saturday they were playing in a golf tournament.

What would she say if Ken admitted he was having an affair? She didn't know.

Should she perhaps have done what they do in films and have him followed by a private investigator? A private eye? She wouldn't know how to start, who to approach, what to do.

The truth was that, although this sort of thing was common, happened all the time—to other people that was—when it happened to you, you were at a loss.

Adultery was commonplace, but to everyone when it happened the first time their experience must have been similar. Man or woman, they would not know what to do or which way to turn.

263

The flat looked clean, impersonal. The block employed a firm of cleaners who cleaned twice a week or as often as you wanted, because it was not part of the general service charge and tenants had to pay for it themselves.

Lois never felt at home in the flat; it reminded her of a hotel. Everything just so, nothing out of place, like in a proper home. There were a few books, the regulation vase or two of flowers—though Ken hardly ever bothered with these—and a few of the less valuable pictures she had inherited from her father.

When they had first bought the flat she was quite interested in it, thinking that it would be fun to have a pied-à-terre in London and that she'd make regular use of it, but she hadn't. She only ever went up for formal 'do's', usually connected with the bank. Or, occasionally, Ken might get special tickets for the opera or a theatre and she'd go up then.

Lois put her handbag and overnight case down in the sitting room and went into the bedroom. This merely had a double bed, now neatly made, a dressing table and chest of drawers, a television and an armchair. The wardrobe and cupboards were built-in.

Lois stood by the side of the bed and slowly, deliberately drew back the cover. Then she rolled back the duvet and stared at the white bottom sheet.

No telltale stains, no suspicious crumples, nothing. No clue as to whether Ken had spent the night before, or any other night, with another woman in their bed.

She felt tired. For the last two nights she'd slept badly. She didn't quite know how she would handle things when Ken returned. She went into the sitting room and brought her things back into the bedroom, unpacked, undressed and, slipping on her light robe, went into the bathroom and ran a bath.

As she lay soaking she wished she hadn't come.

*   *   *

Ken put his key in the latch of the flat and let himself in. He sensed immediately that the flat was not empty. He threw his briefcase on the sofa and went into the bedroom, saw Lois's things and then put his head round the bathroom door.

'Hi!' he said, unable to conceal his surprise. 'Fancy seeing you.'

Lois, busy soaping her arms, looked at him.

'Were you expecting to see someone else?'

'No.'

'I thought you might.'

'We need to talk, Lois,' Ken said and, abruptly leaving the bathroom, went back into the bedroom and took off his jacket and tie. Then he went into the sitting room, got himself a drink and shook out the evening paper.

It was about twenty minutes before Lois came in and joined him. She wore a pretty striped cotton dress with a round neck, buttoned down the front, and a plain white belt. It was as though she'd done her best to look attractive, but she was attractive anyway. Her curly hair, naturally springy, bleached by the sun, was brushed back from her forehead and secured with a bandeau of the same material as the dress. She had on, as always, a modicum of make-up and looked extremely youthful, scarcely her age. Hard to think she was the mother of two adolescent boys.

'Drink, darling?' he asked, getting up but careful not to kiss her as he would normally have done.

'Please.'

'The usual?'

'Yes.'

As she sat down he poured a gin and tonic then went into the kitchen for some ice. Returning, he put the drink into her hand and took a chair opposite her.

'Miranda told me that you phoned here.'

'Oh!'

'She was very upset.'

'Why?' There was a challenging note in Lois's voice and she put her head on one side. The blue eyes, usually full of merriment, were steely.

266

'She thought you might have misunderstood.' Ken cleared his throat and went on rapidly. 'We are not having an affair. We're both married.'

'I see.'

'That's what you thought, isn't it?'

'Can you blame me?'

'I can see why you'd think that—and I'm not saying the possibility hadn't occurred to me, purely on a physical level. I'd be dishonest if I said anything else.'

'But she said "no"?' Lois gave a mocking half-smile, as though to say she disbelieved him.

'No. It hadn't got to that stage. I see now how wrong and foolish it would have been, and I'm glad you phoned and found out when you did.'

'At least you're honest.' Lois laughed nervously and took a sip of her drink, her hand a little unsteady.

Ken got up and came across to sit beside her.

'Lois, I love you very much. I'm not saying I could never have an affair with another woman—I was tempted with Miranda. Half my friends, if not more, are having affairs. It's all rather sordid. Everyone gets hurt. There are messy divorces, the children suffer. We, you and I, have a good life. I don't want to spoil it.'

'You are being honest,' Lois said. 'But I wouldn't expect you to be anything else, Ken.'

'I'm laying it straight on the line, as it is. But you see, I do get lonely up here during the week. I mean, there's plenty to do, but my reality is the weekends and I look forward to them. Miranda happens to work at the bank. A group of us meet after work for a drink and occasionally she joins us. One night we were the last to leave the wine bar and I asked her out for dinner. We went to a restaurant and chatted. I told her about Oliver and Wendy—she knew anyway—and she told me about her unhappy marriage. I knew then that I was tempted.'

'So you gave her the keys of the flat.'

'She said she'd make me a meal. She's good on curries. I forgot to tell her I was going to Norwich.' Ken lowered his voice and stared at the floor. 'I don't know what would have happened had you not rung, but nothing did, and if it had it would not have been important.'

'Except to me.'

'Quite ... if you'd found out, but I would naturally have tried to keep it from you and ... hell, there would have been all that deception.' Ken shook his head vigorously. 'I hate it all; the whole idea, and then another woman getting involved. No, not for me. Definitely not.' He rose and, hands in his pockets, went over to look out of the window. It was not a spectacular view because of the cantilevered lines of the building, but you

268

could see a gleam of water: the outlines of some City buildings. For most of the day the room didn't get any sun.

'Ken,' Lois said, 'why don't we sell up and get a place in London?'

Slowly Ken turned round.

'I'm not just saying it because of this.' Lois rose and went over to stand beside him. 'I've been thinking about it for a while. This Oliver business has unsettled me terribly.'

'I know. It has me too.' He put an arm around her waist and was pleased that she didn't move away.

'I thought we could make a fresh start. I mean, I thought it before the other night, before I heard Miranda's voice. I'd had a row with Madge. Beverley told me she and Neal are leaving . . .'

Ken stopped her. 'My God! Why?'

'They want their own place. Somewhere in Scotland.'

'That is a blow.'

'It's a huge place.'

'But we love it so.'

'I know, but we could love something else. If we didn't have the farm we wouldn't need another couple. Frankly,' she looked around, 'I hate this flat.'

'I do too. But would you like to live in town?'

He seemed excited by her idea, she could tell it from his voice.

'It needn't be "in town". It could be Richmond or somewhere north of the river.'

'That would be wonderful. We could do so many things during the week. And we could have a smaller place in the country.'

'That's it—a weekend cottage.' Suddenly, instead of feeling depressed she began to share Ken's excitement. Instead of feeling lost and alone she felt now that she was the most important person in the world to Ken. His life. It was quite something to be all in all to somebody else.

'What would the boys say?' Ken's expression grew grave.

'I don't think they'd mind at all. Anyway, we're not going to do it next week.'

'It's an idea,' Ken said. 'An excellent idea. This Wendy/Oliver business has been ghastly, darling. I haven't been as understanding as I might. I realize that.'

'And I *was* idiotic. I was obsessional. That's why I think a change, a complete change, might be the answer . . . for us, Ken. We want to stay together, don't we?'

She had such lovely limpid blue eyes, she emanated such a powerful, erotic aura that he felt more in love with her than ever. A lucky man who had nearly made a terrible mistake. Imagine being hooked up to Miranda with her lousy marriage, and in no time she'd say she was pregnant and start demanding that he leave Lois and marry her . . .

270

He leaned over and his lips brushed Lois's cheek. Their mouths met in a long, lingering kiss. In each other's arms they were grateful for the familiar; for a feeling now that they never would, never could, grow apart.

Later, instead of going out for dinner, he got a Chinese takeaway, and then they went to bed.

*   *   *

'And now,' the presenter said, 'we come to the mystery of a woman murdered in a remote Cornish cottage. Who is she and where did she come from?' An artist's impression of a woman with black hair appeared on the screen.

The presenter then proceeded with the details: the discovery of the body, hideously mutilated, and the subsequent recovery of the dog which had belonged to her, found wandering in the countryside nearby.

There was a picture of Rusty and footage of the cottage nestling away from the water, amidst trees. Its beauty and picturesqueness were in stark contrast to the horrible death of the last person known to occupy it.

The presenter went on: 'The link with the dog is a man whose only known name is Oliver. Oliver has disappeared and is believed to be travelling with a woman, and possibly another dog resembling the one you've just

271

seen in the picture. For legal reasons, we cannot give the name of the woman, who is entirely innocent of any involvement in the crime, but this is a picture of her.'

And there followed a photo of Wendy, supplied, reluctantly, by Lois. She and Ken had been quite adamant that Wendy should not be identified, and their solicitors had made this clear to the programme's makers. It was however an excellent likeness of her.

'The couple were at first travelling in a red van'—a picture of the red van appeared on the screen—'which has been dumped. Where are they now? Any information, please, to the studio or the police ...' The number of the police station in Cornwall appeared in large figures on the screen.

'It should also be emphasized,' the presenter concluded, 'that at present the man is only wanted for questioning in the hope that he can assist the police in identifying the murder victim.

'Now, our next case concerns ...'

*   *   *

Gwen Davies looked over at the figure of her sleeping husband. It had gone ten and he invariably fell asleep in front of the telly. She was tired too.

She got up and switched off the television and nudged her husband awake.

272

'I say, Dai. Time for bed,' she said.

Dai opened his eyes, yawned, scratched himself and lumbered out of his chair.

'There was a funny thing on the TV just now,' Gwen said, puffing up the cushions and emptying Dai's ashtray full of tobacco ash. 'Someone looking just like that woman who was here, oh, several weeks ago now. I would say it was her spitting image.'

'Was she an actress?' Dai asked.

'No. She's wanted for questioning over a murder.'

'Gracious me!' Dai said, stopping to look at his wife. 'Who did she murder?'

'No, she wasn't the one who did the murder. It was the man with her.'

'And when were these people here?' Dai, by now fully awake, looked shocked.

'A few weeks ago. I can't remember exactly; but she was a good-looking woman. He was attractive too, but younger, I'd say, and strange.'

'And you mean they were *here* in this house? You must call the police at once.'

'Don't be so daft, Dai.' Gwen was a bit sorry now that she'd spoken. 'They can't do us no harm.'

'They could come back.'

'She didn't look like a murderer.'

'How do you know what a murderer looks like?'

'I suppose you're right. He didn't look like a
273

murderer either; he was so quiet. Didn't say anything and when I asked them for coffee he didn't want to stay. Anxious he was to get away.'

'You best phone the police,' Dai said. 'And make sure you keep the bolt on the front door during the day.'

'Oh, I can't do that. Anyway, what do I tell the police?'

'Tell them they was here.'

'They'll be miles away by now. Besides, it sounds so far-fetched, doesn't it? And it was a long time ago. Really, Dai, I wouldn't know what to say. Afraid of making a fool of myself, I'd be.'

CHAPTER THIRTEEN

Wendy opened her eyes and lay for a moment not quite sure where she was. She'd had one of those dreams when everything happened. She'd been by the seaside and there had been an accident in which someone either drowned or nearly drowned. A man had been taken away on a green stretcher. She didn't know whether he was dead or not.

As usual she had the feeling of time rushing by, of there being so much to do. She had to leap out of bed and brush her teeth and take a shower and swallow some coffee . . . No, no, no. She didn't have to do any of these things. She had absolutely nothing to do at all. No one waiting for her, no meetings to attend, no fractious author needing to be mollycoddled and flattered, no budgets to prepare, or jackets to pass, or editors to pester.

She sat upright and everything fell into place. She was in the country, by the sea, miles from any big city, even a medium-sized town. Oliver lay sleeping on his side, face turned to her, while Chump stretched out at the bottom of the bed, nose twitching.

How they slept, the pair of them!

And far from there being so much to do, there was nothing to do. She stretched her arms luxuriously above her head, then snuggled back against the pillows.

Nothing to do. When she thought back to her busy life she realized she could never have envisaged a Sybaritic lifestyle such as the one she had now.

Even her social life had been frantic. She and Tim were always partying, going places. A night in was a rarity. If she had one, she couldn't stand the isolation and had the television on all the time. Now the only time she saw TV was occasionally in a pub or the window of an electrical shop.

And then there was the silence. She had never been aware of silence before. Silence so profound it muted their senses and brought its own kind of peace. And then it accentuated the nice sounds, like the calls of cattle or the song of birds, or the wind sighing in the trees.

A lot of this sense of peace had to do with Oliver. He was an extraordinarily restful man. Nothing fazed him; he worried about nothing. She wasn't sure if this was the kind of person he was or if he'd become like that. She thought the latter. He read a lot. She read a lot too, but he was voracious in his reading, mainly the classics: Tolstoy, Dostoevsky, Turgenev, Dickens. He was astonishingly well-read; reading and re-reading paperbacks bought in places they passed through. She felt positively uneducated beside Oliver, and she had a university degree.

Occasionally, like Peer Gynt peeling the onion, she uncovered layers about his past. It turned out he was almost completely self-taught. He had spent a lot of time in libraries trying to get away from the cold. He had been a poor student and his frequent bouts of truancy had been the reason most of his foster parents had returned him to the residential home.

They never sat down to have a heart-to-heart about his past, or hers. It just came out in odd remarks, odd moments of reflection, odd musings aloud. Sometimes she thought he wasn't interested in her, nowhere near as much as she was in him.

She realized she loved Oliver. Loved and was in love. She didn't know if she was loved in return or merely fancied, or desired. It was so hard to plumb his real feelings.

She was less sure now than she had been that it would end, or that she would let it.

But how could they make permanence work? And was permanence a thing Oliver understood? She couldn't live in a van all her life. It was fun; it was an adventure. But there would come a time when it would pall, probably in the winter when it got cold.

She could imagine herself longing for the comfort of a permanent dwelling; central heating or a warm fire, a shower, a loo that flushed ... Somewhere to live, but not necessarily her old way of life. What would she do? Would she resign from work? How would they live, and where?

And what would they live on? She could sell her flat, that would fetch a bit, and her car. She had savings, stocks and shares. Her father had left her and Lois quite well off. Really, with all her investments, she could probably live quite simply, and support Oliver too, for the rest of her life.

Oliver stirred and Chump opened his eyes at the same time. Dog and man were extraordinarily attuned to each other. Oliver lay there for a while blinking, as if he too didn't remember where he was.

'What time is it?' he asked.

'About ten.'

'Oh, quite early.' He closed his eyes as if he

277

intended to go to sleep again.

'It's a bit cloudy, but I think it's going to be a lovely day,' Wendy said, drawing back the curtain and looking out across the sea. The surface of the water was flecked with a fishing boat, one or two yachts, and several buoys bobbing about.

'Mmm.' Oliver's eyes were still closed.

'I really feel I should phone Lois,' Wendy said, putting her feet over the side of the bed.

'Then why don't you?'

Wendy didn't reply but went over to the door and let Chump out. She was sure he must be bursting. He leapt down the steps and out on to the patch of heath they were camping on beside the sea. They moved from time to time so that they would not become too obvious, but no one bothered them. Sometimes they only moved a few yards.

Oliver seemed to have this thing about the police. He always imagined they were looking for him, and when she joked about it he said it was because the rozzers were always after him when he'd absconded from the home. He really had had a wretched childhood.

If anything had made him haunted and unsettled it was that.

Wendy left the door open and went over to fill the kettle and put it on.

'Are you too ashamed about going off with me?' Oliver asked from the bed.

'What do you mean?' She looked over at

him.

'To ring your sister?'

'Of course not.'

'Then ring her.'

'All right, I will. Tonight.'

She made the tea and, bringing his mug over, sat on the bed with hers.

'I love you,' she said.

'I know.'

'I thought this would end, but now I'm not sure.'

'I don't know either.'

'That's really why I don't want to ring Lois. I think it will bring things to a head.'

'Why?'

'There'll be a fuss.'

He smiled in the slow, reflective way he had, not showing too much emotion. 'Oh, there'll be a fuss, all right, especially from your sister's husband.'

'But there's nothing they can do. I'm nearly thirty-five. I'm independent.' She paused and finished her tea. 'Yes, I think it's the thought of the fuss that's stopping me. It turns you into a coward, doesn't it?'

Oliver nodded but said nothing. Then he snuggled down again as if preparing once more to go to sleep.

*   *   *

The sun was slow to come out, but towards

late morning it began to show promise of a hot day. Wendy, sitting outside the van drying her hair, saw people carrying bags, lilos and deck chairs drifting towards the sea.

Really, one could stay here all day. She spread the towel out on the grass and lay on it, closing her eyes. Chump came up and nuzzled her and without looking she threw him a ball. But in no time he was back again.

Idleness, simply idleness.

They had brunch, which they often did, Oliver cooking. Oliver had scrambled egg and beans on toast and Wendy bacon and egg. Then, carrying the rugs and a flask of tea, they put Chump on a lead and, after locking the van, set off for the sea, going carefully down a steep, narrow, winding path that led to a more sheltered part of the beach. This was full of large rocks and boulders where they could sunbathe almost naked and then leap from there into the sea.

It was a blissful day. The sky was now completely cloudless, a haze almost obscuring the cliffs, leaving them with the feeling that they were cocooned in a world of their own. They lay on their backs on the hot sand, sometimes linking hands, occasionally embracing when there was no one in sight.

'Peace,' Wendy murmured, 'perfect peace.'

At five they had their last swim. By then it had begun to get a little cold, so they took off their wet suits and put on shorts and T-shirts.

They had their hot tea from a thermos and then they packed up. Instead of returning the way they had come, they took the main path up the cliff because Wendy wanted to get cigarettes from the village shop near the top. Oliver, taking Chump, carried on past the shop to go back to the van.

*　　　*　　　*

The shop was quite full, people buying cigarettes, papers, postcards, fishing nets, bottles of coke, lemonade. Wendy waited her turn patiently, purse clasped in her hand.

She had been staring with a certain fascination at the picture on the newspaper hoarding for some time before she realized that she was looking at a photograph of herself.

It must be a mistake, she thought. But as the queue diminished she was able to get a closer look at the stack of evening papers on the counter.

MURDER HUNT SHIFTS TO WALES

This was some dreadful mistake. It couldn't be her.

Nevertheless, she was glad she was wearing dark glasses as she bought her cigarettes and a copy of the paper, turning away as soon as she'd got her change.

No one seemed to recognize her, not even the friendly man across the counter who by this time knew her quite well.

Once outside, Wendy drew the paper from under her arm and, finding somewhere to sit, began to read:

A couple featured on television a few nights ago are thought to be in Wales. They are wanted for questioning by the police in connection with the savage murder of a woman in Cornwall.

The man, known simply as Oliver, is believed to have been the last person to see the murder victim alive. He and the woman accompanying him were last seen on the first of May, election day. She is not wanted on any charges, and it is emphasized that the police, at this juncture, only want to question the man to see if he can assist them with their enquiries.

After the programme there were several phone calls to the police and TV studios from people in the Principality who thought they had seen the couple. They are thought to be travelling in some sort of caravan or camper van.

Anyone who sees the couple or has knowledge of their whereabouts is asked to contact the nearest police station.

Wendy sat crouched on the bed, as if she had a

pain in her stomach, watching Oliver carefully as he read the disastrous news that she'd brought in with the cigarettes. Why was it that joy was so often and so quickly followed by pain?

Oliver hardly ever sat or stood when he could lie, so he now lay on his side on the bed, the paper spread out in front of him. When he'd finished, he flicked over the pages as though looking for other interesting items of news and then, with a rueful smile at Wendy, he closed the paper and threw it on the floor. Finally he lay on his back, hands under his head, and stared at the ceiling. Being Oliver, he said nothing. But she thought he looked immeasurably sad.

'Did you know her?' Wendy asked after a while, able to endure the silence no longer yet not wanting to do or say the wrong thing.

'Yes . . . but I didn't kill her,' he added after a pause.

'I didn't think you did.'

'Really?' He raised his head and looked at her. 'I liked her a lot. I'm really sorry she's dead.' He seemed to choke on his words and the expression on his face was melancholy, bitter; something she hadn't seen since she first knew him. She realized then that her influence on Oliver had been as beneficial as his on her.

They had both done each other good. He had become happier—he often laughed now, whereas before he seldom did. He had put on weight and the sullen, anguished expression of a few months before had been replaced by one of contentment.

'I know you didn't kill her, but I'd like to know more about her, if possible,' Wendy added diffidently, knowing that Oliver liked to do things, if he wanted to do them at all, in his own time.

'Her name was Sarah. I thought she might be my sister. You know I've spent a long time looking for my family. It seems I might have had a sister who was put into residential care too, but in Cornwall. For some reason my mother went to the West Country. She was following the hippie trail in those days, the glorious sixties.'

'And was she your sister?' Wendy felt she hardly dared ask the question.

'No, not a chance. I liked her, though. She was a very laid-back, careless kind of person. Also, she was a bit like me, physically and temperamentally. But she wasn't as interested in finding a family as I was. She lived alone in this cottage miles from anywhere. She wrote songs and painted a bit. She had a brutal husband whom she'd left and she wanted shut of the world.'

'Then that's the person who killed her.' Wendy's voice was slightly breathless. 'We must go to the police.'

'I'm not going to the police.' Oliver's tone

284

had a note of finality. 'No blinking fear.'

'But, Oliver, you must, if you're innocent.'

'No, I am not going to the police. I've spent a lot of my youth getting away from them. They frighten me. Once they get their hands on you, you've had it. They never let go. You can't get rid of the bastards. They know I've got a record and they'll make that charge stick. You've no idea what a lot of corrupt shits they are.'

'I didn't realize you had a record.' Wendy bit her lip.

'Nothing serious. Not murder. I was up a few times before the magistrates, petty theft, possessing hash, that kind of thing. I was only young, but the records will be there.'

Wendy gnawed cautiously at the corner of her finger. 'I'm sure there must be justice,' she said.

'I'm sure there must be, for those who can afford it; but the drop-outs and the has-beens in society haven't a chance.'

'Oliver, with me behind you ...' Wendy pleaded, putting out her hand. He took it and squeezed it but said nothing

They cooked themselves a meal. They shared a bottle of wine, but the light and laughter had gone out of their lives. Wendy noticed that Oliver, who normally had a hearty appetite, played with his food. Much of it he put on the floor for Chump who'd eat anything.

'You realize that at any minute', Oliver said when they had finished eating, 'we could be surrounded. They even mentioned a camper van. Any number of people in Wales have seen us.'

'I thought of that,' Wendy said. 'If you go to the police it could all be over in a couple of days. You'll be released.'

'Little do you know the workings of the policeman's mind,' Oliver said, grimly helping himself to a cigarette from Wendy's pack. This in itself was a sign of unusual tension as he hardly ever smoked. 'I shall be sent to Cornwall and charged. They'll find some excuse to keep me. Then my records will be raked out. They won't bother to look for anyone else.'

'But they have ways of telling these days. DNA . . .'

'I am *not* giving myself up!' Oliver thumped the table and stood up. 'And that's final. I would rather kill myself.' He looked at her strangely then, whistling for Chump, he walked out of the door.

Wendy watched him from the window. Then she put her head in her hands, not knowing what to do.

*　　　*　　　*

Later they went to bed and lay there, each grappling with their own thoughts. They knew

286

this was the end of one chapter and the beginning of another. Finally, Wendy said:

'I have a plan.'

'I am not—'

'No, I know you're not going to give yourself up, and I would never betray you, you know that.'

'Yes, I know.' He clasped her hand. 'You believe in me and I believe in you.'

'We should move away from here tonight, while it's dark. We'll go as far as we can, if possible out of Wales. I think we should make for Scotland.'

'Why Scotland?'

'It's kind of remote too. We could lose ourselves there. I'll leave you in some remote glen, go to London and come back with my car. That way we can abandon the van and try and get to the Continent, where we'll have time to decide what to do.'

'I haven't got a passport.'

'Mmmm. That was a point I hadn't thought of.' After a while she said: 'But this way we're running away. It just makes us look more guilty.'

'I have another plan,' Oliver said. 'You go to the police, tell them what you like, and I disappear.'

'No, I will never do that.'

'It's easier for you, Wendy. The paper made it clear they have nothing against you. If you go to the police you can say you had no idea I was wanted, and you hadn't. You can get on with your life. Resume where you left off.'

'You know I can never do that, Oliver. Logic tells me that we can get out of this mess. We must not panic. But tonight we must get away from here, if only to give ourselves time.'

So, rising from the bed, they quickly dressed themselves again and, under cover of darkness, left the beautiful coast of Wales where, if only briefly, they'd known such happiness.

*   *   *

'There's a call for you, Simon,' Brenda Howard, his secretary, called from her desk outside Simon Kemp's office.

'Who is it?' Simon put his hand on the phone.

'Won't say. A woman.'

Simon picked up the phone. 'Hello?'

'Hello, Simon.'

'Ah . . . It is you.'

'Please don't say my name.'

'OK, but it is, isn't it?'

'Yes, it is. Simon, have you seen the papers?'

'Yes.'

'Did you see anything about . . . me?'

'You?' Startled, Simon nearly shot out of his seat. 'No, what has there been about you?'

'Do you think we could meet?'

'Sure.'

'In London? Today?'

'Yes.'

'In a few minutes?'

'Where are you?'

'Shepherd's Bush. I'll meet you outside the tube. All right?'

'OK.'

'Thanks, and, Simon, don't tell anybody.'

'No. But give me an hour. I don't want it to look too mysterious.'

*   *   *

When Simon got to the tube at first there was no sign of Wendy. He wondered if this was some sort of set-up, and then he saw her standing with a scarf round her head and wearing dark glasses. She also wore a light raincoat, though it was a bright, sunny day.

'Simon, thanks,' she said as she ran up to him. 'I didn't know where to turn, and I thought of you.'

'But what on earth has happened?'

'I'll tell you. Let's find somewhere where we can talk.'

'The pub?' Simon pointed across the road. 'We can also have a drink and get a sandwich.'

'Good idea.'

As they crossed the busy road she clutched his arm, as if hanging on to him for dear life.

Inside the darkened saloon bar of the pub the atmosphere was noisy with a jukebox playing, a fruit machine clacking away and a thick cloud of smoke rising to the ceiling.

'Perfect cover,' Wendy said, grinning conspiratorially as they pushed their way to the bar.

'Is it as bad as that?' Simon looked down at her.

'It is bad.'

'What will you drink?'

'Shall we have a bottle of wine?'

'Good idea. Red or white?'

'I think red.'

'And to eat?'

They looked at the menu chalked up on a board and Simon ordered beef and ham sandwiches and a bottle of the best Burgundy. In due course a bottle of Nuits St George arrived with two glasses and he took them over to the table where Wendy waited for him.

'I see you're smoking,' he said, sitting down and pouring the wine into the glasses.

'I'm afraid so.'

'Wendy, what has been going on?' He leaned over the table, whispering to her urgently. 'Thank God you're safe. Your sister's worried sick.'

'I know that now. I didn't realize we were being hunted.'

'You didn't know that the bloke you ...' Simon didn't quite know how to put it.

'Went off with? Yes?' Wendy looked askance at him.

'They say he's wanted by the police. Ken

had to go and identify a dead woman. They thought it might be you.'

'Oh, my God!' Wendy put her head in her hands. 'How perfectly foul. Of course it couldn't have been me.'

'Well, they thought they knew that, but they had to be sure.'

'Oliver didn't kill anybody,' Wendy said heatedly. 'If you knew him, you'd know he couldn't kill anybody.'

'That's what Lois said. They were still worried. Have you rung Lois?'

Wendy shook her head. 'I didn't dare. After this thing on the TV, in the papers, I thought her phone might be tapped. That's why I rang you. I want to see Lois. I feel awful about not getting in touch with her, now that I know what she was going through; but I didn't think.' She glanced shyly at Simon. 'That is, I *did* think, but I was too happy. I didn't want anything to spoil it and I wasn't sure how Lois felt about me going off with Oliver. I knew Ken wouldn't be too pleased.'

'You can say that again.'

'Can you arrange for me to see Lois?'

'Sure.'

'But Ken mustn't know. He'll go to the police.'

'But aren't *you* going to contact the police?' Simon stopped abruptly as their sandwiches were brought over. When the barman had left Wendy shook her head.

'Oliver doesn't want to. He has a record, just from when he was a juvenile. He's distrustful of authority. I told him he shouldn't be afraid if he is innocent, but he's convinced the police will frame him.'

'But the woman was raped. There's DNA . . .'

'I know, I know. I told him but he's been traumatized. He's led a terribly hard life.'

'And giving you one, by the sound of it. Wendy, what made you . . .'

Wendy, mouth full of sandwich, held up a hand. 'Please don't ask. I can't explain it. It was a *coup de foudre*.'

'Tim came to see me.'

'Did he, now?' Her voice hardened.

'He was upset. He said the bloke exercised some strange fascination over you and Lois.'

'Maybe,' Wendy shrugged. 'Anyway, I love him and I'm doing all I can for him. That's all there is to it.'

'Even if he's a murderer?'

'He isn't.'

'Did he know the woman?'

'Yes. He thought she might be his sister. He was abandoned as a baby and never knew his parents. Apparently there was some record that he may have had a sister. It's really quite sad. He was looking for her.'

'And was she his sister?'

'Apparently not; but he liked her. She was a hippie type and so is he. He left one of his

292

dogs to look after her because she was a bit nervous, living in this remote cottage. She had a husband, and Oliver thinks she was afraid of him. Oliver certainly didn't kill her. He wouldn't hurt a fly. Simon, can you ring Lois and arrange for us to meet? Maybe in a pub or restaurant in the West End? We kind of feel the need to move on. My picture was on TV and in the Welsh newspapers.'

'I haven't seen anything about it.'

'Perhaps it hasn't made the nationals yet. It's not such an important case, but you know what they're like when they get their claws into something.'

'I certainly do. I wish they'd get their claws into some of our authors, but it's not quite the same thing, is it?'

Her hand closed over his. 'You are a dear. I trust you, Simon. Please, please don't tell a soul that we met.'

*   *   *

The sisters embraced for a long, long time. Then they took their seats in a restaurant off Wigmore Street, one of the many that proliferated in that busy part of town.

They sat for a while looking at each other, both shy, as if not knowing where to begin.

'I've got to apologize.' Wendy put a hand across the table. 'I'd no idea there was this hue and cry. I'd have got in touch at once; but it was difficult. I behaved badly, running off like that. I guess I felt a bit ashamed of myself.'

'And did Oliver feel ashamed of himself too?'

With a half-smile, as though she didn't expect an answer, Lois looked up as the waitress came over with the menus and they both ordered.

'I think Oliver did feel slightly ashamed of himself. He's always said how good you were to him; but you know Oliver, he's a bit like a leaf blown on the wind . . . he doesn't have a very developed social conscience.'

'Where is he now?'

'He's . . . somewhere. I can't be specific. He didn't murder this woman.'

'I never thought he did.'

'So there was no need to worry about me, was there?'

'Not as far as I was concerned, but most people thought otherwise. Mummy was terribly worried. And Ken . . . well, Ken never liked Oliver. Madge was prejudiced. I've had quite a hard time.'

Lois raised the glass of water to her lips. To her chagrin, her eyes filled with tears. 'I think you could have let me know, Wendy.'

'Actually, I feel horrible about it. As soon as we saw this thing in the local paper I got in touch with Simon. I know it sounds a bit dramatic, but I thought your phone might be tapped. One gets such grotesque ideas when

294

one is on the run.'

'But you aren't on the *run*!'

'We are, in a way. Although Oliver says he's innocent, he refuses to go to the police. I've got to find some way of convincing him that he'll be quite safe.'

'Where are you staying now?'

'Actually, I'm staying at the Dorchester.' Wendy smiled at Lois's expression. 'I wanted somewhere big and anonymous and luxurious. I couldn't go back to my flat. A big international hotel is the last place they'd expect a wanted woman to go. I went home and packed a suitcase, sneaked out while no one was looking, got my car, which I've left in the garage under Hyde Park, and heigh ho. But I had to see you. I had to tell you I was OK.'

'Wendy, if you don't go to the police you may be considered an accessory. I can't tell you how serious your position is.'

'I am quite aware of my position and I'm going to convince Oliver that it is in his interests too.'

'He must give himself up. If he's innocent, he has nothing to fear.'

'He won't.'

'Ken saw photographs of the murdered woman. He said it was ghastly. I've always maintained it wasn't Oliver, but you know Ken. Incidentally, we're thinking of selling up, moving back to town. Bev and Neal are leaving—nothing to do with Oliver, but they are. All in all, it seemed the best thing to do. Everything had changed. We've all been terribly unsettled by Oliver. Sometimes I wish we'd never met him.' She looked earnestly into her sister's eyes. 'Don't you?'

'No!'

There was a pause as the waitress approached with their food. Wendy also asked for a glass of wine, so they had half a bottle.

'Lois, you didn't love him, did you?' Wendy looked anxiously into her sister's eyes.

'It was a kind of love, I suppose, but not sexual. With hindsight, I think that I acted stupidly. I did it out of kindness, but I upset so many people. I let him stay on our land without consulting Ken. I bought him a new van—I know it wasn't much good, but . . . I did go a bit over the top. I overdid the Good Samaritan bit. I can see that now.

'Because of what I did, your engagement to Tim is over, and he's bitterly hurt. And if you and Oliver think you have a future together, what sort of life will you lead? How will he fit in with your friends? Have you thought about that?

'I upset Ken and I do love him. That's partly why I think we want to move away.' Lois paused and, for a while, concentrated on what was on the plate in front of her. Then, putting her knife and fork neatly together, she folded her hands on the table and leaned towards her sister so that there was no possibility of being heard.

'I'm sorry to say this to you, Wendy, but I'm not sure I'd ever want to see Oliver again. It's not entirely his fault but his influence was so harmful and ... sometimes I wondered ...' her voice faltered, ' ... sometimes in the middle of the night when I was feeling low, I would have doubts. Supposing ... just supposing, we're both mistaken about his innocence? What then?'

CHAPTER FOURTEEN

The hum of vehicles coming and going, the chatter of voices as people went up the steps to the motorway complex frequently disturbed his rest. It seemed to go on all night and by the time dawn came Oliver felt he hadn't slept at all.

Chump, too, had appeared restless and uneasy and now was in desperate need to go out.

Oliver prised himself from his warm bed, pulled on his trousers and a jacket to cover his nudity, slipped the leash on Chump and, cautiously descending from the van, looked all round before he took the dog over to a stretch of open grass at the side of the complex.

It was a chilly morning, just after six, and

297

the smell of food emanating from the surrounding restaurants was enticing. After he had dressed he would go over to the lorry drivers' café and have scrambled eggs with tomatoes and lots of hot toast, dripping with butter.

Chump finished doing what he had to do, scratched the grass and looked eagerly up at Oliver as though asking for a good long walk.

'Later, boy,' Oliver promised him. They climbed back into the van, which was parked close to the complex but next to some trees. They had, after all, decided to leave the van in a crowded place where it would be less likely to draw attention to itself than in an open and otherwise deserted space. Each day since Wendy had left for London, Oliver managed to drive it to a fresh part of the service station. He managed with difficulty. It was nearly six months since he had broken his arm and he knew that all was far from well. It ached continually. He had moments of severe pain. It was awkward and difficult to move. In his heart of hearts he knew that something needed to be done to the arm, but with the situation as it now was, getting medical help was out of the question.

He couldn't go near a hospital or a doctor's surgery. He was a man on the run. So he made do with pain killers and sometimes they didn't help.

Oliver gave Chump his breakfast and made

himself some tea, then climbed back under the warm duvet. He propped himself up on the pillows and put the mug to his lips. Deep, satisfying, hot, sweet tea. There was nothing like it for clearing the head, causing the blood to course through one's veins, induce, perhaps, a feeling of optimism and well-being.

But not today.

Today he felt horribly, foully depressed. It had been creeping up on him ever since a taxi drove Wendy away from the service station to catch a train at the nearest station. He had felt so bereft when she left him that he imagined himself like a small boy parted from its mother—except he had never known a mother, and no one had ever taken the place of one. He hadn't slept well and he didn't think he would until this was over.

And he could never see it being over: whichever way he looked there seemed to be waiting for him an open chasm into which he would fall, never to resurface. He would go on falling down, down, down.

Oliver jerked himself back from his cogitative state, a sort of half-waking, half-sleeping. The mug had slipped in his hands, nearly spilling the contents on to the bed. He finished his tea and put the mug on the window ledge. He rubbed the steam off the window and looked out at the people briskly entering and leaving the complex: happy, busy people with things to do, homes to go to, loved ones to take care of them, without a stain on their characters.

Oliver felt terribly isolated and alone. He missed Wendy. He missed her much more than he had imagined he would.

He didn't just miss her doing things in the practical way she had, taking charge; he didn't just miss being looked after and spoiled in a way he never had been before. He missed her, he thought, because he loved her. Finally and ultimately he had to face up to it. Parting, it was said, was dying a little and he was half-dead without Wendy: his other half. She was without doubt the most important thing in his life ... And what future did they have, now that he had discovered this love?

How awful to realize you really loved someone who you might be separated from, possibly for years, perhaps for ever. Never to see each other again ...

He couldn't bear the thought of not seeing Wendy, but he knew that to stay with her was to abuse his love. To stay with her was to bring her trouble, maybe a prison sentence if she knowingly hid a man who was wanted by the police. He was not sure about the law. If he went down he might drag her down with him.

And he felt he would go down. He had no doubt at all that if arrested he would be tried and found guilty, banged up for life.

That was the hideous way the police dealt with these things. Once they had their man, their victim, they wouldn't let go, however much he might protest, however innocent he, or she, might be.

Oliver had a profound sense of pessimism about the world and those who inhabited it. He felt that disaster always lurked round the corner; anything good that came to pass wouldn't last; nice people would become nasty; good luck turn to bad. Hadn't this been the case now? He and Wendy had been so happy, isolated from the world in a beautiful place, utterly content, bound up in each other. Then, by chance, she saw her picture in the paper and discovered that he was wanted for a crime. What worse thing could you imagine than that? No wonder he never read the papers.

He didn't trust anybody because he'd seldom had occasion to. He had learned that from the many mistakes he'd made as a child and in growing up. He was deeply suspicious of people with apparently kind motivation, which was why he had been so cautious with Lois.

Lois had treated him well and he had abused her kindness. He hadn't meant to, but he had. He hadn't wanted to tell her about himself even though the only reason she wanted to know was because she was so kind. But her kindness jarred on him, as though it wasn't real. There had been too much of the goody-goody, the lady bountiful about Lois.

But because of her wild streak, Wendy had been different. Despite their different

301

backgrounds, he had sensed immediately that she was a fellow spirit. Something in her had reached out to him, as partners, equals.

In Wendy he had at last—only slightly at first and then with increasing conviction—found someone he could trust, who over the weeks they had been together came to matter more to him than he mattered to himself; whose love for him was unselfish and altruistic. He felt that she would give her life for him, and he would gladly have given his for her.

But now he had lost her. It was only fair that he should disappear from her life instead of dragging her down into the bowels of the earth with him.

*   *   *

Oliver had not suddenly reached this conclusion in the time it took him to wash, shave—the last shave perhaps for some time—and dress in clean underclothing, jeans and T-shirt. It was the culmination of a process that had begun soon after Wendy left him on the motorway, promising to rendezvous there with him in a few days' time. She had left him money and a number where he could contact her.

It was then he had begun to make plans that would leave the van empty when she returned.

Oliver no longer wanted any breakfast, his stomach felt too tense. Instead he packed carefully into a small rucksack the things he needed. The basics. Other clothes that Wendy had bought him in their time together he left. He took fifty pounds and left the rest in an envelope. He didn't leave a note because he didn't know what to say that wouldn't sound trite and sanctimonious. He thought that she would know the reason and would understand.

Oliver cleaned the van, put everything away, made the bed and left it tidy and neat.

He took a couple of tins of food for Chump, clipped on his lead and opened the door, looking, as he always did, carefully around at the large open space in front of him.

The truth was that he was scared, petrified of that knock at the door, the van surrounded, the men in blue beckoning him to come out. They wanted to incarcerate him and they always had. They would be determined to get him now and, with every day that passed, he knew that moment was getting nearer. Someone would say, 'That van has been here a long time. Something funny about it.' And they would phone the police. If they hadn't already.

Oliver started to panic as a man in a boiler suit emerged from the transport café and began to make his way purposefully towards the van.

He knew he'd left it too late. Any moment now others would appear from round the sides of the building, behind the trees, out of the petrol station. They would hail him and tell

303

him to give himself up and, because he didn't have a weapon, never had carried a weapon, he would do that. With his hands up, in an act of surrender, he would walk into oblivion.

'Take care of my dog,' he would say.

But instead of approaching him, the man veered to the right and jumped into the cab of a petrol tanker which stood a few hundred yards from the van. He gave Oliver, who had been staring fixedly at him, an odd look, then raised his hand in a cheery wave and drove off.

The sweat broke out on Oliver's forehead. He pulled a reluctant Chump, who seemed to sense what was happening, down the steps, turned and locked the door and put the key under the mat where he hoped Wendy would find it. He wasn't sure that she had a spare.

He was behaving logically, yet at the same time selfishly. Yet, paradoxically, he was for once thinking of somebody else. He'd wanted to write a note saying 'Wendy, I love you', but it wouldn't have been fair. It would have been banal too, and he hated banality. The best thing to do was to make her angry by his desertion, so that she would quickly forget him.

Chump, happier now at the prospect of a walk, jumped up and licked Oliver's cheek. Oliver bent and nuzzled the face of the dog. There were hot tears behind his eyes. He stood up, blew his nose and set off at a brisk pace, rucksack slung over his shoulder,

304

heading away from the van, away from the complex, across the open fields, once more out into the unknown.

*   *   *

Wendy hummed in tune to the music on the stereo as she drove along the motorway, sometimes with reckless speed as she ignored the restrictions, praying that there wasn't a police car about or a camera concealed somewhere on the side of the road. She felt exhilarated. She'd enjoyed her three days of luxury in London. She'd bought some new clothes, including a few bits and pieces for Oliver, she'd dined at good restaurants, she'd loved the luxury of the Dorchester, her room overlooking the park high up above London. It was great to have her car again, a fine-tuned BMW that seemed as eager as she was to be once again on the open road.

But it wasn't so much the past that made her happy as the future: the thought of being with Oliver, seeing his face again, feeling his body next to hers. What was more, she had a plan. If they toured in the BMW and stayed at pricey hotels, no one would suspect that they were a couple on the run. She would have her hair dyed by some hairdresser in whichever big town they came to. They would dress smartly, behave extravagantly. That way they could go on, at least until the real murderer of Sarah was found.

In a way it would be fun.

The only trouble was, as Lois had pointed out, the police were not looking for anybody else. Only them. Until Oliver was eliminated he would remain the prime suspect.

It seemed so silly. Wendy still couldn't believe it. She was so anxious to see Oliver again that she didn't stop until, at around four, her car slid into the motorway car park where she had left Oliver and the van.

She looked expectantly around. At first she couldn't see the van. It wasn't where she'd left it, but she had suggested that he move it from time to time. For a ghastly moment she thought it wasn't there and he'd driven away. Then, to her relief, she saw it at the edge of the car park, between the petrol pumps and the transport café, gleaming in the sun, waiting for her. All was well.

She drew up a few spaces away, got out, locked her car and went over to the camper van. The door was shut and she tapped on it. No reply. She hoped she was wrong, but it had a deserted air. She must be wrong. Oliver wouldn't have left. He had nowhere to go.

Feeling suddenly panicky, she ferreted in her bag for the spare key and found it, put it in the lock, turned it, opened the door. Stepped inside. She knew at once that he had gone. The place was deserted as if his spirit had left it. Chump's bowls were empty and upended on

306

the sink. Everything was terribly tidy and clean. There was an envelope on the table between the stove and the bed, with no name on it. She picked it up and, opening it, drew out several banknotes. At first she was puzzled. Then, absentmindedly, she began to count them. There was about £250. She thought she'd left £300 for emergencies.

How like Oliver to take the minimum.

No more.

How like Oliver to go without a word, leaving no trace.

*   *   *

Sergeant Thompson of the Dorset Police and Sergeant Greaves of the Devon and Cornwall force sat in the Hunters' drawing room facing Wendy. On either side of her were Lois and Ken. They also had Michael Routledge, the family's solicitor, who had rushed over from Salisbury to be present.

It had been a curious meeting. No dramatics, no tears, just facts.

The solicitor clarified the situation. He explained that Miss Cartwright had not realized that Oliver was wanted for questioning. As soon as she read about it in the papers she suggested he should go to the police. He said he was innocent and she believed him. She told the police about the supposed sister and the sister's husband—who was most probably the real culprit.

What was the husband's name? Wendy didn't know.

Neither, unfortunately, did she know where Oliver was.

'Don't you think the fact that he has disappeared, Miss Cartwright, points to his guilt?' Sergeant Greaves suggested, speaking in the gentle tone of a benevolent uncle.

'No, I don't.'

The policeman exchanged a sceptical glance with his colleague.

'He was afraid,' Wendy went on. 'He had an absolute phobia about the police, about any kind of authority.'

'That in itself is a bit suspicious, madam, don't you think?'

'No, I don't.' Wendy, pale but composed, looked straight at the officer. 'In the three months we were together I had the chance to get to know him, probably better than anyone else ever has. Oliver was a damaged man, psychologically. In his youth he was always in and out of care and residential homes. He became solitary, inward-looking. He didn't trust people. His best friends, his only friends sometimes, were animals. He loved dogs.' Her hand curled around Rusty, sitting by her side, who had taken to her immediately, maybe because the smell of Chump, his long-lost brother, lingered about her, despite several baths and fresh changes of clothes.

'Just because you're a dog lover, madam,' the policeman began gently, 'it doesn't mean you couldn't, if severely provoked, murder another person.'

'But that murder was savage, Sergeant.' Ken became animated. 'It wasn't an attack in the heat of the moment. It was a wicked, murderous assault.'

'I agree with you, sir.' The policeman inclined his head. 'We're talking about someone who was probably a psychopath. Miss Cartwright might have been in very real danger.'

'I was never in danger for a moment,' Wendy declared loftily. 'Oliver was not a psychopath. He was a caring, feeling, loving person.'

'You loved him, madam?' The policeman avoided her eyes, writing something in his book.

'I did, and I do.'

'An unusual relationship, if I may say so.' He raised his head as if taking in the expensive cut of her trouser suit, the soft silk shirt she wore underneath, the chunky gold necklace at her throat, the well-groomed hair, the air of opulence and affluence.

'Oliver was an unusual man, Sergeant.' Lois came to her sister's aid. 'He might have been begging, but he wasn't what you'd consider—well, I wouldn't anyway—a typical beggar.'

'He was well-read,' Wendy intervened. 'He

read the classics over and over again.'

'But not well-spoken, madam? Not what you'd call an educated voice?'

'He had a northern accent, if that's what you're referring to; but a lot of members of parliament have accents like his. You yourself, Sergeant, have a regional accent, if I'm not mistaken. Does that make you more likely to murder somebody?'

The sergeant flushed, looking annoyed.

'That's quite unnecessary, Wendy,' Ken said angrily. 'You're not doing your cause any good at all by being rude to the police.'

'I'm sorry.' Wendy lowered her head. 'I'm rather over-wrought. But you see, Sergeant, Oliver didn't go to public school or university, but that doesn't make him more likely to commit a crime, does it? I feel that such a lot of this is about class.'

'No, madam, it's about someone who has, or might have, done wrong, regardless of class. People who choose to opt out of society frequently turn to crime, or have criminal convictions. It's a fact, Miss Cartwright. If your friend is innocent, he has absolutely nothing to fear, I can assure you of that. But, really, all this talk about class and family origins is getting us nowhere.' The officer, still clearly irritated, thought this aspect of the conversation had gone far enough. 'What we really want to know is where this Oliver is and whether we can eliminate him from our enquiries. Until we do that, we must consider him as a suspect. Now, can you give me any hint, any clue at all, as to where he might be?'

*   *   *

For a long time after the police had gone Wendy stood looking out of the window, watching Rusty scampering about with Lucy and Sally in the garden. He reminded her so much of Chump that a lump came into her throat.

She was utterly at a loss as to what to do next. Her impulse to jump in the car and look for Oliver was stupid. The possibility remained that he would go to ground, she would never see him again. There was a movement behind her and a hand was placed on her shoulder. She turned and leaned her head against her sister's breast.

'I'm so sorry,' Lois said. 'I feel so helpless.'

'I just wish I could have persuaded him to go to the police. I thought I might eventually. He was so terrified of them in a way we can't understand.'

'I can understand it.' Lois produced a tissue for Wendy, who blew her nose and then perched on the arm of a chair. 'I've seen so many people who are petrified in court,' Lois went on. 'Police forces may have changed, but in the past they helped to create such a bad reputation. They jumped to conclusions. Just

311

because Oliver was a beggar they assume he could be a murderer too.'

'I know he's not,' Wendy repeated firmly and looked speculatively up at Lois. 'But you're not sure, are you? You said in London . . . You've lost faith in Oliver, haven't you?'

'I don't *know* him as well as you. I thought I did, but as time has passed I realize I didn't know him at all.' Lois sat by Wendy, clasping her knees. 'I've come to understand that, despite being a magistrate, I am after all not a very good judge of character. I make an awful lot of mistakes.'

'Ken has put you off Oliver.'

'Ken *may* be right. He's quite astute.'

'I don't think much of Ken's astuteness in that case.'

'Ken's been deeply concerned about you. Most unhappy. Darling . . . Ken and I think you should try and put all this behind you. Look, we're thinking of going over to France next week. Now that you're back there is no need for us to hang on here.'

Wendy put her hand on her sister's arm. 'That's a really excellent idea.'

'We'd like you to come with us.'

'Out of the question.'

'I thought you'd say that, but I wish you'd think it over. Wendy, I don't think you will ever hear from Oliver again. He's gone to ground. If you wait here hoping for the phone

312

to ring, hoping against hope, your life will fritter away.

'I know this is an awkward thing to say . . .'—Lois put a hand to her head and ruffled her hair—'but people like Oliver really *aren't* the same as us. I mean, he can't help it, but he isn't. He had the gross misfortune to have the sort of childhood he had, and it has distorted his values. He behaved so selfishly— taking advantage of me, going off with you. We were all so good to him and he did nothing but practically ruin our lives . . .'

'He gave me a lot of happiness,' Wendy said. 'He helped me to understand a lot of things. He had a philosophy I found very moving. He had no possessions; they meant nothing to him. I agree he wasn't one of "us", but he's not one of anything. He is simply Oliver. Unique.'

Lois saw that it was futile to pursue the matter. Six months ago she would have defended Oliver the way Wendy was defending him now. In six months' time, Wendy might have gone the same way as she had, reaching the same conclusions. Undoubtedly in time this would happen. But, momentarily, she was a woman in the grip of a strange obsession that defied logic and reason. It was a kind of disease.

Lois let a few seconds pass then, holding out her hand, she said on a lighter note: 'Come with us to France for a couple of weeks. Mum and the boys would love to have you, you know

313

that. We would too. Let's all go off and try to forget this business with Oliver ever happened.'

'You go off,' Wendy said with a tremulous smile. 'I shall never forget that Oliver ever happened.'

*   *   *

Tim said, 'Despite everything, you're looking very well.'

'Thanks.' Wendy tossed the hair back from her face and gave a wry smile. 'I thought you'd never want to see me again.'

'Of course I want to see you again.' He reached for her hand across the table, but she kept hers firmly tucked under her arm.

'Tim, we just can't go back, you know.'

'I know. You don't want me now, but in time ... you might change your mind,' he concluded, looking unhappy.

At first Wendy had been reluctant to accept Tim's invitation. Indeed, she had been astonished to hear from him so soon after her return. But she decided it was very decent of Tim and here they were lunching at a restaurant in Soho, one of their favourite haunts in the past. The manager was discreet as he welcomed them, placing the menus before them with a flourish, asking if it was their 'usual' to drink. You'd think they'd never been away.

314

September. This was to have been the month of the wedding. With about a fortnight to go to the appointed day, there would have been frantic fittings for her dress, last-minute things to do at work. Lois and her mother would have been knee-deep in preparations, consulting caterers, checking the guest list for changes, unpacking the presents, clucking away.

How different life would have been if they had never heard of Oliver.

It was almost as though Tim could read her thoughts. He had such a sweet, sympathetic expression on his face.

'I don't know how you can be so nice,' Wendy said, tucking her hand under her chin, avoiding his eyes. 'You should be bitter and hate me. What I did was dreadful, but I couldn't help it. I mean, I could help it. I acted selfishly, but I was in the grip of this passion, the urge to get away, to be alone with Oliver.'

'I know; but what you did wasn't normal. It was like an illness. That's the way I look at it. If you'd had some disease I'd still want you, and I feel you did have some sort of disease . . . of the mind.'

Instead of being offended, Wendy felt amused. Trust Tim to find a good old psychological explanation for being jilted. Maybe it helped massage his ego. She looked at him with affection, thinking what a nice straight guy he was, what a great husband he would have made. They would have been secure. They had so much in common; they came from the same background. Or this was the theory.

Now she could never contemplate settling down with Tim, or anyone like him.

'Will they, do you think ...' he began tentatively, 'find Oliver?'

'I hope so, because he is innocent and he has to prove his innocence—which he can with the DNA.'

'Maybe that's what he's afraid of.'

Wendy looked surprised. 'Why should he?'

'As you say, it would clear him ... So why won't he take it?'

'He has a phobia about the police. He was in care as a child and always getting into trouble. When he sees a policeman he feels the way I do about spiders. I go rigid and I can't think. My whole body undergoes a complete physical transformation, my mind becomes paralysed. I can't act rationally, even though I know they're not dangerous. Even if the police can clear him, Oliver just can't face them.'

Tim remained gazing at his plate.

'You're not convinced, are you, Tim?'

'I find it hard to believe that someone who is innocent would not wish to clear his name. He even ran away from you, and you wanted to help him.'

'I imagine he thought I might make him give

himself up. Or he couldn't face being on the run with me. He would have an explanation, but I don't know what it is.'

'Lucky for you . . . I mean, being on the run would have been hell.'

'Oh, I don't know. It might have been a bit of fun.' Wendy's face twisted into a smile. 'But then, I always say that, don't I, whenever I get into scrapes? It's all a bit of a lark.'

*   *   *

Oliver leaned against the wall of the shop, Chump's lead wound tightly round his hand. He felt absolutely hopeless and helpless, terribly weak. He was in great pain. His arm throbbed from morning till night and had begun to swell. He knew he should go to a hospital, but he didn't dare.

It had been a desperately hard few weeks on the road; much, much harder than before because now there was an alternative: Wendy at the other end of the phone. The longer he stayed away from her, the more he missed her, but the more frightened he became of betrayal, of being turned over by the fuzz. By now Wendy would have talked to Lois and Ken, and they would have converted her. For all he knew, she might never want to see him again, glad their relationship was over. To her it might have been an interlude, a lark—her favourite word. The point was that you could

317

never trust people, never know what they really felt.

Oliver looked down at Chump, who was trembling, not so much because it was cold—the month had been something of an Indian summer—as because he was frightened and undernourished. His coat no longer gleamed and he shook with fear. What he was doing to Chump was not fair. Soon he would take him to an animal shelter and leave him there, and then ... Well, one day he might jump into the murky waters of Manchester's canal and let them close over him. Looking at the water was comforting. It also reminded him of Wales and the sea, and Wendy.

No one took any notice of him, passers-by coming and going in busy Market Street. The great new city centre, demolished by an IRA bomb, was being rebuilt a short distance away. If his arm hadn't been so bad he could have got work as a builder, some sort of navvy; casual work where no one would ask questions. At night he slept in doorways and hung about the backs of restaurants hoping for scraps of food.

Sometimes he thought he really was going out of his mind, so ... wouldn't prison be better than this? Wendy said they could prove he hadn't done it by DNA testing; but he didn't believe her. To her, the police were nice, fair, helpful people, but he knew better. He knew the police. They would pin it on him,

318

innocent or not. They would fiddle the samples and falsify the reports. They would find him guilty and he would be banged up for good.

A man stopped beside him and pressed a note into his hand.

'Good luck, mate,' he said and Oliver, clutching the note in his palm, could have burst into tears. A policeman walked slowly past and looked keenly at him, and he froze again. The policeman's gaze lingered on the dog and then he moved on.

Panic. The rozzer would go straight to the station and check up on wanted people. Then they'd come chasing back for him in a Black Maria. Time to move on.

Oliver moved away from the shelter of the door. The pain, shooting up his arm, seemed to be reaching his head. He felt strangely giddy. He lurched sideways and bumped into someone who pushed him sharply away with a foul oath.

Oliver felt his head hitting the pavement and the light exploded into stars. Chump's lead was still wound tightly round his hand so that he would be safe.

*   *   *

The telephone rang in the Dorset Police headquarters and a call went out for Detective Sergeant Thompson. Thompson was in conference with his superior and asked if he could ring the caller back.

He was told the message was urgent and his superior nodded and gave him permission to answer the phone in his office.

'Hello?' Sergeant Thompson said.

'Jim, it's George Greaves.'

'How are you, George?'

'I'm fine,' George answered, a chortle in his voice, sounding pleased. 'Jim, we've got the man we want for the Mylor murder. Oliver's been caught.'

They spoke for a while longer and then Jim Thompson put down the phone with an air of satisfaction. 'Another catch, sir, and this one's in the bag. Oliver, the beggar wanted for the murder of that woman near Mylor Bridge, has been apprehended in Manchester and is on his way to Cornwall to be questioned. He's got a record as long as your arm.'

CHAPTER FIFTEEN

Wendy hovered behind the author in the bookstore, looking as patient as she could. There were not an awful lot of people coming to have books signed and the author's temper was fraying, along with her *amour propre*. She seemed to think that Wendy was personally responsible for keeping away the hordes who

320

should otherwise have been gathered there.

The shop assistants were flapping too, waylaying browsers and pointing to the desk where the author sat with piles of unsold copies in front of her.

The trouble was that this was only the start of a nationwide tour, and if shoppers in the fashionable West End store with its large book department and its affluent clientele wouldn't buy, who would?

Not only that, but Wendy had one meeting after another scheduled for the day, another in the evening, plus a party for this disgruntled author, who would be sure to express her discontent at the inefficiency of her publisher's publicity machine. Simon, she knew, would support her. She now had an assistant and the PR department ran like clockwork; but it was still tedious, especially as the author's latest novel was a piece of hopeless drivel that had long since gone out of fashion. The publishers now tried to trade on her name and her name wasn't enough.

The store manager's assistant arrived with coffee in a silver pot, Sèvres china, nice little lace doily on the tray, *petit fours*.

The author refused to be mollified. If these were the only people who were going to be here, she was wasting her time. After all, she was a busy person with a lot to do. The thing just hadn't been properly advertised—she glared at the manager. Or organized—she glared at Wendy. To save any further humiliation she was going to go. There were so many more important demands on her time.

A customer who had been browbeaten into buying a copy was hustled up to have it signed. Even the store's assistants had been mobilized into buying copies, at the store's expense of course. But it was still a trickle compared to the avalanche of faithful fans that had been expected.

At noon, the author was shown into her waiting car where she sat frostily in the back without speaking to Wendy until it was time to alight at Claridges.

'I shall be speaking to Paul about this, Wendy,' she said as she prepared to get out of the car. 'I have nothing against you personally, in fact I like you, but it seems to me that you, or your department, are falling down on the job.' She peered at her closely. 'Are you getting enough sleep?'

'I think so,' Wendy answered.

'You look tired to me. Maybe they're overworking you, and if they are, they're not giving important authors like me the time and publicity we deserve. After all, I have made a fortune for your company, and if today is anything to go by I shall be telling my agent to move me elsewhere.'

Without saying goodbye she got out of the car and went quickly into the hotel, leaving the concierge to close the door.

As it moved away, Wendy leaned back against the car seat and closed her eyes. What a ghastly day. She'd known it would be. The advance sales were poor and there had been precious little press interest in the author, whose annual visit to London had previously been considered a highlight if not of the literary year at least of the fiscal one. It was hard to tell a woman who had worked hard and earned a lot of money, but was still primarily motivated by her ego, that the fashion for her books was waning. Nitty-gritty realistic stories written by beautiful people, preferably under the age of twenty-five, were now *de rigueur*. They didn't sell in anything like the numbers the famous author had previously sold, but they got interviewed in the newspapers, they got reviewed, their faces appeared on the TV, and at parties written about in the glossies. They were showbiz, they were feisty and streetwise. They employed the fashionable agents who knew the best way to squeeze as much out of book and film and TV deals as they could in order to make small fortunes before they became unfashionable and the next fad, the next 'personality', took their place.

Publishing wasn't what it used to be.

Wendy kicked off her shoes. God, she was tired. In the time she'd been back she hadn't stopped. Because she'd been away so long the workload had doubled. The assistant was good, keen, but she was young and new and she had little publishing experience.

Wendy rushed from one meeting to another, an eye always on her watch. She ate scratch meals at her desk, usually washed down by more coffee than was good for her and helped along with an increasing mountain of cigarettes. Dinner was a handful of nuts and some crisps left over from the party or reception. She knew she looked awful and she had lost weight. She flopped into bed too late and she was exhausted.

She never stopped thinking of Oliver. Work was no compensation for missing him. She slept badly and she didn't eat. Maybe she drank too much; she certainly smoked too much.

Lois said if she wasn't careful she'd crack up. Simon was concerned about her.

Wendy looked out of the car window as it came off Westway, went round Shepherd's Bush. She remembered that meeting with Simon in the smokey little pub. What a heady, exciting adventure it had been. One looked back almost with nostalgia now, whatever the dangers. Back then, although she was not going to see Oliver again (she refused to use the word 'never'), she didn't know it. She thought they were a number, that instead of being at the end of a big adventure they were at the beginning of one.

If she'd never met Oliver the wedding would

now be over. She and Tim would have completed the purchase of the mews house in Chelsea and would probably just be returning from honeymoon in the Bahamas. She would be starting work with her new wedding ring on her finger beside the large sapphire and diamond he'd given her for their engagement. Each night they'd eat out at trendy places, attend smart parties or have cosy little intimate dinners at home. At the weekends they'd go to Lois or to his mother or her mother and would probably be looking for a little weekend cottage in the country, not too far from London.

It would have been a perfectly safe world with Tim, a familiar world. She would be rushed at work as she always was but there would be a cushion of stability, of security. Now she never knew what the next day would bring.

The car left her at the door of the vast, futuristic building. She rushed inside and took the lift up to her office. Heavens, the meeting would be half over, and she had promised . . . She skimmed through her fax messages, scanned the e-mails on the computer screen, grabbed a pad and hurled herself out of her office, bolting along the corridor. She threw open the door of the meeting room and a sea of faces looked up, startled, as she came in.

'So terribly sorry I'm late,' she said, searching for an empty seat.

Simon murmured something to the person next to him and, getting up, came over to Wendy, his face unusually grave.

'Simon, I'm so *sorry* . . .' she began, but he shook his head, manufacturing a smile so as not to frighten her. Then he took her by the elbow and steered her out of the room, closing the door gently behind him.

'Simon, if Agatha has *already* talked to Paul . . .' Agatha being the disgruntled author and Paul the managing director of the organization. But Simon shook his head.

'Wendy, Oliver has been found. I'm afraid he's been arrested and taken in for questioning. Good news and bad news, eh, Wendy?'

Wendy leaned against the corridor wall, felt her legs go weak, burst into tears.

* * *

His name was Oliver Pearson. Born in Manchester in 1964, he was now thirty-three years of age. His mother was Mary Pearson. There was a blank on his birth certificate where the name of the father should have been.

The reports of social workers at the time provided evidence that his mother had another child, a daughter. As she lived in reduced circumstances, probably from prostitution, she'd felt she didn't want another baby. No

326

one knew why she hadn't had a termination except that it was before the Act that made abortion legal.

Oliver was taken as a small baby to the children's home, but his mother wouldn't allow him to be adopted. She always thought she might wish to claim him back. He was fostered to a couple until he was about three. They wanted to adopt him, but at that time no one knew the whereabouts of his mother.

When the social services failed to trace her, the couple who had fostered Oliver rejected him because they said they couldn't face the prospect of losing him when he was older. Anyway, they now had a child of their own, which they hadn't thought they would be able to have, and Oliver had accordingly ceased to be so important to them.

From the age of three, Oliver lived for some periods in the residential home and for others in foster homes. He was a sensitive, affectionate child who was desperately looking for love, but either he couldn't show that love or no one could respond to it, or at least not enough, and all the attempts at fostering him ended unhappily.

He grew restless at being constantly moved about, shifted from pillar to post, trying to settle first in this place and that, wanted and then finding he wasn't wanted, and soon became a problem. He was first up before a juvenile court when he was eleven and then at various times until he was nineteen. His offences varied from petty theft to possession of cannabis, and he served time in remand homes. He was considered intelligent but truculent, unruly and undisciplined at school and he frequently played truant.

When he was twenty he seemed to take a hold of himself and under one of the numerous government schemes began to train as a carpenter and cabinet maker. He got a City and Guilds Diploma and seemed to be making good. He loved his work, but he was restless and moved from one digs to the next. He was unable to form permanent relationships with women and had few male friends. He moved all around the north of England and developed a taste for mobility, living in various ramshackle vans which enabled him to get about. He liked this style of life, and he managed to keep clear of trouble and the police.

In an effort to belong, he had made various attempts to trace his mother but with no success. Then his researches turned up, by chance, the existence of a sister, possibly living in Cornwall. He had never been further south than Manchester, but one day he set off in a small battered brown van with two mongrel puppies he had saved from drowning. Their legs had been tied together and they had been thrown into the Manchester Ship Canal into which he dived fully clothed to save them. He loved them because they seemed lost and unwanted, like him.

Sergeant Greaves ran his hands over his face and turned off the recording. He asked Oliver if he wanted a cigarette but he said he didn't. He seldom smoked. He was pale, but he'd shaved and had a good rest. Above all, he'd had a bath and some decent meals. He'd been given clean trousers and a shirt and underclothes. He'd spent the first night in hospital, where he had emergency treatment for his arm. It was now heavily bandaged and immobilized in a sling. It was a matter of urgency for the police to get the questioning over because he had to have an operation to save his arm. He'd been stuffed full of painkillers.

He hadn't resisted the police. He'd been so glad to be clean and warm and, above all, free of pain that he had co-operated with them and told them everything they wanted to know. It all spilled out of him. Above all, he knew that Chump was safe, though still in an animal shelter in Manchester.

They'd been so nice, gentle with him, even friendly. He wasn't taken in. He knew this was the softly softly approach in order to get him to confess.

He had nothing to confess, but they hadn't got to that yet.

Sergeant Greaves switched on the recorder again, made a note of the time and began.

'Now we come to the time you were in Cornwall, Oliver. Tell us about it.'

Oliver leaned back, his memory sharp and clear despite the drugs.

'I left Stinsbury with my two dogs.'

'Someone had been kind to you there. Mrs Hunter . . .'

'Yes.' Momentarily Oliver's thoughts lingered not on Mrs Hunter but her sister.

'But you didn't want to stay?'

'No. Also, the police had asked me to move my van.'

'And did you make your way to Cornwall, stopping, as you had in Stinsbury, to beg?'

'Yes. I made my way slowly down to Cornwall. The van was in very poor condition.'

'And had you any idea how to find this woman you supposed was your sister?'

'No, except I knew, or thought I knew, her name was Sarah Pearson.'

'It seems a long shot.'

'It was.'

'Pearson is quite a common name. How did you go about trying to find her?'

'I used to ask the travellers. I asked everyone I met. There's a bond with travelling people. It was pure chance and coincidence I found her. But if she wasn't my sister then it was an unlucky break, on my part.' Oliver grimaced. 'Another unlucky break. She'd been kind to a couple of travellers who'd lost their baby, it had died. They were telling me about her and they thought her name was Pearson. She was about the right age: five years older than me. Pure coincidence, but these things happen. I got quite excited about this and managed to find the house where she lived near Mylor.'

'This would be about, when?' The sergeant looked at the calendar on the wall.

'About January.'

'January of this year?'

'Yes.'

'So Sarah would be nearly forty?'

'Thirty-eight or so. Yes.'

'That figured with the autopsy report.'

'Oh, it was the same woman. I have no doubt of that.' Oliver had been shown the pictures which had nearly made him physically sick. Very hard to get something like that out of your mind. He'd noticed how keenly the sergeant had watched him as he inspected them.

'How did she take the suggestion that she might be your sister?'

'She knew she wasn't. Pearson was her married name.'

'I see. That must have been a blow to you?'

'It was a blow.'

'Did she tell you what her maiden name was?'

'She did, but I've forgotten. It didn't seem important at the time. It was nothing like Pearson. However, I didn't altogether lose hope, because there was a similarity. We looked alike. We had the same colouring, dark hair, blue eyes, same noses.'

'But there was little chance she could have been your sister?'

'None at all, really. She had been born in Manchester though she hadn't lived there all her life. She'd lived in London for a long time, I think. She went to Cornwall when she left her husband. He was cruel to her and she was afraid of him.'

'I see.' Sergeant Greaves scribbled something on his pad and underlined it several times.

'She must have been worried that you'd found her when she'd been trying to hide?'

'I think she was, though she'd lived there for a bit and he hadn't showed up.'

'Did she own the house?'

'No. She rented it.'

'And how did she live?'

'She was quite an accomplished artist and wrote songs. She made a bit on the side, I expect. I don't really know how she lived.'

'But she didn't seem to know many people?'

'I don't think she did. She was a bit of a recluse. She'd led an odd life. She and her mother had roamed about all over the place on the hippie trail. Sarah more or less had to fend for herself. She also spent time in a children's home. She'd married Pearson when she was seventeen.'

'And did she have any children?'

'I don't think so. She didn't mention them.'

'The autopsy showed she hadn't had children.'

'That's it then.'

Sergeant Greaves looked steadily into the eyes of the man opposite him. 'Did you, er . . . Did the two of you become lovers, Oliver?'

'No. There was nothing like that. Absolutely not. I liked her very much, I . . .' Oliver began, but his voice broke and while he attempted to recover himself Sergeant Greaves leaned back in his chair and studied the surface of his desk as though his mind was miles away.

'I have to ask you this, Oliver. Did you kill Sarah Pearson at some time in February, or early March, of this year?'

'I did not.'

'It may have been done on the spur of the moment, in anger. Perhaps you wanted to go to bed with her and she resisted. One could understand that sort of thing.' The sergeant's tone was kind, wheedling.

But Oliver wasn't deceived.

The bastard, he thought, up to his tricks. Maybe he should have had a lawyer, after all. He had waived his right to free legal aid and a solicitor because he disliked lawyers almost as much as policemen. They had never been the slightest use to him when he was a youth in trouble. They'd had no time for him at all, so the feeling had been mutual.

333

All forms of authority were best avoided, in Oliver's opinion.

'I did not kill her. I did not want to go to bed with her, nor did I try, despite the fact that we got on well. She didn't attract me.' Oliver's voice broke again. 'She was a good, kind person. She didn't deserve such a horrible death. I did a few jobs about the house and she asked me to stay, but I wanted to go back to Manchester.'

'Why?'

'I just did. It was my home.'

'But you had no home.'

'It was familiar. Anyway I thought I could get work there. There was no work in Cornwall and we were short of money. I knew Sarah was nervous, living in this remote place, but it was beautiful and, as she was artistic, she liked living there. She was careful to lock up at night. She had made it all nice and cosy. I offered to leave her one of my dogs. I had two and she had become fond of them. I just made it sound a sort of joke, that he would look after her and protect her.' Oliver's voice broke again and he paused for a long time, thinking about that sad, lonely, beautiful woman who was dead. They'd formed a bond. One of the few he ever had, before Wendy. Sergeant Greaves tossed a paper tissue over to him and he blew his nose. 'I really was very fond of Sarah and I'm sorry about what happened to her. I think if I had stayed on she would still be alive. But one couldn't know that, could one?'

'I'm afraid not.' Sergeant Greaves shook his head. He leaned across the interview table, his expression grave.

'Now, Oliver, there is a simple method we can use to determine whether you killed the woman you knew as Sarah Pearson or not. You have probably heard of the scientific technique called DNA?'

Oliver nodded.

'We require a sample from you. This can be saliva, blood or semen. We have DNA of the semen found in the body of Sarah Pearson but we don't need to take any from you. We can get the same result from blood. Are you willing to give such a sample, Oliver?'

'And if I don't?' Oliver trembled.

'On the evidence before me, you will be cautioned and held in a police cell on suspicion of the murder of Sarah Pearson. We are obliged either to release you after thirty-six hours or we can apply to the magistrates to detain you for a longer period. We shall probably charge you with a lesser offence while the sample is being tested, something to do with the vagrancy laws. We will oppose bail and, in view of the seriousness of this charge, we are empowered to take a DNA sample without your consent. If this proves positive, you will be charged with the murder of Sarah Pearson. Now, Oliver, what do you say?'

He knew that they had him. His nightmare

had come true. They would take the sample and it would prove positive. They would make it positive. They would fix evidence, as they had in the past, as they had threatened to do in order to detain him. Some vagrancy charge!

They were completely unscrupulous and they always had been. No matter how nice they seemed, they were pigs. He looked at Greaves and the sergeant, unsmiling, looked back. He knew that Greaves, however gentle his approach, thought he was guilty. He had been aware that the effect of the painkillers was beginning to wear off and a sudden pain shot up his arm into his head. He felt giddy and sick.

'I don't have much choice, do I?' he said at last.

'That's great.' Relieved, all smiles and amiability, Greaves switched off the tape recorder. 'I'll make the necessary arrangements.'

'How long will it take . . . the result?'

'About ten days. As we can't detain you, and as you are co-operating, we will release you on police bail, to return to this station when we have the result of the tests. I understand the hospital want you in urgently, anyway. They need to operate on you and that way you'll get a good rest.'

'I'm not guilty,' Oliver said in a strange, uneven voice.

'We shall see,' Greaves replied. 'The tests

don't lie.'

*   *   *

Oliver lay in a white bed in a white hospital room. He was propped up against a white pillow and his right arm, heavily bandaged, lay against his chest. He slipped from waking into sleep and back again, still recovering from the effects of the anaesthetic. It was a very pleasant feeling, as if he had left the rest of the world, allowing it to slip by him.

He was safe, warm, free from pain. There was no policeman by his bed, or outside the ward. It wasn't necessary. He wasn't going anywhere. He was never going to run away again.

He opened his eyes and saw a vision: she was standing by the door looking at him, not smiling but concerned, tender, loving. The vision came towards him, sat on his bed, gently ran her hand over his forehead, lightly kissed it.

No vision; flesh and blood. Wendy.

He slipped his good arm round her waist and drew her towards him, and they stayed like that for some time, aware of what it meant to be together, of how agonizingly long the separation had been.

'How's the arm?' she asked prosaically, looking at him with a hint of amusement in her eyes, as though she'd seen him yesterday

337

instead of weeks ago. 'I must say you're making an excellent job of being a patient.'

'Can't feel a thing,' he said.

'They say the arm had a crack in the bone which caused all the pain. It had never mended properly, probably due to the silly life that you led.'

'They've put a pin in it,' he said, choked with emotion but not wanting to show it. 'They've been absolutely marvellous.'

'Pity you ran away.' She kissed him once more on the forehead. 'Don't do it again.'

'I shan't. Don't worry.'

'Or I shall make them put leg irons on you.'

'They probably will anyway. They've taken the blood, for the test . . . the DNA.'

'Good, then it will soon be over.'

'They'll find out it was me.'

For a moment Wendy felt shock, disbelief. She stared at him for several seconds. Had Lois, had Ken, all those people been right after all?

'I see I've shocked you,' he looked at her askance. 'So, you really do think I did it?'

'I don't, unless you tell me you did.'

'I might have deceived you all the time about what sort of person I really was.'

The chill round her heart didn't go away.

'It wasn't me,' he said.

'It's not funny,' she said angrily, getting up.

'What I mean is, they'll fiddle the evidence. The fuzz, the rozzers. They always do. They plant things. It would be convenient for them to find me guilty. All wrapped up with no need to look elsewhere. I know Sergeant Greaves thinks I did it.'

'I believe the police are straight and honest.' Wendy went back to the bed and took his hand. 'And so must you.'

'I remain to be convinced,' Oliver said. 'You can't break the habits of a lifetime.'

*   *   *

They'd found a buyer almost as soon as the estate went on the market. The buyer was so anxious to complete that the Hunters had agreed to move out at once, put the furniture in store and camp in the Barbican flat while they looked at leisure for a property.

Events had moved so fast that Lois was in a perpetual state of bewilderment. Oliver had been found unconscious on a street in Manchester and promptly arrested. Now he was in hospital in Truro having voluntarily given a sample of his blood for DNA testing. Wendy had rushed to join him and, despite all she had to do, Lois had volunteered to go up to Manchester to collect Chump from the animal shelter.

She had recognized the dog even though he was so thin, emaciated and afraid. He knew her at once. But now, a few days later, joyfully reunited with his brother, rested, given some good food and checked over by the vet, he was like a new dog. At the moment he was racing around the lawn with Rusty. Sally and Lucy had retreated in the face of this male onslaught, perhaps out of jealousy.

Arms akimbo, Lois gazed out at the garden, lit by the mellow autumn sunshine, and realized—not for the first time since they'd made the decision—how much she would miss Higham Hall, its peace, beauty and serenity. Had it been a decision that was too impulsive, made in the heat of the moment with all that uncertainty? Maybe. But it had been made.

The telephone rang and she answered it. It was from Wendy. The police had asked to see Oliver. He was to go to the station the following day.

Soon they would know.

*   *   *

Wendy was not allowed into the interview room with him. Sergeant Greaves had been most affable in his greeting, asking almost tenderly after Oliver's arm. Oliver was apprehensive, pallid; inwardly shaking, she knew, with fear. He was convinced the police were out to frame him. She gripped his hand as the policeman led him away, and then she sat down to wait.

*   *   *

In the interview room, Sergeant Greaves did not turn on the tape recorder. Oliver imagined the bastard didn't want anyone to hear what he was going to say. He steeled himself, wishing he had Wendy with him. He needed her strength. Sergeant Greaves joined his hands, leaning slightly forward.

'Oliver Pearson, I have to tell you that the DNA report on the sample of blood taken from you is negative. In the opinion of the police expert, you did not murder Sarah Pearson. You are free to go.'

'And that's all?' Oliver asked when he had found his voice.

'That's all.' Sergeant Greaves relaxed and stood up, smiling. 'You are no longer a wanted man, and we now have to turn our attention to another line of enquiry. Any help, incidentally, that you can give ...' he paused slightly, 'would be invaluable.'

'How do you mean?' Oliver asked suspiciously.

'Any recollections you may have of your conversations with Sarah, any clue as to the whereabouts of her husband, would be most helpful.'

*　　*　　*

Sergeant Greaves watched them from the window of his office as, after a prolonged embrace, the couple got into the car and drove off. Shaking his head, he turned to the detective constable who had been in at the original interview with him. 'That man doesn't know how lucky he is that this DNA technique is available. If it weren't for that we would have made a cast-iron case against him. Put him behind bars for life. I would have sworn he was guilty. I can't believe he didn't sleep with her. I thought that story about a sister was all eyewash. A vagrant finds a woman living on her own . . . what conclusion would you come to? Robbery, rape? We only had his word she had no money.

'Now he gets not only a new life but a good-looking and wealthy woman. What has he got that I haven't?' He turned to his subordinate, who also shook his head. 'Exactly,' Sergeant Greaves said, as though in a comment on the unfairness of life. 'On the other hand, if what he told us of his past is only half-true, maybe he deserves it. Good luck to him, I say.'

*   *   *

The cottage stood well back along a track through the woods, away from the main road. Through the trees was a glimpse of sheer water, the Carrick Roads which, with its many tributaries and branches, continued on eventually to Truro. It was a beautiful spot on that bright autumn day. Not the least bit spooky, despite the dreadful event that had happened there. This thatched cottage with its whitewashed walls and mullioned windows, the fading hollyhocks a last echo of summer in the pretty garden, had a story-book appeal.

They stood outside for some time looking at it. Then Oliver put the key in the door and, pushing it open, they went in.

It had been emptied, scrubbed and repainted. It was for sale and, in view of the position and despite its history, which most viewers, unless they were in the know, would not be told about, the asking price was a high one.

They said little as they wandered round opening doors, peering into cupboards. There was a large downstairs living room with an inglenook fireplace, stairs leading to a fairly spacious landing off which there were three bedrooms. The cottage had a downstairs loo and bathroom, a good-sized kitchen with a newly installed Aga.

'Do you really *want* to live here?' Wendy asked at last, throwing open the back door that led into the garden, which had also been nicely done up, the soil turned over and fresh lawn laid. On all sides was woodland and further glimpses of water. She turned and looked at Oliver, who stood behind her. He nodded:

'As far as I want to live anywhere.'

'You don't mean you're going to get into some battered old van again and take off?'

'Not unless you come with me,' Oliver said and, reaching for her, he took her in his arms. As she snuggled up against him, he knew at last he'd come to rest.

THE LADY AND THE TRAMP

An extraordinary romance has developed between a beggar who earned his living on the streets and Wendy Cartwright, a high-powered PR lady from London who says she will probably give up her job to live in the West Country. The vagrant, who just wishes to be called Oliver, has recently been cleared of any connection with the murder of a woman in Cornwall earlier in the year.

Miss Cartwright is the daughter of the late Mr P. E. Cartwright, an eminent surgeon, and Mrs Margaret Cartwright of Brighton. She first met Oliver at the home of her sister who had helped to rescue him from an unprovoked attack in the small Dorset market town of Stinsbury.

Wendy and Oliver embarked on a three-month fling during which time he was, unbeknown to them, being sought by the police . . .

The article from a prominent national tabloid then went on to narrate the adventures of Wendy and Oliver until he was apprehended in Manchester.

Lois didn't know how they got this sort of stuff. She was sure Wendy hadn't given it to them. Maybe one of her PR colleagues had done it in order to make a bit of extra cash.

Lois stuck the paper in her holdall and made a final tour of the house. She felt lonely, restless and ill at ease. Ken had had to hurry back to London because there were jitters on the stock market. If they lost too much money they would have to consider a smaller property than the one they had their eye on.

Sally and Lucy were temporarily in kennels until the move was over, and Chump and Rusty followed her disconsolately round the house as if they couldn't quite understand why everything was so bare. They ran in and out sniffing in the old familiar places, but all the nice smells, as well as Sally and Lucy, had gone. Even the garden wasn't the same. They didn't know what was going on. First one ran back to her and then the other, as if seeking an explanation. She bent to stroke each in turn. If only one could tell dumb animals, but one couldn't. It was so unfair. She looked into their eyes and they gazed uncomprehendingly back at her. She would miss them, but they weren't hers. She was thankful for Sally and Lucy, with whom she would soon be reunited.

As if on cue, there was the sound of a car coming up the drive and she went quickly to the front door pursued by the dogs, who ran ahead of her through the open door and greeted with exaggerated enthusiasm the couple who descended from the car, as if they had come to rescue them from a life of misery. Oliver seemed to be trying to hold back tears as he took first one head between his hands and then the other, nuzzling them fondly. Wendy stood back as if she wanted this moment to be between him and the dogs he'd rescued from a cruel fate. She raised her eyes and looked smilingly at Lois, and at that moment Oliver also looked up; as if seeing her for the first time, he came over to her and put his hands around both her arms.

'Lois, hi!' He kissed her firmly, first on one cheek and then the other, and she was acutely aware of the strong clasp of his fingers.

'Hi,' she said looking up. 'At last.'

'Are we very late?' Wendy, glancing at her watch, walked over to them.

'Not at all,' Lois shook her head, smiling. 'I meant at last I am Lois. Oliver always used to insist on calling me "Mrs Hunter".'

'I was an awkward bastard in those days.' Oliver released her and, stepping back, reached for Wendy's hand. The dogs still scampered around them, begging to be caressed first by one then the other. It was as if Lois, who had looked after them both for many weeks, no longer existed.

And she didn't exist for Wendy and Oliver either, she thought, feeling a sense of exclusion as the lovers exchanged glances, and she saw how their knuckles whitened as their clasped hands became more tightly entwined.

There was an aura about them that was slightly awesome. Oliver all freshly shaved, the inevitable thick check shirt with the display of white at the neck replaced by a button-down royal blue Ben Sherman, more handsome than ever. Wendy beautiful now, yes, really beautiful, in a way that Tim had never made her. They no longer looked like the same people. It was all slightly unreal.

'Let's take you out for a pub lunch,' Wendy said suddenly, hunching her shoulders as if suppressing a shudder. 'It seems so creepy here with the house all deserted and no curtains at the windows.'

'Really, I can't.' Lois looked over at her car packed with all those little bits that one discovered after the removal men had left. 'I was just holding on until you came.'

'But, darling, we've hardly *seen* you . . .'

'Yes, but you will, once we're all settled. We'll see lots of one another. Besides, I promised Ken I'd be back soon as I could. This collapse of the Far East market has shaken him. If the bottom does fall out of world markets we may not be able to go ahead with the house purchase.'

Oliver seemed to find this vaguely amusing and a sardonic smile flitted across his face. Wendy, interpreting his expression, said quickly:

347

'Oh, dear. I am sorry . . .'

'On the other hand,' Lois interrupted her, 'it may not be as bad as we think.'

Of course Lois had to say that. It was expected of her. She was the brave one, the stoical one who always looked on the bright side, the person who didn't give in, the one with the stiff upper lip. The archetypal British female who tramped through African jungles, bore babies in clearings, stood at stockades with their men.

She was the support to all creatures, animals or human, who needed her. Then she was dispensable.

Good old Lois, always came bouncing back.

'Well, if you're sure . . .' Oliver and Wendy exchanged glances, the sort of intimate glances of lovers who wanted to be alone, who had time only for each other.

'Quite sure.' Lois paused. 'And your cottage? You're really going ahead with it?'

'We hope so. We really do.'

'But how can you want to live in a place where . . .'

'We want to make it a good Karma for Sarah,' Oliver said gravely. 'We want to banish the evil of what happened there and bring back happiness and light.'

'It *is* a lovely place,' Wendy said firmly, as if to forestall any sense of misgiving on the part of her sister, or, just possibly, herself. 'I agree with Oliver. We want to make it beautiful, fill it with love.'

Oliver nodded approvingly. 'Sarah would have wanted it.'

Wendy went over to Lois and, kissing her, looked steadily into her eyes.

'Thanks so much for everything. Above all for giving me Oliver.'

Lois, embarrassed, flicked the hair back from her forehead. 'I really don't know what to say.' She looked across at Oliver standing behind her sister. His smile was warm, almost intimate, as if they were already related. He put out a hand and as she took it he drew her towards him.

'Thanks,' he said and, once again, he kissed her.

*   *   *

More effusive goodbyes were said—it was as though they were emigrating rather than being separated by a few hundred miles. The dogs, who didn't seem the least upset to be leaving, were hugged once more and jumped excitedly into the car. When the car doors had been shut behind them, Wendy, still at the wheel, gave a couple of toots on the horn and made a sharp U-turn in the drive.

Lois stood waving and, as the car disappeared down the drive, the feeling she'd had of loneliness and isolation returned. It wasn't, she was sure, so much that she envied

Wendy, it was that she envied *them*: the new start, the heady idiocy of a fresh love affair.

The whole thing was in many ways unreal. It was unreal to want to live in a place where someone had been brutally murdered, in circumstances, moreover, that had affected Oliver. It seemed bizarre to her, but then they were a bizarre pair. Wendy was obviously getting on to Oliver's wavelength. Soon it would be beads and a kaftan instead of the snappy dressing, the power suit.

Karma indeed!

Certainly they were bizarre, but they were happy. Oliver seemed like a different man, and Wendy was different too. Of course, it wouldn't last, and God forbid that she marry the man, but still . . . one couldn't help being just *slightly* jealous, much as she loved her sister.

Because Oliver was such an attractive man. Undeniably. He had an extraordinary quality Lois still couldn't explain. It was illogical, as Ken had always said. After all, they'd found communication between themselves awfully difficult: those stilted discussions, those attempts at small talk over coffee. Today when he'd said 'Lois' was the warmest he had ever been. He'd hugged her. She'd treasure it, the feel of his fingers clasping her arms.

She didn't quite know what his fascination for her had been—philanthropic, altruistic? Yes, but had it also been partly sexual? In her

350

heart of hearts could she deny it?

In her heart of hearts she could not.

Well, whatever it was, or had been, it was over. She was sure of that. In the same way as for her sister, it had been an adventure, something different, a little exciting, out of the ordinary, unconventional. She could understand why Wendy went off with him. In different circumstances, so might she.

The cruel fact was that she was thirty-seven years of age, children nearly grown up, and just Ken for company. What was she going to do with the rest of her life? Ken had already confessed to nearly embarking on an affair. Nearly? Maybe he had, and he'd lied to her. Maybe there'd be another and another. She'd never know unless he asked for a divorce. This was a terribly gloomy way to confront the future, Lois thought, but she was aware of an anti-climax, a watershed in her life. That was why, she suspected, she'd wanted to move.

She drifted restlessly from room to room checking that the windows were shut. Nothing remained, not a curtain rail, not a lampshade; the taps were turned off, all that sort of thing. Next week the place would be humming with workmen expunging the last traces of the previous owners.

The house bore the usual air of depression, of being deserted, as if one were ruthlessly abandoning a place where one had been happy. And they had. Fifteen busy, fruitful years.

Now the place was empty. The furniture had gone, the telephone had been disconnected. Bev and Neal had departed for Scotland, the dogs were in boarding kennels, the horses had gone to new stables, the boys had gone back to school, her mother back to Brighton. She'd resigned from the bench. The church flower rota was now in the hands of someone else.

She hadn't said goodbye to Madge, but then she hadn't intended to; they'd never got over their tiff. But, because of the haste of the move, they had been too busy to say goodbye to most of their friends. They'd write and send Christmas cards instead.

She went out into the hall, opened the front door, shifted her few bags outside and relocked it. Then she put her bits and pieces into the car and stood looking up at the house, then at the grounds once so full of people buzzing about, horses, dogs and cats—full of life and activity. There was a curious stillness in the air, a sense of time having irrevocably passed, a question mark over the future.

It was, she thought, as though Oliver had never been. Yet Oliver had been, and he changed their lives—all their lives—for ever.